ENEMIES OF MAGIC

ENEMIES OF MAGIC

THE LEIRA CHRONICLES™ BOOK 7

MARTHA CARR

MICHAEL ANDERLE

DISRUPTIVE IMAGINATION

LMBPN Publishing
PMB 196, 2540 South Maryland Pkwy
Las Vegas, NV 89109

Version 2.00 July 2020
Version 2.01, October 2020
eBook ISBN: 978-1-64971-065-9
Print ISBN: 978-1-64971-066-6

THE ENEMIES OF MAGIC TEAM

Thanks to the JIT Readers

Joshua Ahles
Micky Cocker
Kelly O'Donnell
Larry Omans
James Caplan
Edward Rosenfeld
Sarah Weir
Peter Manis
Thomas Ogden
Erika Everest

If we've missed anyone, please let us know!

From Martha

To everyone who still believes in magic and all the possibilities that holds.

To all the readers who make this entire ride so much fun.

To Louie, Jackie, and so many wonderful friends who remind me all the time of what really matters and how wonderful life can be in any given moment.

And finally, a special thank you to John Nelson of the Austin, Texas Police Department who patiently answers all of my questions. I hope I made you proud. Thank you for your service.

From Michael

*To Family, Friends and
Those Who Love
To Read.
May We All Enjoy Grace
To Live The Life We Are
Called.*

CHAPTER ONE

Harkin barreled through the far reaches of the Dark Forest near the coastline, far from the Light Elves kingdom. The floating islands of Rodania appeared above the treetops in the distance over his right shoulder, helping him to track his location.

Wolfstan Humphrey had managed to slip away from him in the market, but Harkin wasn't going to give up so easily. He had made his way quickly out from under the tents and the press of energy churning around inside, getting far enough down the road.

There the energy began to subside, and Harkin could focus, searching for the clues he knew were there. He was going to need every advantage he could grasp. Wolfstan was clever at hiding his tracks and there was almost no trace of him anywhere in the market or just outside. *Almost.*

Harkin knew better and kept searching, willing himself to focus. He had spent too many years locked in the narrow stone cell with the Light Elf and had learned too many of his tricks. There were crumbs there if someone knew what to look for and what they were seeing when they found it.

He tramped down into the woods, looking for the small particles of neutron stars that were contained in Wolfstan's magic. They pulsed with a concentrated energy that made it nearly impossible to completely obliterate.

Harkin moved around in a circle, breathing hard, sweat forming on his forehead, not getting anywhere. The bushes and vines closest to him, swayed in rhythm with his movements making it look like a herky jerky dance of one.

"Enough! You know better." Harkin clamped his hands on his head in frustration, his long braid swinging across his back and stopped himself in mid spin. "You can do this. Focus. There's enough time. There's always enough time. Work with the elements. Trust that everything is working with me." His old mantra from a long time ago. Another lifetime. "Where would Wolfstan be heading? Away from the road." He turned toward the forest and turned in fractions till he saw the tiny thrum of light. "Got you, you bastard."

Harkin stepped forward, repeating the exercise till he spotted another pulse and then another till he saw a pattern like constellations along the dirt floor. His breathing was steady, and he picked up speed, moving faster, steadily making his way. He glanced up at one point and saw the looming mountain ranges of the Gnomes appearing gray against a deep blue sky.

A herd of curious deer followed alongside him staying behind the first screen of trees, breaking off after a while and running deeper into the forest.

The humid sea air reached him just as the piercing bits of light abruptly came to an end the closer Harkin got to the water's edge. He turned and searched over and over again but there was nothing. A painful ache filled his gut at the realization. "Wolfstan has taken a portal out of here. Correk." He kept walking, tearing at the vegetation hoping for one more neutron spark until he emerged at the edge near the water. There was nothing.

He stretched his arms out wide and bellowed, the sea air filling his lungs with a familiar scent.

He looked over the water at the horizon and the island where Trevilsom Prison sat. He stood frozen in the sand, sucked back in time. *All those years.* He winced and ducked at the unseen weapon being swung at his head by a prison guard from a long time ago. The memory of the dull ache it had left passed through his head again.

A lion roared and was quickly followed by a loud blast of noise. Harkin rubbed the heels of his hands against his eyes, willing away the images.

The Gardener of the Dark Forest broke through the treeline astride the lion, holding aloft a large conch shell. A snake wound itself around the lion's antlers, dropping to the ground and burying itself just underneath the soil.

"I heard your distress call," said Harkin still looking toward the sea.

"Damn your distractions!" yelled the Gardener, startling Harkin.

Harkin turned around, his brow furrowed. "Wolfstan has escaped to the other world. He must know I left a copy of the plans with Correk."

"I told you that ring was a bad idea from the start. Now,

Correk doesn't even know he's got something that needs protection. But there are more problems closer to home. Peyton has broken out of that thing you called his home." The Gardener's voice roared through the forest, shaking the trees. The ground shook from the animals moving further away from the fury.

Harkin shook his head, surprised. "That's not possible. There was a ward on that room."

"Sometimes desire can overcome even magic. And without those wards, his magic is no longer contained. You saw what happened the last time. He won't be able to control it. This all has to come to an end." The lion reared back on its hind legs and the vines in the Gardener's hair turned black, twisting in and out. "I bear responsibility for this one. I listened to your ideas and I gave you refuge. Find Peyton and bring him back safely and then you tell the world the truth, including Correk. I'm done with the secrets." He lifted the conch shell to his lips and blew again, a low, deep sound that echoed long after he stopped. A tall chestnut colored stallion came bursting through the trees and stopped next to the Gardener, pawing at the ground and shaking its large head.

"Take the horse and ride toward the Light Castle. I will look to the west. Find him before he can harm someone. Then we will find Correk and you will take back that damnable ring."

"Wolfstan won't get anywhere near it. I know my son. He'll sense trouble coming." Harkin took hold of the horse's mane and leapt up, swinging a leg over the stallion's back, sitting up tall.

"You had better be right. That machine should have been dismantled and buried a long time ago."

"I have to rescue Peyton."

"You have to accept Peyton's fate."

The Gardener gave a nudge to the lion's ribs and turned toward the west, quickly fading into the treeline. Harkin took one last look back at the prison and pressed his knees into the horse's side, ducking his head down low as they galloped through the trees.

Mara stood at the top of Enchanted Rock, her hand shielding her eyes from the bright sunlight. Toni stood to her right, crouching down to pick up a delicate gold necklace with two gold moons hanging from it. "They were definitely here," said Toni, the necklace dangling off her fingers, twisting around in the Texas wind.

Jack was standing at the edge looking down the side trail, searching for any signs of the Elven girl. "Yeah, well there's no sign of them now."

"There has to be." Mara pulled in the energy through her feet and let it spread out across the ground, searching for something, anything to tell her where they had gone.

Toni clambered over a tall boulder, her foot slipping and kicking against a jagged dead tree stump. Dragonflies poked out of every corner, flying off in different directions. Steam blew up in a straight plume, startling Toni. "What the hell..."

"Look!" Jack was pointing in the air, high over Toni's head at the steam. It was twisting and turning into a string of ponies chasing each other in a tight circle. The wind picked up over the edge of the bluff and blew into their eyes, scattering the images.

"What was that?"

"I think I know," said Jack.

"A carousel," said Toni, a sly smile on her face.

"What am I missing?" asked Mara.

"I should have known Cousin Petie was mixed up in this." Jack waved to the others, already making his way down the trail. "He's not really my cousin. It's what we all call him. Baddest wizard in these parts. He runs the Carousel Lounge on the north side."

Toni wrapped her arm around Mara and smiled, heading behind Jack. "Goes to the tune of his own weird circus drum."

"And that's saying something for our people." Jack slid down part of the path and slowed down, waiting for Mara and Toni.

"He came to this world as a ten-year-old runaway and one of the first things he saw was the circus. Made quite the impression on him."

Mara's eyebrows went up. "He was a refugee," she said with a gasp. "How did I not know this?"

"He's a magical version of off the grid, which is not easy to pull off," said Jack.

"Makes sense they would run there. Cousin Petie is part of an informal underground of his own making." Toni let go of Mara's arm to make it down a steep part of the trail. "He is *way* under the radar where no one knows to look for him. The whole place has wards around it." She patted Mara on the arm. "Unless someone told you about it and personally introduced you to Petie you would never even sense it."

"Huh, how did a transplanted Elven kid find it?"

"I have a feeling I know who moved them there," said Toni.

"The Fixer." The witch and wizard said it in unison.

"Of course, a magical was in danger here. It doesn't answer who was after them," said Mara.

Jack looked back and smiled. "Well, we're off to see the wonderful Wizard of odd. He'll know more."

Correk felt the last shivers of magic drain away from Leira. He looked at the smile on her face and thought twice about saying anything. "Fuck it." He took her by the arm, walking away from the others across the grass of Turner's velvety lawn.

Leira's smile grew broader. "Correk, did you just say *fuck*? Wow, I am really rubbing off on you." She put her hands on her hips, standing straighter as the bracelet slid down her wrist, resting against her hand.

He was flustered, searching for the right words. "You didn't cure a disease, you can stand down. No parade is coming."

"No, but I managed to remove a stick." Her laugh came out easy and relaxed, the images of the distorted Elf fading. "Why are you still holding on to my arm, big guy?" She looked down at her arm and up at Correk, a crooked smile on her face. Correk's fingers were pressing into her arm.

Jackson watched them from afar as Turner went on

about the present state of magic on Earth. He was barely listening, giving an occasional "Uh huh." His focus was on his newly found daughter and the way she looked at the tall Elf.

Correk reluctantly dropped his hand, letting his fingers graze her hand. "You heard what Turner Underwood said. This is only a temporary fix." He leaned in closer to make his point. "And one that could fail." *Please take it seriously.*

"I can read your mind by that wrinkle across your forehead. I'm taking it seriously." She tapped the side of her head. "Well aware that things could go south at any moment. That's been the message from the very beginning when you and the King made a sudden visit at the hospital." The smile faded a little from her face. "Frankly, long before that day. Remember, I grew up with a mother that was supposed to be crazy and then had my grandmother disappear without a trace one day. I know things can suddenly change." She took a step back, holding her hands out wide at her side. "For this one moment, right here, I'm going to enjoy this feeling because the reverse is also true. Dammit, things can also weirdly go right. I'm not asking you to give me this one, Correk. It's mine and I'm claiming it."

Correk smiled despite his growing concern, the wrinkles deepening around his eyes. "A form of deadly optimism."

Turner snapped his fingers in front of Jackson's face, close to his eyes, startling him. He stumbled back a step and blushed right up to his pointed ears, visible through his long hair. "Snap out of it! She's grown already and probably better at handling tricky situations than you are."

Jackson rubbed the back of his neck, feeling sheepish. "That goes without saying. She's a marvel but that's what I'd expect from a Berens woman."

"One more reminder for you. Eireka is happy, finally. She's earned it." He held up his hand to stop Jackson and tapped his cane hard against the floor. "Doesn't matter that this wasn't exactly your doing. Fifteen years in a mental hospital because she told the world that magic is real. Let her have this peace."

Jackson took in a deep breath and let it out slowly. "It will take some time to adjust to having so much more and all at an arm's length."

Turner clapped his hand down on Jackson's shoulder. "Well said, my friend. What, you're surprised? Yes, we're friends, we have been all along. Your stubborn streak got in the way but in the end, I came to see that you made the right decision. You were never meant to be a Fixer."

Leira's ears perked up and she caught the last words. "You were supposed to be a Fixer?"

Jackson walked closer toward Leira despite Turner clearing his throat in the background. "Once upon a time I was a rising star in Elven land. It was a long time ago in a land far, far away." Jackson swallowed hard, watching his daughter laugh. His eyes shined for a moment, wet with tears as he blinked, hiding the sadness rising in his throat. He smiled and looked at her. *At least she's happy. Now, if we can all help her learn how to be safe.*

"I was a student of Turner Underwood's, much like you," said Jackson. "I'm afraid I flunked out at some point and went my own way. It was a moment in time when Turner was still willing to mentor the occasional Elf on

Oriceran. Never liked venturing too far from home. My dog needs me." *And I met Eireka and thought my life was going in a completely different direction.*

"If we can break up the storytelling and get back to the work at hand." Turner leaned forward on his cane as he grew solemn. "There are a few troubling developments that can't be overlooked and are out of the Silver Griffins purview. The first being the local population's desire to grab artifacts and use them to create a Frankenstein kind of magic."

"You mean the people of Earth. Quite a large local population." Leira ran her hand through her dark bangs. The bracelet glimmered briefly, unnoticed as Leira felt a pang of something strange pass through her from somewhere else. She gave a slight shake to her head. *What the fuck was that? Ignore it for now. Too many helping hands right in front of me.* "You wave something like unlimited power under human beings' noses and they tend to go gaga. It's an aphrodisiac to them. Mix in the possibility of living a helluva lot longer and their motivation goes through the roof in a very dark way. General Anderson has been filling me and Hagan in on reports that a few rogue companies think they can come up with some magic elixir or machine. It's the Sneetches come to life."

All three Elves looked at her with puzzled expressions.

"Oh, come on. Sneetches? Dr. Seuss? Horton hearing that Who. Thought for sure that guy was an Elf or some kind of Wizard. You're playing with me, right? Some have stars on their bellies. When the dude couldn't make something rhyme, he made up the word! All that weird shit he came up with and none of it was from magic. Wow..."

"It's like you stroke out on occasion." Correk hid his smile behind his fist as he pretended to cough.

"I know what I'm getting all of you for Christmas. Hell, I may not wait that long! You are missing out on Yertle and green eggs and the pants with nobody inside of them." She said the last part in a spooky voice, holding up her hands by her face and waggling her fingers, her eyes wide. "Okay, I give." She dropped her hands. "Bottom line is human beings have a strange fascination with living longer that stretches way back to when they first showed up on this planet. That wrinkle may be tougher to pull them away from than any other."

Correk crossed his arms. "Then the idea needs to be contained and squashed as fast as possible."

Turner finished the thought. "Before the idea leaks out to the populace at large and takes hold as even a hint of a possibility."

"And becomes something on the 'as seen on TV' aisle," Correk added.

Leira gave him a crooked smile. "I really have rubbed off on you. Taught you a few valuable things about my world. Yes, this is my world. Doesn't matter where my ancestors came from. This planet has a way of growing on you and then there's Texas... But this particular fight is not yours, gentlemen. Not one of you comes from Earth in any way shape or form. Closest would be Turner, and you have other things to do." Leira nodded in Correk's direction. "This is PDF business, at least for now. There are already too many beings of every kind wrapped up in the artifacts war. This country actually does have a dog in this fight and

General Anderson is already expecting the PDF to spearhead the battle."

"You'll ask if you need help?" Jackson wrinkled his forehead even as he marveled at Leira's calm command.

"Cross my heart," she said, making an X across the left side of her chest.

"We have other things to attend to, Correk. There's a lot to learn if you're to be the next Fixer and not as much time as I'd like." Turner took out a linen handkerchief from his back pocket and wiped his forehead, sliding it back into his pocket. Leira saw a glimmer of how tired the elderly Elf was becoming but knew better than to say anything. *Let him call his own shots. If he needs help, he'll ask.*

"I could help you two, you know," said Jackson. "It's either that or I'm going sightseeing around town."

Turner looked him up and down. "You have a point. There's still enough people who think the idea of magic is just a reality show headline without much merit."

"I'm honored that you think I could be the tipping point into the truth all by myself."

"Wouldn't be the first time," huffed Turner.

"I can tell there are a few good stories I'd like to hear," said Leira. "That will have to wait for another father and daughter moment. Maybe we can cook up s'mores by the guest house one of these days."

"Finally, something I'm familiar with. A good s'more. I've made my share of those over a campfire."

"Of course, you know what those are... What is it with cheap and easy food and Elves?" Leira tilted her head and smiled. A surge passed through her again. A feeling she didn't recognize. The jewel in the bracelet dimly glowed.

She let it pass through, not calling on magic but casually took a look around them. Nothing seemed out of place. *No need to alert the forces and let my eyes glow. Dead giveaway there's a ghost in the system. What was that? Felt like something was reaching out to me for help.*

Turner doffed his hat and dipped it as he said goodbye. "We will meet again, Leira for another lesson. Till then, gentlemen follow me."

Correk hesitated, wanting to say something to Leira but he could feel the eyes of Turner and Jackson watching him. "Pizza later?"

"Sounds good. We can ask my mother and Nana if they want to go."

Correk opened his mouth to say something but stopped. Jackson let out a snort of laughter behind him. "Why was I worried?" he muttered to himself as Turner poked him hard in the side with the head of his cane.

"Sure," Correk finally said, as he patted Leira's shoulder. She looked at him puzzled and patted him back, tapping him on the shoulder.

"Okay, then." She shrugged, waiting for him to say something more.

"Interesting mating rituals on Earth," Jackson whispered. "Battling dark forces with moments of terror followed by awkward jokes. Not sure which one inflicts greater pain. It's like they're each other's chastity belt." He let out another snort. "I suppose that should make me feel relieved."

"Come on, Correk. We're burning daylight. Leira, you're distracting my pupil. Time for you to go." He waved his hands at her.

Leira looked from Correk to Turner, her brows knit together. "Pizza later," she said, and turned to go.

Jackson rolled his eyes and slapped Correk on the back. "I know what lesson we should start with or you're going to be a very lonely Elf. Not a good look on a Fixer."

"Fuck off, Jackson."

Turner rocked back on his heels and let out a deep, throaty laugh. "You'll be just fine, Correk."

"Huh?" *There it is again.* Leira felt a tug at her core, barely noticeable. A frail, thin tendril of magic was reaching out to her, wrapping around her own and leaving a trace of sorrow in its wake. "What is happening?"

Correk and Jackson were already following Turner across the expansive green lawn toward the house. Leira pulled in a low amount of energy and saw Turner's head give the slightest turn in her direction but he didn't stop walking. Instead, he slowed down enough to put his arms behind the two Elves, ushering them inside his old manse.

Leira kept her breathing steady, observing the trail and followed it down the grass toward the azaleas along a row of red bud trees. She crouched down as a mouse backed away from her under the bushes, quivering even in the warm air, its whiskers twitching. Leira pressed her hand to her chest, connecting with the pain. "I won't hurt you," she whispered. She slowly put out her hand as the mouse furtively turned to the left and the right.

"No!"

The abdomen of the mouse was replaced with gears and a tiny motor covered by a thin membrane.

The energy coursed through Leira lighting up the symbols along her arms as she fought the surge of anger.

Let me help him. The magic responded and curled around the furry creature, easing its discomfort and numbing the pain. She rocked forward on her knees and reached her hand out further, scooping up the mouse and easing him out from under the bushes. "Who did this to you?"

The mouse trembled in her hands, its dark grey eyes looking up at her blankly. "Fuck me, what am I supposed to do?"

"Let the magic tell you." Turner Underwood had returned and was standing behind her.

"You need a cat bell."

"That would make it harder to be the Fixer. Set an intention," he said, his expression drawn.

Leira rubbed the soft fur on the mouse's head and took in a deep breath. "Ease his pain," she said softly, her eyes shining. The mouse stopped struggling and lay down in her hand, shutting its eyes till the gears slowed and finally stopped. Leira swallowed hard and let the energy subside within her. An echo of the suffering ricocheted through her and down into the ground. "We really have to stop the bastard who's doing this." She choked out the words, her other hand curled into a fist.

"Let me see the creature," said Turner, tapping his cane angrily against the soft ground. "Come on, put him there." He cradled the still mouse and peered more closely at the gears holding the mouse together. "This was done for a very specific reason, I suspect. He was meant to be a listening device."

"Why not use a damn ball of light like the rest of us?"

"I would have known immediately, exposing them. The genius of technology. Magic is not able to detect it. But whatever evil is behind this doesn't realize the connection a Jasper Elf would have with his abominable creations."

Turner let his cane fall to the ground and placed his other hand over the mouse, closing his hands and whispering into them. He opened them again and all that remained was a small pile of ashes that rose into the air, spiraling out over the lake, eventually scattering with the wind. The Fixer put his arm around Leira's back and squeezed her shoulder, pulling her closer. Her magic hummed just beneath the surface, vibrating with anger. "We will find them and make this right, Leira. Even the smallest creature deserves better. Whoever the demon is though, he's aware of us. Perhaps we can use that to our advantage."

CHAPTER TWO

The black SUV with the tinted windows sat just down the block from Turner Underwood's circular driveway. Wolfstan Humphrey was sitting in the front seat in a narrowly cut dark blue suit with an open collar shirt and a large platinum watch on his wrist. The timepiece no longer kept time. It was an old artifact that could sense when an enemy approached. He was staring at the house and cursing under his breath, pounding on the teak and rosewood steering wheel. "Damn rodent," he growled. He started the car and drove as close to the estate as he dared, watching Correk pass by one of the tall windows, closely followed by Jackson heading in the direction of a side door.

He pulled away, gradually speeding up, unaware an *Oriceran* rodent had noticed him and climbed aboard for the ride. Yumfuck Tiberius Troll had situated himself underneath the car and was on reconnaissance. "Batfuck is on the job." He was wearing his red mask and matching cape.

The small troll held on to the chassis with one paw, ducking his head out when the car slowed down at a light to let the wind catch the cape and lift it behind him. "Aloha motherfucker," he yelled to a cyclist next to them, startling the rider. The man scowled and turned in time to give Wolfstan the finger as the light turned green.

Yumfuck swung back inside where the metal curled under, wedging himself in and resting his back against the frame. "Let's find out why you've been following us, motherfucker," he chirped. "I know bad cheese when I smell it, and there's something rotten going on here. No one messes with my family."

The car rode down the interstate, eventually crossing over into Williamson County and down FM620 until it got to the sleek campus with Fleeker spelled out in greenery out front. The SUV bypassed the circular driveway and went around to the left and parked in a reserved spot in a side parking lot. Wolfstan got out, still grumbling to himself. "I need those plans. This would go a lot faster." He was lost in thought and didn't see the faint glow from his watch.

Yumfuck dropped down to the pavement and pulled his cape around his body, scurrying under the car and behind a wheel, waiting. Wolfstan punched in a code on a pad next to the metal door, still scowling. He pulled the door open and went inside, letting it close without looking back. Yumfuck saw his chance and raced behind him, squeezing through just before the door clicked shut with a tight seal.

The troll stayed back in the shadows along the dim

hallway, following just close enough to keep Wolfstan in sight in his private entrance. The watch let off another small glow, partially hidden by the white shirt sleeve. Wolfstan was already busy ignoring the heavyset young man with slicked back hair, nervously shifting his weight from side to side.

"Good to see you again, sir. How was your flight from D.C.? My name is Jeffrey and I will be helping out today. Lovely weather we're having." The junior assistant was waiting for him by the private elevator holding a satchel and offering a bottle of water. Wolfstan swatted it away without a word, knocking the bottle out of the young man's hand. The aide's face warmed as he put down the satchel and ran to grab the bottle before it rolled too far away. He scooped it back up and mumbled an apology giving an awkward bow.

Yumfuck saw his chance and dove into the satchel that was just behind Wolfstan, his shoulders hunched, restlessly waiting for the soft whoosh of the elevator doors. Jeffrey picked up the satchel by the handles, not noticing the slight increase in weight and stepped onto the elevator still mumbling. "I uh have your morning meetings here. No? Okay, well, there are a few people in the boardroom waiting for you. No, not that either. Okay, tenth floor. Sure, we can stop there." A shudder passed through the young man. The tenth floor was his least favorite part of the building. He dreaded going there and took a step back, deeper into the elevator. "I could just stay on the elevator and let the others know you'll be coming soon. Would that work? Sir?"

Wolfstan sneered and held up his hand, snapping his

fingers and magically silencing the jumpy young man. Jeffrey continued to sputter but no words were coming out as he grasped his throat, his eyes widening.

The doors finally opened with another soft whoosh and a ding. "Tenth floor," said a silky female voice over the intercom as Wolfstan stepped out onto the gleaming tile floor. The assistant followed dutifully behind him, gagging and sticking out his tongue, still swinging the satchel. Yumfuck peeked over the edge and saw the long hallway, ducking back down inside before he was spotted.

Wolfstan strode down the hallway to a doorway with no handle and punched in another code as the door slid silently inside the wall. He walked inside, ignoring Jeffrey's flailing behind him and stopped at a row of observation windows into the sealed and sterile laboratories. Inside were rows of surgical stations neatly lined up, empty and waiting.

Wolfstan jammed down a button on an intercom and barked into it. "What are you doing? Why are all the stations empty?"

A surgeon dressed in blue scrubs turned around, his eyes wide above his mask. He went to the intercom, pushing the button. "Mr. Humphrey, I didn't know you were coming."

"Obviously."

The surgeon stepped closer to the intercom. "There's been a delay in obtaining new animals. It's gotten harder to import them from that alien forest. We expect to resolve that later today."

Jeffrey watched with his mouth open, picking up the satchel and clutching it to his chest, occasionally still trying to squeak out a word. He hated this floor. Yumfuck came crawling out of the top of the tote and stood on the edges, leaning back against the young man's chest. He looked through the windows as the fur along the ridge of his back stood up and his tiny chest heaved with anger. Jeffrey's brow furrowed and he looked down to see a five inch furry creature with green hair holding up its sharp little claws. He swallowed hard and looked up at Wolfstan Humphrey's back, opening and closing his mouth.

Yumfuck looked up at him and put a claw to his lips, giving Jeffrey a wink. "Not a word," he whispered.

Wolfstan glared at the expensive surgical room and let out a low, angry growl, rubbing his chin. The watch on his other wrist pulsed with another brief green glow.

"But there is some good news," sputtered the doctor. "We've made some progress on the modified CAT scan." Beads of sweat were forming on his forehead. "Of course, we aren't quite there yet. We just can't get the right combination..."

Wolfstan turned his back without listening to the rest, barreling his way back through the sliding door and toward the elevator. Yumfuck took one last look and grabbed onto Jeffrey's tie, pulling his head down closer to his furry face. "Learn from your mistakes motherfucker. Friendly warning."

The elevator doors were opening and Wolfstan was already stepping inside, not waiting for anyone. Jeffrey looked down at Yumfuck and shook his head, blinking a few times but the troll was still there. He tried yelling to Wolfstan, but no sounds came out of his mouth even as he took off at a run. Yumfuck dropped back down into the satchel just as Jeffrey got to the doors, closing in his face. Wolfstan's lip curled up at the edges and he snapped his fingers just as they shut.

"Mr. Humphrey!" Jeffrey shouted, but it was too late. The troll climbed out, hooking his arms over the top and hoisting himself up till he could drop to the floor. Jeffrey's eye twitched and he looked back toward the sliding door that had already shut and at the closed elevator doors.

He was alone in the hallway with the troll. "I hate this job," he said to Yumfuck.

Yumfuck carefully took off the cape and mask, laying them on the ground. He growled as he grew to his full height of eight feet tall, leaning over Jeffrey. "It's time for a career change, Jeffrey."

Jeffrey looked up toward the ceiling and down at the floor. "Did they spray me with something? Am I hallucinating?"

Yumfuck held up a large paw and scraped it along the wall, digging in with his claws and leaving behind thin jagged lines of torn drywall. "Not a dream. More of a nightmare." Jeffrey's knees shook as he pressed the elevator button over and over again, staring up at the oversized troll.

Yumfuck roared, blowing hot air into Jeffrey's face, rustling his hair. "Tell them we're coming for them. Their time is short. Tell them Batfuck is coming back and I'm bringing reinforcements."

"Bbbbbatfuck," babbled Jeffrey. He fell back against the wall, banging his head as his eyes rolled back and he lost consciousness. He slid down the wall and crumpled into a heap as the doors slid open and a silky female voice said, "Tenth floor."

Yumfuck picked up his tiny mask and cape and squeezed onto the elevator, pressing the button for the first floor. He was bent over, humming to the Muzak, waiting for the elevator to finish descending. "Barry Manilow, not bad," shrugged the troll. "First floor," the detached voice announced.

The troll worked his way out of the elevator, bending a door and lumbered toward the locked exit. He ripped the door open, setting off alarms and stepped out into the executive parking lot. Yumfuck trilled at the sight of the sleek black SUV and stomped over to the side, pointing a lone claw and carefully etching, *Batfuck was here.* He stood back and admired his work, shrinking back down to five inches tall. "Sweet. Bob Ross would be proud." He slipped the cape and mask back on and ran across the blacktop to make his escape.

Lily Sharpton slurped up the last of the soda, sucking on the straw as she trudged up the driveway. "Lunchbreaks always go by too fast," she said to her friend, Claire.

"I know what you mean. I shouldn't have eaten that last taco," said the girl, pressing her hand against her belly and blowing out air.

Lily smiled and went to throw away her cup, looking out over the manicured flowers. Her favorite part of the campus. A tiny red cape fluttering above the flowers caught her eye and she stopped, puzzled. Yumfuck's head bobbed up, wearing his mask before he ducked back down again, making his way toward the end of the driveway. "That's a troll," muttered Lily, catching herself and looking for Claire. But Claire was already halfway up the stairs. "Are you coming?" she asked, smiling.

Lily looked back but the troll was nowhere to be seen. "Uh, yeah," she said, shaking it off. She caught up to Claire, a steady smile on her face but she was barely listening. *What was a troll doing at Fleeker? I wonder if I should tell Aunt Lois.*

Peyton pressed his knuckles against his temples, squeezing his eyes shut. He opened them and looked around, hopelessly lost in the far reaches of the Dark Forest near the mountain range and the Gnomes territory. He thrashed about picking up stones and clods of dirt and throwing them at the nearby trees.

A band of Gnomes came running from a nearby tunnel, ready to take on the trespasser. They stopped short when they saw Peyton and his oversized body and bulging forehead.

"Two moons," gasped a balding gnome with a long wiry gray beard, doing his best to circle Peyton from a distance and get a better look. "What in all of Oriceran? What kind of magical are you?"

Peyton cried out, the energy pulling up through him in fits and starts, surging out of his hands and sparking the air around him.

"Stand back!" said a worried Gnome, pushing back the others.

Peyton stopped flailing for a moment, even as the magic continued to swell in fits and starts. Crackling blue lines of energy billowed up out of the ground around him, coming together in a knot and ripping open a hole. Swirls of dark mist curled out the edges, framing a vista of bald cypress trees growing out of a wide creek.

Hands reached out, grasping at Peyton, pulling at his shoulder, faces appearing, pushing against the thick goo that made up the veil between the two sides.

The Gnomes gasped in chorus, some instinctively reaching out to help the tortured Light Elf. "Not that. The world in between," gulped a Gnome. "No one deserves that."

Peyton railed against the intruders, crying out again and staring into the eyes of the oldest Gnome. "Help me," he screamed, falling backward, tripping over a tree root. The Gnome shuddered and threw up his hands. "Help him!" he shouted, rushing forward, but they were too late.

The hands reached out to take him, but his weight carried him over to the other world, barely escaping. He slammed against the packed earth, knocking the wind out of his lungs as he lay there looking up at the blue sky before shutting his eyes and passing out into welcome relief. Peyton had escaped to McKinney State Park, free at last on the southeast side of Austin.

"Much better out here." Turner smiled, working his way across the slate tile. "Shake it off, Correk. Feelings may fuel magic, but they can also distract." Turner's pocket buzzed and he reached inside his suit jacket for his phone, holding up a finger to Correk. "Hang on." He turned his back and listened closely.

Jackson had draped himself over one of the heavy patio chairs, his leg hanging over the armrest. "The Fixer gets phone calls to alert him. Not quite as glamorous as you expected, is it?"

Correk studied Jackson, his muscled arms folded across his chest. "I don't see the resemblance. Any chance Mara made a mistake?"

Jackson swung his leg around to the front, a scowl growing on his face. He curled his hands into fists as Correk arched an eyebrow. *Let him go first.*

"Break it up! Nothing worse than Elven hormones." Turner put his phone away, shaking his head in frustration. "One of the problems with a thousand years of life. You can be a juvenile ass for so much longer. Jackson, stay here if you want and my chef will feed you some of the best TexMex you're going to find while you're on this planet. He has some brisket from Full House BBQ in Georgetown. Melt in your mouth."

"I know that's your way of saying, keep my ass planted right here."

"If I wanted your ass to stay here, I'd make it happen." Turner raised his voice as he waved his arm in frustration, a stream of blue light jetting across the lawn of his estate, knocking Jackson back against the chair. He whipped around and glared at Correk who held up his hands, pressing his lips together and easily seeing it was in his best interests to stay silent.

Jackson's eyes immediately glowed, and anger swept through him as he whipped out his hands to create a fireball but quickly thought better of it and pulled back, his arms vibrating from the effort.

"Still a short fuse, I see..." Turner shut his eyes and lifted his chin, breathing in deeply.

"More of your chai?" Jackson felt a dull ache in his back but did nothing to let on he was smarting.

"I think he calls it chi." Correk's eyes were narrowed.

"Don't assume you can help me or know anything about me," snapped Jackson. "You and I have nothing in common."

"Except a very clever Elven woman named Leira." Turner opened his eyes.

"I always could ruffle your feathers better than most. That has to be worth something," said Jackson.

"That's not magic. Just an astute eye mixed with your strong desire to play the jackass most of the time. You were a gifted student."

"Not healthy to live with regret, Turner." Jackson felt the wince from his own words. Turner noticed but chose to look away.

"Jackson, those words are very true. We may possess great magical power literally at our fingertips." He held out his hands and lit up the tips of his fingers in different colors, tapping each one as they played out a different chord, creating a soothing tune. "But even we can never change the past. If you have regrets about what came before, your part in it, then I suggest you make an amends to everyone, including yourself."

Jackson let out an annoyed snort as Correk quietly watched the two Elves, interested in the answer to healing the past. *Where are you Harkin?*

Turner adjusted the lapels on his suit, taking a moment to let Jackson take in the possibility. Turner understood his old student and knew it was better not to rush him. He looked up at his large mansion, admiring the spires on the top and felt a wave of gratitude pass through him for all the years he had been granted within its walls.

He gave a satisfied smile and said softly, "Make the amends, Jackson by how you choose to live the hundreds of years you have left. If you want to be a father to Leira, be one but recognize it's of a grown woman who just met you. There's a role for you there but you'll have to be open to learning it just like any new father. If you want to be a friend to Eireka, be one. But realize she has moved on and is happy. Support her decisions. If you want to be happy as well, be happy and stop living in a cabin in the Dark Forest and go looking for a mate of your own. Hell, friends even. Get up every day and ask yourself what you can do to live the amends that day."

"Sounds like you've had to take your own advice." Correk shifted his weight and clasped his hands behind his back.

The old Fixer shook his head gently and chuckled. "More than once, Correk. You will see that being the Fixer carries its own perils that you never expect. So many decisions to make with no time to spare. There are hundreds of years with hundreds of thousands of our kind to help.

Once in a while things do not go as planned." Turner grimaced and cleared his throat.

Jackson stood up and headed toward the mansion. "Go and help the needy, you two. I'll check out how the better half lives and put your chef to good use."

"Help yourself to whatever you need," said Turner, his mind still distracted by the memories.

Jackson lifted a hand and waved but didn't turn around. He didn't want anyone to see that his eyes were shining as he curled his hand into a fist. *An entire lifetime, missed. That's going to be a large amends to make.*

Correk waited patiently for Turner as he sucked in his lower lip and watched a crane settle gently on the lake. "A good reminder," the old Fixer said at last. "Come, we have a task. A good project for your first time in the field. A Witch must be saved from one of her own spells."

Correk tried to hide his surprise and failed.

"We don't select only those who need our help through some virtuous act or peril, Correk. Get over that notion," Turner said, brusquely. "The Fixer doesn't offer forgiveness or impart punishment. Fuck..." He rubbed his face with his hands, feeling the weight of nearly a thousand years of work. "We fix things and leave the petty judgments to others."

"Like the Silver Griffins."

Turner shrugged. "They serve a vital purpose. It would be chaos without them. But our paths do not always align. They are the reason why we must get a move on this morning. If they get there first the Witch will think a misguided spell was the least of her concerns." Turner hunched his shoulders and swiftly created a ball of light in his hands, opening a portal to a suburb in Seattle, Washington.

Correk looked through the rapidly growing portal at the tall pines and realized it wasn't Oriceran. "A portal used across Earth," he said in awe. "The Silver Griffins must not fully appreciate you either."

"There is a mutual admiration and wink and a nod to keep our hands off each other. We came to a kind of agreement a long time ago long before I was the Fixer, and it has been abided by to this day. Come on, step lively." The Fixer quickly followed Correk, stepping more easily through the portal than Correk expected, pulling his cane in behind him. *Tricky old dog.*

At the corner was an ornate cement sign painted white with black lettering practically hidden by bushes and pines. Fay Bainbridge Park. The street was full of large homes with neatly trimmed front yards and large SUV's in the driveways. The older houses were set back from the road and hidden by old growth.

"We are going to the newer section. To that dark grey Colonial at the end of the block. The one that has a green noxious cloud emanating from it at the moment. Not good. Like a smoke signal for humans to worry and the Silver Griffins to rush in and erase everyone's memory while dragging off the Witch. Not that she hasn't given them reason." Turner kept walking even as he lifted his cane and aimed it at the cloud like a rifle, whispering into the handle. The cloud curled around itself till it resembled a putrid green icing from a cupcake. He shoved his cane forward in the air and back again as the curl unfurled and raced toward the tip, disappearing into the cane.

"Pretty neat trick, wouldn't you say? Part one, done." Turner was pleased with himself as he hustled down the street with Correk easily keeping stride alongside him. "Keep watching and this will all make sense shortly."

"Is that how you know when to show up? You get a phone call?"

Turner let out a laugh. "Fuck no! Did you think that was the Witch calling me for help? That was a dinner reservation for later. I got a table at Uchi's. Not easy to do but I have a lady to impress. Can you imagine if I had to wait for a phone call to know a magical being was in trouble? Then I'm just a magical 911 operator." He tapped the ground with the cane, pushing it along the ground. His focus was on the destination as he looked for the next sign, picking up his pace to a slow run.

They got to the house and Correk followed Turner down the side of the house, past a row of azalea bushes. They got to the back door off a covered cement patio and Turner pulled in just enough magic to unlock the door, his eyes glowing briefly. Correk took a look around to see if anyone might see them and noticed a mother pushing a stroller along the sidewalk, a small terrier on a leash leading the way. She was busy cooing to her child and passed by without looking up just as a minivan pulled up to the curb. Correk slipped into the house behind Turner, whispering, "The Silver Griffins are already here. We only have a few minutes at best."

"Thank goodness they are such rule followers. They'll start by knocking on the door." Turner shut the door behind them and locked it. He sent out a current of energy ahead of them, easily finding where the noxious gas was coming from.

They found a Witch in the family room in the back of the house wringing her hands over the remains of a large egg and a large dark red lizard rubbing its face. There was a gooey sheen still surrounding most of its body. Correk stepped closer, his eyes widening. It had been awhile since he'd seen one.

"A gargoyle..." he gasped. The thin, wet membrane was clinging to the gargoyle, pinning back its wings but not for long. "What the hell..."

"I was just trying to keep it safe for my cousin. It wasn't supposed to hatch for weeks!" The Witch's voice came out in a squeak.

Turner let out a sharp laugh. "What part of that story makes it okay that you brought a live gargoyle's egg to an American suburb? Tell me, dear Anne, how many gargoyles have you taken care of before?"

The Witch looked like the suburban Mom she was on most days wearing jeans and a cable knit turtleneck, her long brown hair cut in layers around her face. "This is my first one. Look, my cousin was desperate. She said they were stealing the eggs and she wanted to save as many as possible."

"There are more? How many, where?" Turner let the energy flow through him as the symbols on his arms appeared, floating into space and hovering over the gargoyle, soothing it.

"I don't know. Maybe a dozen. The rest of them were buried somewhere. I... I don't know where. Am I in trouble?"

There was a hard knock at the front door.

"Not if we move fast enough. Don't answer that. Correk, gather up the gargoyle. Don't worry, he's in a magical torpor."

Correk looked around and grabbed a pale cream blanket off the back of the couch, ignoring the faint whimpers and protests from Anne. He shook it out and gently gathered up the gargoyle, careful to not rub against the sharp talons and jagged teeth. He held the gargoyle close, holding it tight. "There, there little warrior."

The gargoyle looked up and opened its jaws wide, letting out a long yawn and another puff of green gas.

Correk's head whipped back from the smell and he squeezed his eyes shut. "That is worse than a troll fart. I didn't realize that was possible." His eyes watered from the stench.

The knocking grew more insistent and a woman's voice shouting, "Anne, we know you're in there. Answer the door, please. Don't make us come in there after you. That will only make it worse."

"Thank the two moons they're so damned polite," grumbled Turner. He moved his fingers around, manipulating the gold, sparkling symbols in the air as the shells of the egg lifted up, floating in the air. They came back together as an egg with the slime along the floor sliding inside just ahead of the last piece fitting into place.

Turner churned his hands, one over the other creating a miniature hurricane of swirling, sparkling light that grew into a portal, opening swiftly to the size of a door, perfectly placed against the ground. "Time to go! Anne, get the door as soon as we're gone before they enter by magical force.

Remember, nothing ever happened here. Let them look around as much as they want but you stay here. Go Correk!"

Correk didn't have time to think and stepped through the portal, still holding tight to the swaddled gargoyle. He found himself standing on a large estate and could see a tall black iron fence on the far side of the trees marking the property line. He turned around to see a startled grounds keeper in green coveralls holding a gas leaf blower. Correk looked at Turner coming through behind him. "Is there more trouble?"

"What?" Turner looked over and gave a wave. "Thank goodness! Jimmy, just the man I'm looking for today. I have a special delivery. Correk, hand him the package."

Correk gently moved across the uneven ground, still softly talking to the gargoyle. "There, there. Welcome to the world."

Jimmy set down the leaf blower, tilting his chin down and looking at Turner Underwood. "Can't keep storing all your problems here. What is it this time?" He took the bundle from Correk as the frustration faded and his eyes opened wider. "If this don't beat all. Is that a gargoyle? You brought a gargoyle here? After the last time? You know dragons and gargoyles don't mix well. You have some real balls there, Turner."

"I trust you know what to do, Jimmy."

"Don't I always." He said it like a fact and not a question. "Man, this is bigger than the time you brought the nest full of harpy eggs. At least they were still in their shells. Gave me a chance to get them back to the Dark Forest with no one the wiser." Jimmy looked at the long, red narrow face and smiled. "Where's the large momma gargoyle that is usually close behind one of these little things?"

"There was no time to question the nervous guardian. We will have to circle back on this one."

Correk looked up at the large, old oaks and looked through the trees, trying to figure out where he was standing. "Some of your rescues don't clean up as easily as others..." he muttered.

"Often the case, Correk. Come on, we need to get back. Jimmy knows what to do from here."

The gargoyle lifted its small head out of the blanket and let out a whimper, looking at Correk and letting out another small, green noxious cloud.

Turner chuckled. "Damn smart little creatures. It's bonded with you. Calm down." Turner held up his hands. "It's not like a troll. But gargoyles are smart. You know that. That's why they make such great postal workers on Oriceran. That gargoyle will remember you forever now. If you two ever meet again hundreds of years from now that gargoyle will remember you."

"You want to name it?" Jimmy held the gargoyle out to Correk.

Correk smiled. "What about Lucky? He escaped the fate of the rest of his nest."

"Yes... troubling. We will circle back. All may not be lost just yet. That's a good name. Sometimes, in the middle of all this magic a little luck occurs and that is what actually carries the day." Turner drew in energy and the symbols lit up along his arms, floating up into the air and spinning around till they created a whirl of light, opening a portal, exactly aligned with the ground again, in the shape of a door.

"You'll have to show me how to do that." Correk looked back one more time at Jimmy. He was carefully chucking Lucky under the chin and laughing every time Lucky snapped at his finger, barely missing. Correk shook his head and stepped through, back onto Turner's land in Austin, Texas.

"That and more, my young Fixer. It's a safer and faster way to open portals to anywhere you need to go. Less chance of a rip in the veil and an eternity in the depths of the world in between."

Correk felt the first real thrill of excitement about the idea of being the Fixer since Turner Underwood had asked him. "When do I start?"

"You already have, my friend. Next stop, I'm going to show you some of the secrets of a Fixer and how I can hear the cries for help."

"Make it so."

Turner arched an eyebrow and scowled at Correk.

"Sorry, too much late night TV with the troll."

CHAPTER THREE

Charlie Monaghan made himself take deep breaths as he paced back and forth in his study. His wife was at a meeting of the Daughters of the American Revolution and he was alone in the large house in Richmond, Virginia.

How could this be possible? No one loses that many employees in another world. "In one fucking day!" He took another deep breath and walked more slowly. Heel, toe, heel toe. "Raaarrrrrhhh!" He tilted his head back and let out a roar, holding out his clenched fists, shaking them with all his might. His head felt like it could split in two from the pulsing pain. The blackouts were increasing and growing longer, and the confusion was only adding to his frustration and misery.

Turning up in Austin, Texas with no recollection of how he got there or what he was supposed to be doing there put a fear in him that settled into his bones. He was unwilling to travel very far from his home after that day and hired a valet to look after him with the added duty of discreetly making sure he didn't wander too far away. *Thank God silence has a price.*

He took in small sips of air, checking the watch on his arm. It was time for the conference call with his board. "Not going to be pretty," he grumbled, rubbing the top of his head with his knuckles, willing the pain to subside. It wasn't working.

Charlie pressed enter on the computer's keyboard, connecting him to the cameras in the boardroom that let him see the entire group surrounding the table, all at once. He was dressed in what he considered casual when he wasn't headed for the golf course. A sports coat made just for him and grey slacks with brown leather loafers. Charlie glanced quickly around the table to see who was in attendance, forcing his trademark smile on his face. All of his pearly white teeth were showing even if the smile didn't quite make it to his eyes. He felt a pinpoint surge of pain as he spotted Pearson Cowley's large figure settling into a chair, a croissant by his steaming cup of coffee.

Charlie still blamed Pearson for the vote that forced Axiom to at least appear to be working with the Feds to recover artifacts. Thank goodness he was always prepared with a Plan B and had set up a rogue board that even Wolfstan Humphrey hadn't discovered. Another thorn in his side. Things were going on as usual. "Until that damnable Wizard," he muttered.

"What's that, Charlie? The sound isn't quite picking up what you're saying."

Charlie startled and stood up straighter, reflexively brushing back his thick grey hair that was already neatly in place. "Just letting Fred know about plans later," he said, making a point to smile harder. The valet appeared at the door but quickly stepped back into the hallway as Charlie flicked his hand dismissively in his direction out of sight of the camera. *Best to get it over with.* "Plans to capture any amount of Oriceran ore to finance our operations with the new world have not moved forward as hoped, yet."

"Capture?" Pearson Cowley sat forward, taking a sip of his coffee.

Charlie did his best to not roll his eyes. "Just a turn of phrase, Cowley. We've been unable to locate a suitable scout and the risks are too high without taking care of that first." *Not a lie. Every man dead. Cost a fortune to pay off their families. What a shit show...* It cost Charlie another small fortune to frame each of the men in a complicated embezzlement from Axiom. Charlie had paid each of the families a personal visit to gauge their willingness to take the money and go away. Only Calvin's family gave him the smallest worry, insisting Calvin was an old Eagle Scout and would never steal anything from anyone. *May have to leak a small story about that one. Leave a trail and put him in Belize or Luxembourg.*

It wasn't like Charlie to get so distracted while in a meeting, especially with his board. He felt the beginning of sweat across his forehead. *Keep it short, Monaghan.*

"If we don't find a suitable guide and can't secure any ore, we will have to find another way to finance looking for artifacts. Axiom cannot keep funding the bottom line, especially if we're going to be helping out the government with what we find."

The members all shifted in their seats, with the notable exception of Pearson Cowley who looked straight at the camera as if he could reach out and grab Charlie by the shoulders.

"There are no new ideas since the last time we went over this." A junior board member piped up, nervously looking around at everyone else.

"Should we even be in an artifacts race with foreign governments? Is it that important?" A long-standing member of the board, a middle-aged woman with brown helmet hair that wouldn't flutter in strong winds, pursed her lips tapping an expensive pen against her iPad.

"The two worlds coming together is a fact, Marilyn. Nothing is going to prevent that and we're a multinational conglomerate. We circle this globe, already." Charlie emphasized each word, making a small circle with his finger. "First rule of being a company this size is we keep evolving or rot on the vine. The artifacts are going to be dug up by someone and used by someone. We'll either be at their mercy for their designs or we will be creators, moti-vators." Charlie felt the blood rush through his head, and he had a sudden feeling of strength and clarity. *Much better.* The smile came more easily to his face and the lines around his eyes deepened.

"That makes sense," sputtered a younger board member. Pearson gave him a hard stare, making the young man look down at his phone as if he were checking for messages. Pearson gave a slight shake to his head and looked up at Charlie's face on the large screen. *Something is off, which is saying something about Charlie Monaghan. Can't quite put my finger on it.* Pearson put his fingers together like a steeple, resting the tips against his mouth.

"What if the Elves are telling us the truth?" A middle-aged man with salt and pepper hair spoke up, concern in his voice. "What if it's true that these artifacts hold the key to longer lives. Much longer lives." His eyebrows went up as he spoke, his eyes opening wider at the thought. "Imagine who could live longer."

Charlie felt the mood swinging in his direction. *At last!* "Imagine if the wrong people found a way to stay on Earth beyond their expiration dates. The hell it would bring to all of us. We are a responsible company. We know how to handle a burden like this and use it for the good of mankind. The Elves have said they'll provide us with locations to acquire the artifacts in exchange for basic technology. We cannot pass up this opportunity or hand it over to anyone else. But..." Charlie paused for effect, looking at each person and waiting for them to squirm or return his smile. Pearson kept his stony expression looking back at Charlie.

Charlie felt a sense of satisfaction. *Pearson will lose in the long run. I win.* "It's up to us to go out and get it. That's the deal we agreed to. In order to fund these expeditions a campaign will need to be mounted to extract some Oriceran ore. We cannot take anything more from our other divisions to pay for it and the government will want too much in return if they fund it." Charlie was enjoying his pitch, rocking back on his heels. *Was a temporary setback. Why was I ever worried? Things will work out. They always do.*

"What about a joint venture with another company?" asked the middle-aged woman. "This would provide some coverage for all of us and still yield a healthy profit without government interference."

Charlie snapped his head around to stare at the woman. *Is she a plant of Humphrey's? This board can never be trusted.* He scribbled a note to himself to look into her background later. A hot surge of pain flashed through his head, making him wince. *Not again! What the hell?*

He turned away from the computer and snapped his fingers, waving agitatedly at his assistant, Fred who came quietly rushing into the room. Fred masterfully hit the button, cutting off power to the mini tower that helped keep the internet connection to the office. Someone was talking but all Charlie could hear was every other word as he turned his back, squeezing his eyes shut, balling his hands into fists pressed against his desk. It was close to unbearable.

Fred watched from the side as everyone waited a moment, eventually shuffling out of the board room as the seconds ticked by. Pearson got up and was about to leave but his suspicions got the better of him and he lingered just by the door out of sight of the camera.

The valet counted to five, standing back from Charlie who was resting his head on the desk, his hands on his neck, and switched the mini tower back on, returning the power. For just a moment, Charlie Monaghan stood up and looked directly into the camera, his eyes completely black and a twisted smile on his face. Fred gasped and stumbled backward into the bookcase, knocking a signed copy of The Age of Turbulence off the shelf, smacking the oak floors with a thud.

Fred found his courage and leaned over just far enough to shut the lid of the computer, cutting off the feed but not before Pearson Cowley got a good look.

Pearson gripped the side of the door, pressing his lips together to ensure he didn't make a sound as his body shook involuntarily. He waited till he was sure he could stand still without shaking before he quickly left the room and headed for the elevator. "In all my years I've never seen anything like it. Never!" He was breathless, his words coming out in a hiss as he jabbed the elevator button. "The Dark Mist is claiming a human... What does this mean? If humans find out this is even possible." Pearson gave a hard shake to his head as a cold shiver went through him. "No... No!" The elevator doors opened and he was relieved to see it was empty. "Have to find Lacey and figure out a solution. We have to contain Charlie Monaghan before the world finds out there's more than one kind of magic and the other one will eat you alive."

CHAPTER FOUR

Leira parked the green Mustang near the front of Estelle's and headed for the gate, ignoring the gaggle of college students standing outside laughing and flirting with each other. A girl in a dark blue Jimmie Vaughan t-shirt and a hoodie gave a tall, skinny guy in a long-sleeved polo shirt a push against his shoulder. He laughed and stuck his hands deep in his jean's pockets. Leira paused by the gate and watched them. She pulled in a small amount of magic, just enough to surround them in the energy. A feeling of goodwill swirled around them as the young man reached out for the girl's hand.

Just behind them, a broad-shouldered man wearing a UT football sweatshirt stepped back, looking around till he spotted Leira by the gate. He gave a crooked smile and a two-fingered salute to her, shading his eyes just long enough to let them glow so she could see them.

Leira's eyebrows went up, wrinkling her forehead in surprise. *We're everywhere.* She gave a small nod and unlatched the gate, heading for the guest house as she looked to the left and saw Craig and Mike tending a small grill near the corn hole toss. Cassidy was standing behind them with a plate full of hamburger patties as Kimberly sipped from a tall neck beer in one hand and held out a spatula in the other.

"Leira!" A general cheer went up from all the regulars as everyone else on the patio turned to see who was causing the commotion.

Curiosity got the better of her and Leira steered away from the path toward her front door and wandered over to the grill.

"Before you say anything, Estelle already knows we're cooking our own food right behind her restaurant. We paid her a banquet fee, I think she called it. Settle down, Lemon!" Mitzi held on to the fidgeting schnauzer. "She's dying to help!"

"Special occasion?" Leira looked at the people gathered at several tables, all watching Mike and Craig fiddling with the grill.

"Not really," said Janice, putting silverware in front of each person. "We decided to start our own Meetup. We call ourselves, *What the Fork*," she chirped.

"Estelle came up with the name. There's t-shirts in the works." Scott passed a pile of paper napkins down the line. "Paul wanted to call us the Cuddle Party..."

"So, Estelle basically rescued us from the ridiculous..."

"And before we went further down the rabbit hole."

"I think I have enough t-shirts now to make a fairly good-sized quilt."

"You staying for a burger? We have two kinds of cheese and a few sides."

"Estelle made those. She said some of this dinner actually had to come from the restaurant."

A Catahoula dog barked sharply, looking through the slats on the fence from the bar next door. Lemon squirmed in Mitzi's arms, whining to be let down.

Leira looked at the three tables full of people. "Looks like you already have some new recruits."

"Yeah, who knew?" Cassidy rested the edge of the platter on a table.

A woman with short brown hair and bangs raised her hand. "Hi, I'm Micky. I live in Pflugerville by way of London," she said in a heavy accent.

Cassidy pointed to the man next to Micky. "That's Peter and next to him is Daniel. Oh geez, I can't remember the names of those guys. You'll have to introduce yourself. Hey, you guys are taking too long. It's charcoal and lighter fluid. How hard can this be?"

"You have to set up the charcoal in a very specific pile or things don't cook evenly." Craig nudged a briquette onto the top of a small pyramid. To the right of it was a similar tower of charcoal.

"Why do men always see anything with fire as an Olympic event? Anyone need another beer?" Kimberly got up, counting the number of hands raised.

Mike dropped a match into the grill as a great *whoosh* arose and the fire flamed into a large ball, up and out pushing the two men back on their heels.

"Anyone lose an eyebrow?" Leira did her best to hide her smile, not too worried about who might see it.

Craig turned around, sheepish, smoke swirling around him. "I think I smell burning hair."

"Bout time you trimmed those nose hairs, however you had to do it." Estelle let out a short laugh as she brought out a large bowl of vinegar coleslaw. Her arms were barely long enough to wrap around the bowl and the cigarette in her mouth jiggled dangerously over the open container. Her cat-eye reading glasses hung from an amber-colored beaded necklace scraping against the outside of the bowl. She let the dish down heavily on the nearest table and stood up, her hands on her hips. "Get this show on the road or take it elsewhere." A fly buzzed near her face and she snatched it out of the air with a quick swoop, throwing it into the air toward the fence. It flew off, making woozy loops, bobbing up and down toward the next yard. "You boys have been playing with the fire long enough."

"What she said." Cassidy stepped toward the grill and Kimberly scooped up the hamburgers from the platter with the spatula, lining them in neat rows. Estelle kept watch from a distance, giving a wink to Leira as she blew smoke out the side of her mouth without ever taking out the cigarette. Leira gave her a crooked smile in return as her phone buzzed in her pocket. She pulled it out and saw a text from General Anderson.

"Looks like I'm going to have to take a pass. Work calls but save me a burger or two, would you?"

"I'll put 'em in the restaurant fridge. You can fetch them later." Estelle was sticking to her own rule of no one going into Leira's place when she wasn't there. She blew out a perfect smoke ring and went back behind the bar.

Leira waved to everyone as another communal shout of "Leira!" went up from the crowd. Even Micky joined in, raising her glass as she shouted.

Leira held the phone up to her ear. "General? Is there a disturbance in the force?"

"I'm surprised I don't hear that joke more often. Like twice a day instead of just the once." The general sounded like he was in his usual mood. All business.

Okay, so something may be blowing up, but the casualties are low. "How about just hello, then."

"Don't mean to bark at you. Time is of the essence and it's the damndest thing. You are perfectly situated to handle this one. What they're calling a sinkhole has opened up in the middle of a subdivision in Round Rock, right near you."

"But I take it, not really a sinkhole." Leira opened her door and went in, dropping her purse on the red velvet upholstered chair by the door. The troll was sitting on the couch watching *Batman Begins*. He was on his feet, gasping and leaning forward as the caped crusader drove through the streets of Gotham. "Scarecrow!" He chirped excitedly.

Leira put a finger to her lips trying to quiet him down but he wasn't paying her any attention. "Some furry dude. No, excuse me, general, unrelated." Leira went into the kitchen and balanced the phone under her chin as she started to make coffee. Almost instinctively, her eyes lit up with a glow as energy pulled in from her feet and the phone moved away from her chin and bobbled in the air, hovering near her ear. *The magic is working for me before I have to think of it. This is new.* The bracelet on her wrist warmed against her skin. *Interesting.*

The sound of the general's voice snapped her out of her observations.

"No, not a sinkhole. Not even a little. Turns out there's

a cave underneath someone's rancher. A main room and two side rooms carved out of the limestone. Looks to be thousands of years old, at least. Maybe older."

"Artifacts in my backyard, practically. Makes the commute easier."

"Better hurry. The sinkhole's all over the news and someone's bound to get curious. Agent Hagan is already on his way and will meet you there."

CHAPTER FIVE

Leira didn't waste any time heading back out the door, scooping out troll kibble from the giant Costco bag as she went. She put it in a bowl and set it down next to Yumfuck as she passed through the living room. He blew her a raspberry and cheered, settling down in the middle of the bowl, and popping back to the edge the next second as the action picked back up in the movie.

"Don't know how late I'll be. Tell Correk when you see him." Leira slid into her favorite leather jacket, ignoring the PDA jacket hanging next to it. *Maybe next time.*

"Aloha motherfucker!" chirped the troll, stuffing his cheeks full of food.

"Use your words."

"Have a fucking nice day!" He let out a cackle.

"See? Isn't that better?"

The troll laughed and rolled over, opening his mouth as he pushed through the kibble he had just been sitting on.

"You really will eat anything."

The troll let out another cackle, spitting out some of the small nuggets as he stood up and balanced on the lip, letting himself fall backward into the bowl.

She scooped up her purse and quickly slid out the door, opening it just enough to get through so no one would see kibble flying into the air behind her.

Mike held up his beer and shouted "Leira" as Estelle aimed a plastic top at his head.

"What? How is anybody supposed to know when it's okay to yell hello?"

"It's an instinct thing, my man." Craig slapped him on the back and picked up the top, tossing it back to Estelle who was perched on her stool behind the bar. "You gotta feel it in here," he said, tapping his chest while holding a Shiner Bock with three fingers.

Leira kept moving, quickly going through the gate and heading for her car. She had the coordinates for the neighborhood and briefly thought about trying a portal but quickly realized that could make a small problem worse if she managed to tear a hole in the veil so close to home by trying to open a portal to move around Earth. "Let's not piss off the Silver Griffins just yet, Leira. There's still some daylight left and a cave to get to."

She opened the door to the Mustang, narrowly avoiding a wiry man on a bike wearing a cropped top and cut off jean shorts despite the cooler temperature. "Damn crotch rocket!" The rider turned around and gave her the finger, smiling through missing front teeth.

"Nice." For just a moment she missed being on the police force. Leira took in a deep breath and blew it out as the jewel on her bracelet lit up. "Not going over the top for a dude on a Schwinn." She slid into the car and pulled out of the space, running the lights and sirens all the way to the scene.

As she pulled up, she saw Hagan talking to the home-owner, his narrow notebook in hand. He looked up, arching an eyebrow as she cut the siren and pulled into a spot along the curb. She got out and saw the yellow caution tape around a hole in the sidewalk that closely resembled the shape of a coffin. Leira went to the edge of the tape, leaning in to get a better look and could see that the bottom was too far down to easily glimpse.

"Thank you, I'll let you know if I have more questions." Hagan shoved the notebook into his coat pocket and ambled over beside Leira. "Not exactly legal using the lights on the local blacktops."

"Not exactly illegal, either. Anderson said this was a rush job. Something about an actual man cave."

Hagan chortled. "Damndest thing. Homeowner still thinks it's a sinkhole and is worried how much of it will gobble up her house. They sent down a spycam and by the looks of it, I'd say maybe a quarter of her yard."

"The builder had to have noticed the large hole when they put in the pipes."

"Noticed, probably and decided to move that problem onto someone else's calendar. Pretty sure he had no idea it was more than a hole in the ground. Not much to look at but if you can see inside it becomes obvious pretty fast that it's man made. Well... Elven made or Wizard or some other magical creature." Hagan waggled his fingers in the air.

"No more magic hands today, okay? Ready to go down inside?"

"Just like that? Sure, why not. I've had my coffee. Let's get to it and do a little spelunking. What could go wrong?"

"Knew you were up for it."

"Itching to go. Can check this off my bucket list if I had one."

"Anyone have a ladder we can put in the hole?"

"Funny you should ask. Tricky part will be holding the ladder up and not letting it rest against the sides. I'm told that will stress the top of the cave we like to call the sidewalk." Hagan patted his belly. "Of course, they may have only been referring to me." Hagan waved to the three-man crew in orange helmets standing in the street nearby with a tall aluminum ladder. "Fellas, it's show time. Like we practiced. No slip ups. This one's tough as nails but I'm more delicate and too close to retirement for shenanigans."

Hagan swung his leg over the side, grumbling as the ladder wobbled. "Son of a bitch, this would be easier if you fellas didn't shake quite so much. I'm the one going down in the hole."

"Might want to cut back on the coffee next time, Hagan." Leira put a finger against the ladder, sending a pulse of energy to steady it.

Hagan disappeared down into the hole muttering, "Yeah, it's the coffee that's to blame."

Leira watched him disappear further down the hole. "Have you hit bottom yet?"

"Almost..." Hagan's voice echoed up faintly from the bottom. "Well, I'll be. Get yourself down here, Berens. You will not believe it."

"Thought you'd never ask." Leira swung a leg over and neatly maneuvered down the ladder. Toward the bottom Hagan was waiting with a small flashlight, shining it on the different walls. The pale light showed niches cut into the walls and a long, wide shelf big enough to be a bed. "Looks like early Elf."

"You really think there was such a thing?"

"No idea. Let's get what we came for if there's anything here and get out. If there's company coming, I'd like for us to be long gone. Cut down on the suburban mayhem."

"Let's try the two rooms. See if anything shakes out on its own. Otherwise this will take a magical assist." Hagan shone the light in the direction of the opening to another room. The room was bare except for another carving cut into the wall. "So far we're coming up bupkis."

Leira followed him into the last room, smaller than the others as the ground shook beneath their feet. Hagan dropped the flashlight and it rolled along the ground sending shadows spinning along the wall, catching the light on something shiny embedded near the top of a corner. "What was that?"

"I saw that too." Leira kept her focus on where she saw the glimmer and moved closer even as the ground shook again.

"Please tell me that if this thing caves in you'll be able to magic us out of here. Buried alive was not one of the options I saw for dying." Hagan scrambled to the flashlight and picked it up, shining it across the wall till it picked up the shimmer again. "Bullet, maybe, but not a cave in." He pulled out his cotton handkerchief and wiped his face.

Leira got up on her toes and scratched at the rock with

her fingernail, exposing more of what was buried in the rock. "It's some kind of metal. Not gold, exactly." She felt the hum of her bracelet against her skin. *Jackpot.* "I think we have a winner." The ground shook even harder under their feet. "What the fuck is that? It's shaking from the top down."

"No telling. Our competitors may be arriving on the scene in something heavy. Better speed this up any way you can. What? I think we both know this part is all you. I'll hold the flashlight and tell myself I'm a necessary part of this operation."

"You can buy the coffee later."

"Deal."

Leira shut her eyes and focused, pulling in energy and setting an idea in motion. *Remove the artifact without destroying the cave.* She could feel the energy coming in through her feet and spreading up her legs and through her spine, out into her arms. Symbols lit up along her skin, flipping over as she took in a long, slow breath. The stone in the center of the bracelet began to hum, turning to liquid as it spun in a whirl inside the setting.

"Never ceases to be an eye catcher." Hagan stood back, watching in awe as the settled dirt and stone around the artifact began to spill out into the room, exposing the oil lamp. "Well, fuck me. At long last, we have Aladdin's lamp. About time something like that showed up. Where do you think the flying carpet is buried?" The ground shook violently beneath them, knocking Hagan off his feet as Leira held steady, rising barely an inch off the ground.

"Looks like your people did their flying without the rug," said Hagan as he mustered back to his feet as fast as he could, brushing off his pants. "Might want to hurry it along there, Berens. Whatever is making the ground shake, it's getting worse. Time to go. Tell me you can hear me inside that magical mystery tour you got going on."

Leira reached out for the brass oil lamp even as the magic flowed through her and pulled it in close. The moment her hands touched it she shot across the room, her back hitting the opposite wall, knocking the wind and the magic right out of her. She fell to her knees, the symbols fading as she gasped for air, the lamp still clutched against her chest.

"What the... Are you okay?" The ground shook again as Hagan made his way over to Leira, his arms out to steady himself. "Definitely time to go." He held out his hand to help her up but Leira gave him her best dead fish look. "So, you're okay, then," he said.

Leira sprang to her feet, hustling toward the ladder that was left leaning against the opening at the top.

Hagan followed closely behind her to hold the ladder, brushing a hand against the wall just in case. "You go first. No need to make it personal. I get it. You're the more nimble of the two of us. Damn doughnuts..."

Leira got to the bottom of the opening and looked up to see no one waiting at the top. She came back down far enough to see Hagan. "Wait here. I'll figure out a way to steady the ladder for you."

"I'll hold onto things for you on this end. What is that noise?" They both looked up and saw dirt and paper swirling overhead in the wind. Hagan grabbed Leira by the arm, his voice stern. "Be careful up there." He let go and grabbed both sides of the ladder, standing on the bottom as he held it away from the edge for her.

Leira tucked the lamp inside of her jacket and zipped it up as she let out a breath and let the energy flow through her, setting an intention. *Lighter than air.* She easily went up each step, rapidly getting to the top, shielding her face against the windstorm with her hand. No one was left standing nearby. Small pellets hit her skin, digging in as she tried to get a look at the landscape. In the distance, at the end of the block she saw a familiar figure just beyond the swirling maelstrom, standing all by himself.

A silver-haired Wizard in a long coat was directing pulsating waves of energy toward the hole. *How the hell did you get away from the Dark Mist?*

Leira rolled out of the hole and across the ground, taking a chance the top would hold. She scrambled to her feet and knelt down by the opening, pushing the edges of the ladder away from the crumbling ground. Set an intention. *Let the ladder stand on its own.* Leira tested it, lightly removing her hands as the ladder held. "Hurry!" She glanced to the right, squinting into the wind as she saw the Wizard slowly approaching them.

Hagan took each step as quickly as he could, grunting as he got to the top and reached for the edge, crawling the rest of the way on his hands and knees. He was pressing his lips together against the dust storm, shielding his face as he pulled his white undershirt up to cover his nose. "We're not in Kansas anymore. Like we went down a hole and landed in Odessa." He was shouting over the roar of the wind.

"Look who's joined us. We need to get out of here." Leira shouted as she pointed down the street. The Wizard was getting closer and she could see the determined look on his face. She didn't want to tangle with him again. Her powers may have grown but his skill set still outmatched hers and they were on what was supposed to be a quiet suburban street. A war of fireballs would be difficult to explain to the neighbors.

The Wizard got close enough that Leira could see the jagged scar on his cheek from Patsy's gold thorns. The pupils of his eyes were deep pools of black that sent a shudder through Leira.

"Motherfucker! The Dark Mist is inside the son of a bitch," she growled. "We may have to make a run for it. Get behind me." Leira pushed against the wind till she was standing upright, her hair blowing straight back.

"Not a good goddamn chance in hell!" Hagan got as far as a crouch and drew his gun, shooting straight at the Wizard. Just as the bullet penetrated his skin it turned to liquid, sliding down the front, leaving only the barest impression.

Hagan dropped his arm, tucking his gun away as he pushed against the wind to stand. "Running it is. You think the troll knows we're fucked right about now?"

Leira put her hand on the bracelet, ready to take it off if it came to that and take her chances on her own energy. *Better than dying at the hands of the Dark Mist... or worse.* The wind pushed against her and she summoned all the energy she could through her feet with the bracelet still in place. Symbols flashed across her arms, quickly sliding up her neck. *Set an intention, Leira. Do it.* A thought occurred to her, left over from the battle on the top of Enchanted Rock. *Send me the* strength of all the women in my line. Push back against this force.

Hagan found his way beside her and got out his old weighted black leather blackjack, ready to fight.

The Wizard's face contorted into a wide grin.

So there's still something left of the asshole inside. Leira felt her mother's energy join alongside her own and it wasn't long before Mara's pulsed down the other side. Leira formed a ball of fiery blue light bouncing between her hands. She looked up at the Wizard and opened her hands wider. "Go where you're needed," she whispered.

The ball shot out in a streak, leaving a sparkling trail behind it and slammed straight into the Wizard, knocking him backward onto the ground. A trail of black mist leaked out of his head and down the back of his body. The wind slowed down around Leira and the roar subsided, leaving a calm she knew wouldn't last. *Round one to me.*

The Wizard got back to his feet, anger across his face as he moved his hands in different directions.

"I thought he needed a wand to pull off any tricks." Hagan held his ground, pulling his undershirt down from his face.

"I don't think he's calling all the shots anymore."

"Fuck me, the magical walking dead. Wizard zombie!"

The black swirl grew around the Wizard almost engulfing him as he crept toward Leira. She put out her hands and sent out waves of energy pushing him back. *Much closer and I'm taking off this fucking bracelet. No way I'm letting Hagan die here.*

Only a few yards separated the two as Leira pushed as much energy as she could against the darkness coming at them. *If it's the last good thing I do...* She reached over to remove the bracelet but felt herself lift off the ground as her back arched, a blast of energy pouring through her back, taking her up on her toes, exiting through the scar on her belly, and pouring out in front of her. The artifact tucked inside of her jacket rattled, burning her skin.

Leira knew at once who it was. "Dad..." Her voice came out in a whisper as her eyes widened. The energy slammed into the Wizard, rolling him end over end down the street. Leira's energy combined with her father's and pelted the Wizard, holding him against the ground as the black mist grew to cover him entirely until it absorbed him into itself, disappearing in a sudden gust into the void.

Hagan and Leira were left standing alone on the street. Hagan blinked a few times, looking around at the quiet street. "I don't think anything was even broken. Usually we manage to bust up a few things at least."

"This will still be tricky to explain." The stone in the bracelet had stopped swirling and solidified again. *Explain to Jackson, for instance. No way he knew what I was thinking...* Leira shook her head and unzipped her jacket slowly, taking out the lamp. She pulled her shirt gently away from her skin and looked at the small blisters along one side of her chest. "Note to self. Don't put artifacts near skin in a battle." She winced as she let go of her shirt, holding out the lamp by the curved brass handle, just in case.

"That was some kind of magic show you pulled off there in the..." Hagan was cut off by a black tentacle wrapping around his ankle, pulling him off his feet and slamming him against the ground, rattling his teeth. More tentacles filled the street, wrapping themselves around

Leira's ankles as others climbed higher, snatching the lamp from her grasp.

"Katie..." hissed Leira, angry with herself for letting her guard down too soon.

The black tentacles surrounded the lamp, carrying it along the ground, scurrying back to their owner. Katie came around the side of a white stone rancher as the tentacles came crawling up her leg, leaving the lamp in her hands as they climbed higher, reattaching themselves to her head. "Makes you sorry you're not an Atlantean, doesn't it? No hard feelings?" she said, walking closer. "This is better off in the Silver Griffins vault, anyway? You have to see the sense that makes? That way no one gets to play with the toy?"

The blackjack flew through the air and hit her neatly on the side of the head, knocking her clean out. The artifact bounced along the road, making a loud, rattling noise before it came to a rest.

"Really tired of getting knocked to my knees by anyone." Hagan walked calmly over and retrieved his blackjack, checking on Katie to make sure she was alright. "That's gonna leave a nice goose egg for a bit." He looked down at her unconscious body. There was a small trickle of blood along the side of his head. "Think about that the next time you send your smarmy pets out."

Leira gave Hagan a crooked smile and went to retrieve the lamp. "Told you, you are necessary. Nice throw back there. All those dart games really paid off."

"It's my eating arm. I keep the muscle toned. Do we leave her here or drag her with us?"

Leira heard the sound of cars approaching and saw the

familiar fleet of minivans. "We leave her this time. Her cavalry is on the way and it's best if we don't get into a spitting contest over this thing. Come on, let's ride. For once, we got the damned artifact."

"Wonder what it does."

"Let's leave that for another day."

"I have a government car here." Hagan glanced back at the Chevy as Leira pinged him with a small pebble of a fireball.

"Ow! Right, let's go. I'll get it later. They can tow it away."

Leira and Hagan sprinted for the Mustang, getting in as fast as they could as Leira gunned the engine and took off down the street in the opposite direction, away from the Silver Griffins approaching minivans. She looked in her rear view mirror as they came to a stop. "Let them do the *never was, never will be* this time."

"What's *that* spell?"

"Really handy. Call the general and let him know the artifact is secure. Let's leave out the part about the dark mist for now. That one's going to take some investigation. Something wicked this way is coming."

"Don't do that. That's not funny. Too much spooky magic." Hagan waggled his fingers.

"I'm going to let that magic hands go but only because you're bleeding, Hagan. We're making a stop at the hospital. No arguments. Rose would take me out if I let something happen to you. I'll get you doughnuts on the way."

"At the very least. I'll wait in the car with the magic lamp and try out a few wishes."

"Deal and don't do that. Just in case. I don't want to come back and find a frog where you're sitting."

Hagan looked at her, surprised. "You think that could actually happen? What am I saying? What hasn't happened? Don't answer that one either. Go get my doughnuts. I'll keep my mitts to myself."

CHAPTER SIX

"You think he's passed out?"

The two hikers stood over Peyton from a short distance, one of them adjusting the straps on his backpack.

"I don't know. He looks like he might be hurt. Maybe we should call someone."

Peyton stirred, stretching out his legs, dunking a foot in the cold waters of Onion Creek, jarring him awake. "Where?" His voice came out in a confused snarl.

"Dig those pointed ears and those suede pants. Was there a Renaissance fair out here?"

"I would have loved to have seen that. Dude, are you okay?"

Peyton muttered incoherently, sitting up on an elbow, blue electric lines still dancing around his body. His magic grew even more unstable, seeking out places to ground itself, circling back through Peyton. He rocked back his head, crying out in pain and pushed himself to his feet, throwing his arms over his head.

"Whoa, what was that?" One of the hikers watched his

phone flicker off and restart. Lights dimmed near the park office and cars stalled out in the parking lot.

"We need to go. We can send back help." He pulled on his friend's arm. "Let's go!"

Peyton shook his arms again, the energy circling around him, bathing his face in a blue light. The brownout rolled through again, cutting off power to nearby houses, making residents look up for a moment, puzzled as the power came back on again.

He stumbled forward, batting at his head as if there were flies buzzing around him, trying to run from the energy that was following him everywhere, disappearing into the park in the direction of downtown Austin.

Jackson was waiting for Leira when she finally made it home. He was sitting at a table just outside the guest house, slouched down with his foot resting on his other knee, sipping an Independence amber beer. He was still dressed in his tall boots, leather pants and tunic, his hair tied back in a leather tie.

Leira hesitated for a moment when she saw him, glancing toward the bar. Estelle was standing behind the bar waiting on a bridal shower, pouring shots.

"Your barkeep put this down in front of me and walked off. Amazing powers."

"She's not magical."

"Agree to disagree. Have you tasted this beer?" He held it up before taking it back for another large sip. "Own kind of magic, knowing what a man wants to drink."

Leira walked by him to the door of the guest house. "You might as well come in. You can bring the beer. We'll return the glass later."

"Privileges of being family, I suppose."

"Don't push it."

Jackson followed Leira into the guest house as she dropped her purse onto the red velvet chair and carefully unzipped her jacket on the way to the kitchen. The troll was tucked into his shoebox with a pair of blue panties tucked under his chin, fast asleep. *I'll bet that battle wore him out on this end.* Correk was nowhere to be seen.

"Troll's asleep early. What do you think that's about?" Jackson took a seat at the kitchen table and watched Leira peel off her jacket. She had left the artifact safely locked away at work before dropping off Hagan. He had gotten out of the car with a yawn, excited to tell Rose about the cave. Leira watched his face light up as Rose opened the front door and felt a pang inside her chest followed by a wince from the blisters.

She draped her jacket over the back of a chair and sat down, folding her hands on the table. The bracelet banged against the wood, the light catching the stone. "How you want to do this?"

"Some of that stubbornness you get from me." He finished off his beer and set the glass down carefully. "It's written in our DNA. You can't tell me what to do. That can be an asset and a chain around your neck, depending on the situation you find yourself in. Today it was a chain." His eyes were half closed, and his chin was raised.

"I appreciate your help."

"Not talking about that but you're welcome. I don't

expect you to think of me first, especially in tight corners. Not yet, anyway. Maybe someday you will." He pointed a finger at Leira, sitting forward in the chair. "And you know what we're talking about here. You had no business even thinking about taking off that damn bracelet." The last words came out choked and his eyes shined. "I'll be damned if I wait twenty-five years to meet you only to watch you get pulled away." He was fighting hard to keep in control. "Shouldn't have to go through something like that twice in a lifetime."

Leira opened her mouth to say something and thought better of it, letting the air hang empty between them for a moment.

Jackson pressed his hands flat against the table.

"I'm sorry," Leira finally said. "I was thinking about my partner..."

Jackson slid his hand across the table, resting it heavily on top of Leira's hand. "You know, I've done a lot of things wrong in my life because I was too stubborn to just ask for help. I wanted to prove something that didn't need proving way too often. I can't change any of that but for once I can honestly say I'm glad to be a Jasper Elf because it means I have hundreds of years left to at least get this right. To be some kind of father to you, if you'll let me." He stuttered, getting out the last words. "If... if you want me to."

So many questions rolled through Leira's mind. But in the end, all she said was, "Sure."

"Then you have to promise me you'll do what it takes to stay here on this side of the veil... with me... and give me a chance."

A tear rolled down Leira's cheek and she brushed it

away roughly with her other hand. "I'll do my best." She squeezed his hand. "I'm sorry, Dad. I was trying to do the right thing."

Jackson blinked back tears. "That trait you get from your mother."

Leira let out a laugh. *Maybe this is going to be a good thing...*

"The badass you get from both of us."

"Well, of course." She shifted in her chair, pulling her shirt away from her skin. *Have to cut down on the battle wounds one of these days.*

CHAPTER SEVEN

The sun was still rising in the sky when Mara got up, determined to leave before Eireka noticed. There was a growing restlessness inside of her and it was time to take things into her own hands and stop talking to herself about it in the shower. "Time to take it all out of theory and put it into action. Find out what chapter three is supposed to be, Mara."

She dressed quickly, putting on a long dress and soft grey leather boots. She draped a deep blue cloak around her shoulders and tied it at her neck. She pulled her long dark hair back with a silver clip that had a row of pearls and slipped a wide leather bracelet on her wrist that had a small pouch on the inside for a few Oriceran coins. "Not bad for a grandmother." She leaned in peering closer at her face in the bathroom mirror. "Getting preserved in goo for four years had one benefit."

There was a soft tap at the door, and she walked quietly down the metal stairs to the door before the tapping could disturb Eireka in the bedroom upstairs. She opened the door and saw no one till she heard the sound of a small raspberry coming from below and looked down at the welcome mat.

Yumfuck gave her a hearty wave and walked on into the apartment.

"Don't feel the need to wait for an invitation."

"Works for me," he chirped. He hopped up on their couch and clapped his hands together. "Tell my future."

"Dim if you don't get out of here. I have things to do."

Yumfuck smiled, showing his tiny razor-sharp teeth and gave the once over to Mara's clothes. He arched an eyebrow and crossed his little arms over his chest. "Take me with you."

"Take you where?"

"Don't kid a kidder. Remember, I know what you've been doing. Take me with you to Oriceran or I start singing. Loud." He opened his mouth wide and took in a deep breath.

"Done!" Mara hissed, holding up her hands and looking up the stairs. Eireka would have too many questions that Mara couldn't answer yet. She had caused enough trouble lately. *Better to gather some information first and then spill the beans.* "If you're coming, come on."

The troll scrambled down the side of the couch and ran into the narrow kitchen.

"Wrong direction. Oh, I see. Road trip snacks, of course. Leira won't drive outside the city limits without them."

The troll came back with a plastic grocery bag and a large bag of Cheetos, a sleeve of peanut butter Do-Si-Dos and a few Twinkies inside.

"Okay, ready." He ran over to Mara and she scooped

him up and put him on her shoulder, forming a sparkling ball of light between her hands. The portal opened in their small living room shining the morning light as small yellow birds with black stripes down their backs sang on a nearby branch. "Here we go!"

The troll hung on to Mara's clothing as she stepped through the portal and onto the soft, damp moss of the Dark Forest. A large animal trumpeted somewhere deep in the forest and a monkey swung overhead, quickly passing out of sight. "I miss being in the middle of this forest all the time."

"Me too." The troll stood up on her shoulder and looked around, breathing in the deep air, his hands on his chest.

"Leira know you went out?"

"In a manner of speaking..."

"So she knew when she saw you weren't in your nest or on the couch or buried in the pantry in the kitchen." Mara let out a short sigh. "At this point, I suppose that's okay."

"She went out of town on assignment. We're good!" He held up his tiny paw for a high-five. "Down low! Too slow..." He let out a cackle and settled down on her shoulder, hanging on as Mara walked through the woods.

"Didn't know the leash on a bond was this long." Mara made her way through the forest following a familiar path. The floating Light Elves castle hung in the distance, a deep blue sky overhead. Spring had arrived on Oriceran and the wildflowers were in full bloom across patches of the forest where the sun broke through the green canopy. Red poppies sprung between large tree roots and small daffodils lined the path. A young rabbit hopped across the path and disappeared into the thick underbrush as a larger doe jumped, easily crossing over behind them.

"It's an inside thing." He beat a little paw on his chest. "Leira is a Jasper Elf. Her magic can travel across the veil. I can travel here without straining the bond."

Mara lifted the troll off her shoulder and held him in her palm where she could see his face. "You've been missing home."

The troll gave a shrug. "It happens. I've gotten little tastes of the place lately. Made it even harder."

She put him back on her shoulder and kept walking, anxious to get to her destination. "I'll drop you at the edge of the forest near the old oak trees. Thousands of your cousins are going to be thrilled to see you."

It felt good to hike through the forest and listen to the tall pines creak in the gentle wind. *Feels good to be doing more... at last!* She got to the edge of the forest and looked up at the castle, the tall spires partially hidden by clouds. "The parties I've been to in that castle, Yumfuck! The dancing went on all night..."

The troll let out a soft trill. "I'm not the only one who needed to come home for a hot minute."

A bronze staircase popped out of the side of the castle and grew, spiraling toward the ground and a young Elven woman with long silver hair came out of one of the lower floors to the ground, heading for the royal gardens, passing right by Mara and the troll.

"Ossonia, it is you."

Ossonia stopped in her tracks and turned, surprised to see Mara. A look of pain and disappointment flittered across her face. A reminder of Correk's absence. "Mara, you're here." She opened her arms to greet her old friend, despite the longing, and smiled, wrapping her in a warm hug. She shut her eyes and held tight for a moment. *Be grateful for the visit. Stay present.* Ossonia stood back, her hands still on Mara's arms. "You look well."

"Getting out of the world in between has done wonders for me." They both laughed easily. "That gelatin I waded through for four years was great for my complexion."

"I'm going to have to take a pass on that one. I'll just stick with magic elixirs from the local Gnome apothecary." Ossonia smiled more easily, the heavy feeling easing from her chest but not before Mara noticed. "It is good to see you, Mara. What brings you to Oriceran?"

"I'm in search of a purpose. I know... kind of a big topic." She shook her head as the troll sat down and let out a sigh, resting his chin on his paw.

"Don't mind me. Just settling in here."

Mara arched an eyebrow. "Hang on, Ossonia. This is somebody's bus stop." She gently lifted the troll off her shoulder and held him in front of her face. "Can you make it from here?"

"No problem!"

"Meet me back here by the time the sun is straight over-head. That give you enough time to say hello to everyone?"

The troll considered it, waggling his paw. "Just about..."

"If I have to go back without you and Leira comes looking for you..."

The troll made a small 'o' with his mouth and let out a cackle. "I'll be standing where I belong. Between you and the people of Gotham."

"Where's Gotham?" asked Ossonia.

"In his fevered little head. Last week he was into reality shows. I'm guessing this week is superheroes and Batman's on deck. It's an Earth thing. They like to make up stories about human beings who have special powers and run around saving people. It's like some part of them remembers there was magic on their world at some point, but they can't quite put their finger on it... yet."

Mara set the troll on the ground and watched him scurry away, into the large ferns. The occasional leaves rustled, and a crow took to the air, letting out a loud *caw*, as Yumfuck made progress on his hike to his village. Mara smiled and looked back at Ossonia who was looking down the path toward the post office.

"I don't want to keep you. I have places to be as well and not a lot of time." On an impulse, Mara grabbed Ossonia's hand and grasped it between her own. "Can I tell you what I'm doing? I'm in search of a new story for myself. I need something to do that gets me excited in the morning and wears me out by bedtime. Frankly, I wouldn't mind if I stumbled over a hunky Elf on the way."

Ossonia looked confused and glanced down the path again.

Mara let out a deep breath she didn't realize she was holding. "I do a lot better at these things when I don't try to be subtle. It's not my strong suit. You're a little younger than I am but not by much. Time to move on with things. Correk may come back, he may not."

Ossonia tried to pull her hand away but Mara held on tight. "I wish someone had said something like this to me when I was younger. Hell, I'm a lot more stubborn than you, though. Probably wouldn't have listened, and for all I know someone did..."

"May have even been me," Ossonia said softly.

Mara let out a loud laugh. "Well, there you go. I'll share this gift with you. We need to create something new for ourselves and stop standing on one foot, waiting around. I need more good ideas in my life before I start looking around at what others are up to."

"You mean, like now?" Ossonia smiled.

Mara tilted her head to one side, sizing up Ossonia. "You're on the way to the post office, aren't you? At the beck and call of the prophets. Is that really what you want? I seem to remember a slightly wilder version of you, and that Elf had big plans for herself. Weren't you a painter? The animals leaped off your paintings... literally."

"That was a good hundred years ago. I'm not sure..."

"Like riding a bike. Never mind. Like floating just above the ground." Mara let the magic on Oriceran lift her off the ground. "If you let it flow through you and don't think too hard, a lot of good things happen." Mara let go of Ossonia's hand. "We're Elven women. We are strong, creative, magical beings." She leaned in closer. "Time to get on with things. I'm off to see the Gnomes about an idea." Mara hugged Ossonia again. "Not really sure where it's going to lead but it's a start to somewhere."

Mara wrapped her cloak around her shoulders tighter and waved goodbye, headed for the castle and the library. "If I can survive the world in between, I can talk some Gnomes into a little help."

Ossonia watched her march determined up the path. A silvery blue butterfly landed on her hand, gently batting its wings. "She's right, you know. I've been telling myself to wait just a little longer for some kind of sign. Didn't think my sign would be Mara Berens." She lifted her hand as the butterfly flew off, letting the wind carry it along. "I can let go and start something new."

CHAPTER EIGHT

Yumfuck Tiberius Troll ran as fast as he could, tumbling over tree roots and pulling at flower petals, breathing in their perfume, happy to be back on Oriceran. He got to the edge of his village and stopped, taking it all in. There were the houses carved out of the sturdiest tall mushrooms, lined in row upon row for as far as he could see. Old stumps had windows carved into them and front doors and were packed with trolls living inside of them, all nestled together.

A nearby troll was busy shaking out a yellow piece of a forgotten Elven dish cloth and another was sitting at a table outside of his home, smoking on a long pipe made from a hollow reed. Two trolls were bartering with each other, happily trading pea pods for corn kernels, helping each other load up their tiny wagons. Most of the trolls were rolling over each other, playing in the tall grass, cackling and trilling under the warm sun.

"Aloha motherfuckers!" Yumfuck waved his arms over his head. "ET came home!"

Every tiny, head topped with colorful green or pink or yellow fur turned at the sound of his voice, looking in his direction. For a moment, the air hung still, and the only sound was a catbird, meowing in the trees in the distance. At last, a gasp rolled through the village as everyone recognized Yumfuck and a loud chorus of "Aloha motherfuckers!" rose from the village loud enough to carry to the nearby path.

An Elf on his way to the post office looked over the field but saw nothing. "Wonder what that was about..." He shook his head and kept going, anxious to pick up a package from the gargoyles.

Yumfuck was quickly surrounded by trolls, all talking at once, taking turns hugging him and squeezing his arms, kissing his head. Yumfuck smiled till his face hurt. "Joy, joy, joy, joy," was all he could get out.

"Is it you?"

Yumfuck stood on his tiptoes to see above the trolls in front of him. "Who said that?" His heart was beating faster as everyone parted, making an opening in front of him. "Mama! I'm home!" The small, round troll with yellow fur standing straight up on the top of her head, clutched her paws to her chest. She sung out a lilting trill. Yumfuck took a slow cautious step toward her till he was standing right in front of her.

The troll took her paws and put them on either side of Yumfuck's face, squeezing his cheeks. "You've come back for a visit! Your siblings will be so happy to see you!"

She curled her tongue, sending out a series of different trills and more trolls appeared, filling the little lane. "Look who came back to see us!"

"What's it like on the other world?"

"Is that Elf as much fun as she looked?"

"Do you go on any adventures?"

"Has anyone figured out how much you know about plants, yet?"

"Have you seen any other trolls on Earth?"

"What's the food like there?"

"What's a motherfucker?"

"What's in the bag?"

"I brought presents!" He chirped excitedly.

Yumfuck opened the bag and let everyone take a peek inside. "Earth magic. Behold." He started with the bag of Cheetos, opening the bag with a round *pop*, pausing for dramatic effect as he slowly pulled out a large, flaky orange noodle as his hundred brothers and sisters and all the villagers behind them gasped and ooohed and aaaahed. "It's called a Cheetos and humans on Earth eat it like food."

He held it out gingerly to his mother. "You get the first nibble." Mother troll ducked her chin and smiled, reaching out with both hands to get a good grip on the Cheetos. Orange dust shook off it, floating to the ground. She stuck out her small, pink tongue, giving it a lick. "Yummmm...."

"That's what I said!" He reached into the bag and hauled out a Twinkie still wrapped in clear cellophane. He lifted it over his head triumphantly as everyone cheered, lowering it down to the ground. It was almost the same size as a troll.

Yumfuck pointed a claw and ripped open the cellophane as the smell of sticky, yellow cake wafted through the air. A chorus of "Yummmmmmm....," echoed across the crowd.

"This is called a Twinkie! More Earth style magical food and this one will even last forever! Never goes bad!"

"That is magic," someone gasped.

He broke off a small piece and gave it to his mother. She popped it into her mouth, rolling it around on her tongue, savoring the sweetness before she swallowed it whole.

The other trolls all leaned in toward the Twinkie and the Cheetos, drooling and licking their lips. Yumfuck cackled as his mother said, "Thank you!"

"They have large castles filled with things like this where you can go and pick out what you want and take it home with you." The trolls gasped, some squeezed their eyes shut in delight while others clapped their hands on their furry faces. A few trolls climbed the stems of nearby flowers, sliding out onto the petals as they held on to the stamens so they could get a better look at the food.

At last, he pulled out the plastic sleeve of Do-Si-Dos, neatly ripping off the end and rolling out one of the cookies. "They send out their girl children to sell these things..." A hush went over the crowd. "Everywhere," he whispered, holding up a paw to the side of his mouth. The trolls gasped as one.

He rolled the cookie toward his mother. She was barely visible behind it. Yumfuck put out a paw, getting a swipe of the peanut butter filling and licking it off. His mother imitated what he did, and her eyes grew wide with delight. "Best one yet!" She let out a soft trill ending in a squeal.

Yumfuck waved to two of his brothers. One was a large, muscular troll with bright red hair and the other was just as large with green hair like Yumfuck's. "Help me spread out all the treasures. Today we feast like the Kings and Queens, but better!"

The two large trolls made a circle with the Do-Si-Dos, pouring the Cheetos in a mound in the center. They built a small wall of two by two with the Twinkies and stood back, admiring their work.

"Mama, you give the call," said Yumfuck, letting out a cackle.

Mother Troll clapped her hands together, curling her tongue, smiling broadly as she hesitated, watching everyone holding themselves back. At last, she let out a loud, high-pitched trill and dropped her hands. The other trolls dove in, rolling all over each other, taking licks and swipes and small nibbles of everything. Everyone got to share in the feast.

Minutes later it was all gone, and the trolls went off in search of a soft, warm place to sleep.

Yumfuck sat down on the stoop in front of his mother's mushroom cottage. She came and sat next to him, still licking the creamy filling from a Twinkie off her fur. "Saw you do a straight dive through the middle of one of those, Mama. Nice work. Couldn't have done it better myself." Yumfuck let out a cackle as his mother joined in, settling down next to her son.

"Your dad's taking the youngest thirty of your siblings out on a sleepover deeper in the Dark Forest or he'd be here too. I'll tell him you stopped by. He'll be happy to know you're doing so well." She patted Yumfuck on his knee. "Tell me about where you live. I want all the details to share with your father."

"I live in a large building made of wood that has its own

kitchen and endless supply of food. My nest is a cozy box with a silky, warm blanket and there's something they call T.V. that works like the Light Elves magic. It shows all kinds of adventures over and over again. It never ends," he squeaked, throwing up his arms in delight.

"You landed in paradise!" She squeezed her son around his neck. "You've made this family proud with your bond. Have you taught them anything about what you know? The hibiscus found on Oriceran or the sweet peapods that regenerate?"

"That hasn't come up yet." Yumfuck gave a shrug. "There's time. There's too much to do there. Botany can wait."

His mother tilted her head to the side. "You're letting them think you don't really understand them, aren't you?" Yumfuck gave another shrug and smiled.

His mother let out a loud laugh and fell over on her side. "You always were the prankster. That's a good one. A troll that can't understand. Wuueeee! Now I've heard everything!"

"Let me show you the dance I've learned. Sing something."

His mother trilled a song as Yumfuck turned around, shaking his small bottom, looking over his shoulder with a smile. He put his paws on his knees and shook some more as his mother laughed. "They call it twerking. It's big over there."

"Your father would be amazed! I'll remember to tell him everything." She rocked back, still laughing, clapping her paws. "When you go back to Earth, if you find yourself in Cincinnati, look up your cousin, Earle. He's bonded with a

Wizard. Oooh, or if you go to a place called Charlottesville, Virginia I hear there's an entire village on Afton Mountain. You have a few hundred cousins there by now. Lily's there with her brood. Show them the Twinkies. They'll be amazed! Hey, your cousin, Balzac was almost eaten by a boar in the Dark Forest last month, but he rolled up into a ball and plopped right into an old gopher hole. That was a close one! I tell you kids all the time to keep your ears and eyes open for boars and harpies. Flying skeletons!" His mother's voice softened, and she took her son's face in her paws. "Your cousin Meer stopped by and told me about your heroics. You're a good troll, son."

Yumfuck sat down next to his mother and squeezed her paw. "Love you, Mom."

"Love you, too. I hear that from you kids at least a couple hundred times a day. Never gets old, I tell you. A troll's life is the best thing to be. What a day!"

CHAPTER NINE

Leira walked with General Anderson down H Street in Washington, DC admiring the budding trees. She was wearing a backpack with the brass lamp inside, carefully wrapped in a soft, cotton cloth. The lamp had proved too powerful for any humans to use and the decision was made to move it to a more secure location and the general was entrusting Leira with the shipment. The general could think of only one place that was capable of being the guardian for something he didn't want to see being used by anyone and had reached out to the Silver Griffins.

Lacey Trader was all too happy to oblige and had even offered a safer mode of travel but not till Leira and the general had both been sworn to secrecy and signed an oath to never disclose the location or anything they saw.

The general's curiosity was piqued, and he insisted on seeing her off even though the beginning of the directions explicitly stated the trip was not for the weary, ill or out of shape.

The directions were handwritten on a piece of paper by

a local Witch and handed over to Leira. "No one else is to handle them," said the Witch, giving a hard look at the general who had stood nearby. Human hands will make the letters turn into a jumble. You've been warned."

"I'm part human," she had been quick to say.

The Witch startled and took Leira's hands, holding them for a moment. Leira noticed a tattoo on her wrist of two griffins facing each other. The crest of the Silver Griffins Order.

"No, we're good. You're not over the limit."

Whatever that means. Silver Griffins love them some drama.

They came to the Metro Station on the edge of Chinatown and waited till the flood of people riding up the escalators was passing by them, using the cover to slip inside a plain, brown metal door to the side of the escalators. Leira took out the brass key she'd been given by a Witch in Austin. The handle was in the shape of a three-leaf clover. She was given explicit instructions not to lose it but not to worry. It always returned to its rightful place after a certain amount of time.

Leira quickly unlocked the door, holding it open briefly for the general as they passed through. Leira was certain that no one would pay too much attention to a man in a military uniform going through a side door anywhere in the Capitol.

Inside the small alcove was an old elevator with a heavy, expandable door that Leira shoved at with her shoulder till they were both inside the small compartment. The general glanced up at Leira and said, "It's been real."

"I have assurances this is used all the time." She pushed the one button on the panel and the elevator took off with a whoosh, plummeting several stories. Leira fell back against the wall behind her, clutching the edges of a ledge to keep herself upright. The elevator slowed as it neared the bottom, gently coming to rest as a soft bell echoed, letting them know they were at their stop.

"You have to wonder if the guy who built that thing had a sense of humor or really hated your kind."

"Supposedly he is my kind. You know, part of me is your kind, too." Leira pulled out the piece of paper she'd been given and studied the directions. "We have to take a flight of stairs still and there's a note here not to be worried about any other stairs we see. Not sure what that means... This must be the door to the stairs."

"It's the only door."

"That's what's giving me a high degree of confidence."

They stepped through and found themselves on a small, black metal platform that gave a distinctive creak as they stepped onto it. It was situated high above the ground, several more stories below and was attached to the wall by a series of iron pipes. A system of stairs wound down from it, crisscrossing with other stairs that led off in other directions, disappearing into the darkness.

"Do those directions say which set of stairs?"

"There's something about follow the green dots, not the blue or the yellow and if we find ourselves staring at orange dots, go back. I heard the words, abandoned line and Kilomeas and its own little Dark Market. Not sure, exactly. That was said with some severity. There was also a mention that I would just know if we're on the right track."

The general raised his eyebrows as he looked over at

Leira. "You mean, you'll get a vibe?" He waggled his fingers in the air.

Leira suppressed a laugh with a cough and looked down at the paper as if she was studying it for more details. "The staircases are permanently illuminated from... what does that say?" Leira read it again as her mouth formed an 'o'. "No wonder this place is kept hidden from human beings. She read part of the directions out loud. "The staircases are permanently illuminated from within and are one long, intact artifact created by an earlier chapter of the Silver Griffins dating from the early 20th century." She cleared her throat and looked at the general. "I suppose you understand this is part of that non-disclosure you signed before I brought you here."

"Perfectly understood." The general ventured closer to the edge of the six foot by six foot platform, peering over the edge. "Amazing. No matter how long I live, there's always something that will cause wonderment inside of me. I live for those moments. Too many dark ones that I can't imagine a moment before I behold them." He turned to Leira just as his foot slipped and he stumbled, his hat falling off his head. He caught it in mid-air just before it fell into the vast darkness surrounding the stairs. "That caught my breath for a second. Would have had to just call that one a loss."

"We should get started. You good with this many stairs?"

"I can still pass an army physical," he said, curtly.

Note to self, do not impugn the general's physical capabilities. Good to know. Leira took the lead and started down the stairs, curving to the left as she kept an eye out for the green dots. She looked down at one point, two staircases below the top and realized she was staring at a blue dot. "Wait here."

Leira took off up the stairs, lightly running her hand over the rail as a guide. She got halfway up to a junction where the stairs split like a spider web with different legs into several directions. She darted down each set a few steps till she saw a dot, running back up when she saw blue or yellow. At the next to last one she finally found green but couldn't resist looking over her shoulder at what had to be a flight of stairs with orange dots.

"Save that curiosity for another time." She leaned over the rail and called to the general. "This way."

He hurried up the stairs, one hand on his hat and they continued on their way down the labyrinth into the bowels of Washington, DC.

Four stories down they passed close to a brick wall that was scratched with different initials and dates. H.W. 1910 and P.A. 1933 or L.L. 1945.

"If these walls could talk..." whispered Leira as she looked at the vast wall, covered in initials.

"Right about now I would not be entirely surprised if it suddenly did."

Leira paused for a moment just to see if it might be possible. A talking wall. She shook her head, wondering how far down the rabbit hole they were actually going.

Six stories down they came across a cape with a wand carefully propped on top. "Don't touch it," cautioned Leira. "It's a trap. Bait for anyone who doesn't know the system. It'll set off alarms and a spell or two. I don't know what kind, but I'd rather skip it this trip."

"Agreed," said the general, as he gave it a wide berth. "Clever, have to admire that."

"Sure, I suppose."

At eight stories down Leira could see a reflection from below and realized they were getting close. Her calves were starting to ache even though she was still keeping up with her long runs through Austin streets. She could only imagine how the general was feeling but he wasn't showing any signs of slowing down. *Now that's something you have to admire.*

She looked down at the last platform as the stairs broke off into two directions. She looked down and realized she was about to put her foot onto an orange dot. Slowly, she eased her foot down anyway. *Let's see what happens.*

A wave of nausea came over her and her bones felt as if they were turning to liquid. She threw her weight backward enough to fall onto the platform, dragging her legs in and curling up until the feeling passed.

The general came and bent over her. "I suppose that's what they meant by a vibe. I take it that packed quite a wallop. Somebody out here has their own alarm system to keep out the Elves."

"Yeah..." she gasped, swallowing a little bile. "I say we go the other way."

"Good idea," he said, smiling, still bent over. He stood up straight and waited patiently till she made it to her hands and knees, pulling herself to a standing position by holding onto the rail.

"Okay," she eked out. "I'm ready." She took in a few good deep breaths and set out again. *Second note to self. Pay atten-*

tion to the fucking directions in magical places in particular. Or run the risk of being turned into Jello or worse.

They headed down the final flight of stairs and at the last few steps, Leira's shoes started to stick and she had to pull her legs harder with each step to make any headway. The general was having the same issues.

"One last test I suppose. Hang on, let me read the directions." Leira let out a snort. "Oh, no... Leftover from an Elven rager. Apparently without permission. There's a mention here of the cleaning bill and some residual effects. Okay, here we are in what feels like the center of the Earth. No wonder Lacey said this would be safe from prying eyes." Leira peered into the darkness, wondering if there might be other eyes staring back. She took out a flashlight and shined it ahead of her to see if anything shined back or skittered away.

Nothing. Why am I disappointed? Hagan would love this part. Stairs might have done him in.

Leira stood in the darkness, holding up the flashlight so she could read the piece of paper in her hand. The stripes along her running shoes glowed silver in the darkness. "Why a Witch needs to write things down on a piece of paper is beyond me. You'd think she could send them to me in a spell, or something."

"What are you muttering?" General Anderson stumbled across the old stone pavers in the tunnel. "Don't you have a little magic of your own?"

"I was given strict instructions by Lacey Trader who gave these to me not to use magic down here. My magic can leave a trail that could attract an unsavory crowd. That's a quote. I think it was some kind of weird compliment about my abilities. And, frankly after the last artifact mission she's probably not that thrilled with the PDF."

The general chuckled, his face half hidden in the shadows of his large service cap. "That was a good one. Finally routed that Atlantean they love to use. Blasted woman has bested us one too many times." The general stumbled again, holding out his arms to steady himself as he kept right on talking. "Mind you, I like her, even if she does play a little rough. She gets the job done."

"Just not for our side, exactly."

"Frankly, if Lacey had asked nicely I might have seen the sense of locking the daggum thing up in her vault."

"You mean, like we're about to do anyway."

"That would be what I meant. That lamp is a little too powerful to take any chances with. Who knew the thing acted like a steady portal, even on Earth? Can you imagine a clever thief using something like that?"

"I can imagine a clever thief going boom using something like that. Hang on! I think I've found it." Leira found the fuse box along the western wall near the old rusted green door just like Lacey wrote down. She opened the box and threw the large handle into the up position, lighting the space. "At last, much better. General Anderson, welcome to the underground world of the Silver Griffins and other magical beings living on this planet."

The general and Leira turned round and round, their mouths hanging open as the light illuminated an old rail car painted a glossy red with the number four-four-one painted in gold on the side. "Will you look at that..."

"That's an authentic Pullman car from the 1900s. I'd

know it anywhere." The general stood as close as he dared, keeping his hands off it, per the instructions.

Nearby was a snack shop, closed for the night. Above it was a sign neatly painted with the words, Washington Metro Station.

"Lacey said thousands travel through here every year." *Another underground world. First Hilldale and now this.* Leira kept the thought to herself. The general was already learning enough about the hidden magic of Earth. He didn't need to know that there were entire cities beneath his feet.

"Seems deserted now. I suppose that's for the best."

Lacey had also insisted if the general was going down to the substation it had to be after hours, so no one got spooked by the presence of a human. "A military human, no less," she had said. "Make sure he doesn't touch anything. He'll leave a trail that anyone can follow, and they'll think the place has been found out."

The general looked up at the curved ceiling at the polished glass and stone mosaic of the constellations. "I pride myself on knowing all the constellations but not all of those look familiar."

Leira looked up at the mosaic and gave a crooked smile. "That's because not all of them are floating over this planet. That one over there is from the skies over Oriceran. I suppose that was their way of bringing a little home to this place without actually giving up any secrets if someone stumbled onto the place."

"We are standing at stop 441 of the underground SGRS. Silver Griffin Railway System." Leira went over to the car and ran her hand along the brass fittings. "This baby runs under most of North America." She walked around the outside. "Not the only one, either. I've heard rumors about this, well... stories from Nana and Mom but they made it sound like actual fairy tales. Imagine what it took to carve out tunnels like this." She touched the numbers on the side of the car, and they lit up, sparkling under her touch. Gas lights inside the car lit, flickering shadows against the tunnel walls, and the engine revved.

"I think your ride is ready for you."

"Was it worth the trek down here, General? You have to venture all the way back up those stairs."

"Wouldn't have missed it. How often does a person get to see the largest railway system on this planet that almost no one has ever heard of? Climb on board, I'll stand back here as instructed. No touching anything for me. Still, she's a beaut. Used to play with trains as a boy. Would have loved to have something like this in my collection. An actual Pullman car. If that doesn't beat all. Jessica would have loved this."

Leira wanted to ask him about Jessica but there wasn't time. The rail car was revving its engines even more, as if it was signaling it was leaving the station, with or without her. She stepped up the steps and onto the car, taking a seat on the side closest to the general. "I suppose this thing knows where to take me. The directions don't say anything about what to do once I'm on here." Leira looked down just in time to see the paper crumble and blow away as if it never existed. "That explains the handwritten notes. Very efficient."

The train started to pull away, steam pouring out of the back as if there was actually an engine. At the last moment, she leaned over the side, rising out of her seat and yelled, "Don't forget about the green dots and don't touch anything!"

The general waved his hat, smiling from ear to ear like he was a kid again.

CHAPTER TEN

Leira sat back against the thick red leather seat tufted with padded buttons, the backpack by her side. The rail car gradually picked up speed till it was sending out sparks from the wheels. The walls lining the tunnels eventually became a blur and Leira found herself pinned against the seat, gripping the armrest. *How fast are we going?* None of the directions had given any clue to how long it would take to get there. *Sorry I didn't bring a few traveling snacks. Feels like I broke with tradition heading this far out of town.*

But thirty minutes later the train was already slowing and Leira could feel a change in temperature even that far down in the tunnel. "It's like this entire part of the Earth is cold in spring." She pulled out the puffy coat that was stuffed under the lamp and slipped into it, zipping the backpack closed again.

The rail car lurched to a stop, letting out a long, low whistle, steam pouring out of the back. "Kudos for authenticity."

"Thank you."

Leira jerked around, looking for the source of the voice. At the bottom of the stairs was a Witch dressed in a blue wool coat and a faux fur collar with a knit hat pulled down over her ears and a thick scarf wound around her neck. "Good, you came dressed for the weather. I brought an extra pair of gloves, just in case. We've had a spring snow upstairs. Not uncommon."

"Upstairs? Are you referring to topside?" Leira climbed out of the car, slipping into the backpack, jumping down from the last step. She could feel the cold through her running shoes. She didn't wait for an answer, following closely behind the Witch as they started up a similar flight of stairs. *No dots, interesting.* She was bursting with questions. "How did the Silver Griffins manage to get the train to go that fast? Who built all this? What do you do if someone can't take all those stairs?"

The Witch turned around and flicked Leira in the forehead, turning back, continuing her patient climb.

"What the fuck was that? Did you really just flick me?"

"It calms down children rather well. I was hoping it would work in this instance."

Listen bitch, I will flick you with a fireball so fast...

"Hurry along, Lacey is waiting, and we have a few flights to go."

An icy wind whistled through the cavernous opening, watering Leira's eyes. She pulled up the collar on her coat and kept moving, hoping they were getting closer to the top, as they passed floor after floor, zigging and zagging.

The Witch suddenly took a turn going down a few steps and across a gangway, disappearing into a tunnel.

Leira had to jog to catch up with her, stopping at the edge of the tunnel. "Are you in there?" She couldn't see anything and put out her hand to make sure she wasn't walking into a wall. *Would be just like this wench.*

"Hurry up, don't want to keep Lacey waiting." The voice echoed from somewhere deep in the tunnel.

Give her this, bitch can really move.

"Here goes nothing."

From deep within the tunnel Leira heard an echo. "Don't be so dramatic. Follow my voice."

Leira stepped over the line into the darkness and felt herself pulled forward, almost lifted off her feet. She ran to keep up with the motion and found herself half running, half sliding along the ground. The light around her gradually grew till she suddenly found herself standing in a lit room with walnut paneling all the way around. *Hello 1980.* She pressed her hand against her belly, working to regain her equilibrium and not throw up on the Persian rug under her feet.

"Do hold it together," the Witch sniffed.

Come a little closer. Leira put out her hand like she was looking for an assist, but the Witch didn't move any closer. *Not the first time someone has wanted to throw up on her, I'll bet.*

"To answer your question, yes, we're above ground again. Well, close enough. We're in the lower levels of the Silver Griffins headquarters in Chicago."

A door suddenly opened, and Lacey Trader breezed in, a smile on her face. "Agent Leira Berens. At last we meet. I don't believe we've ever been in the same room together, but I've heard a lot about you from many different sources. I trust you got here safe and sound?"

Leira tried to gauge if Lacey's concern was genuine. "I have the lamp to turn over to you for safekeeping."

"We will get to that, but I have something else I want to talk to you about first. Now that I have you away from your government handlers, there's a more pressing matter that may complicate the artifacts race. Please, have a seat. Did you ask Agent Berens if she wanted something to drink? What about hot coffee? This room gets so drafty."

"Hot coffee would be great. I take it black." *Here's hoping the Witch doesn't spit in it.*

"Same for me."

The Witch left the room barely taking a glance at Leira but smiling as she passed Lacey.

"Don't take it personally. She's friends with Katie, which is saying something. Atlanteans are not easy to get to know. I'm afraid she's only heard Katie's account of things. However, I've dealt with Katie enough to know there's always another side to the story and usually it starts with something Katie did to get everyone's blood going. Am I right?"

"Something like that. She knocked my partner flat and he returned the favor."

"A human caught her off guard?" Lacey laughed easily. "No wonder Katie was so worked up. She comes off much more heroic in her version."

"It didn't really last all that long. Not that part anyway." Leira shuddered at the memory of the Dark Mist using the Wizard. "You wanted to discuss something else?"

"Yes, thank you for keeping me on task. I've heard that

about you from Lois, an old, dear friend. She speaks very highly of you." Lacey sat down behind her desk as the Witch came in with the coffee. "Leave both mugs here. I'll hand them out."

The Witch hesitated as if she wasn't sure what to do.

"Want to start over and come back without the stinging spell in one of them? Consider this one a test run and a warning. I won't have guests mistreated. Are we clear? Enough is enough." Lacey's voice had an icy edge to it as cold as it was outside. The Witch scooped up the mugs and quickly backed out of the room, mumbling an apology without making eye contact with anyone this time. Her face was ashen.

"I apologize for that. There will be consequences later. This should be a safe haven for anyone we invite inside." She let out a sigh and sat back in her chair. "Times are changing, growing darker I'm afraid. I've read stories in the old books about the same thing happening in the years before the gates started to open the last time. Everyone becomes afraid of what it all means, and power brokers want to make sure they're on a winning team. Leading the way if at all possible, no matter the costs." She looked suddenly tired as the Witch brought back in new mugs of steaming coffee, placing them on the desk next to a shiny black patent leather purse with stiff handles.

The Witch's cheeks were hot as she looked directly at Leira, her hands clasped in front of her. "I wish to apologize for my earlier rude behavior. I let my personal feelings get in the way of my duties, and I was wrong. It won't happen again. You're a guest here."

"I appreciate the effort Jennifer," said Lacey sternly, "but we'll still be chatting later about believing things wholesale and not thinking for yourself. You can go."

The Witch pulled her bottom lip between her teeth as if she was stopping herself from saying more and backed her way out of the room, softly closing the door behind her till it clicked.

"You run a tight ship."

"It's necessary. We don't do brain surgery around here. It's even trickier. The wrong mistake and a powerful artifact gets out into the world or a group of Wizards think it's okay to perform magic or something far worse."

"You were about to tell me about the far worse."

Lacey reached across her desk with one of the mugs and sat back down in her chair, picking up the other and taking a sip, savoring the warm liquid.

"This must really be bad." Leira took a sip and held the mug just beneath her chin, enjoying the warmth of the steam. "You don't strike me as someone who likes the casual pause just for fun." *Or anything fun.*

"I don't intend to draw this out, but it is that bad and it's more complicated than we're used to dealing with but with broader consequences. Everything goes back to the involvement of human beings. The natives of this planet."

Leira sat forward, her hands wrapped around the mug, listening.

"The stunt the prophets pulled has complicated things before we were entirely ready to deal with it. Exposing magic like that got the attention of a lot of powerful and important people. Ordinary citizens may be placated by the suggestion that it's a stunt, which helps, but there are very hungry, large players in the game now that we don't exactly govern but are becoming entangled in our world."

"The artifacts race."

"That's the start of it but I'm referring to the humans who are experimenting with animals..."

Leira instinctively touched the bracelet on her arm as she took another sip.

Lacey glanced at the bracelet and pressed her lips together for a moment. "And looking into the possibilities of eternal youth. A perpetual quest among their kind. Living a long time is not all it's cracked up to be. This is just the beginning. The natives here are very clever and will throw their best scientists at the artifacts to discover all the ways they can be manipulated. It's very possible they will come up with things we haven't even imagined, yet. Some of it may even prove to be a boon to everyone. But when it goes wrong, and it will..."

Leira set the mug down, finally seeing the bigger picture. "There could be a gradual panic."

"We have a few things on our side. One of them is you. Another is that we're early in this game and can still affect real change and put the brakes on the worst of it. But others may not be as patient, while we sort it out. There are families of Witches and Wizards here on Earth that have been here for thousands of years and have acquired a lot of power. Both the kind that humans enjoy and old, dark magic through books and artifacts that have been passed down for generations and they don't like to share. They've also noticed all the human activity and the theft of magical artifacts. We have a few well-placed Silver Griffins among them and they're reporting back that the families are organizing, which they do every couple of hundred years. I suppose they were due for stirring up some kind of trouble, especially with the start of the gates opening getting closer and closer. It never goes well but no one seems to remember that part of the lesson."

"It's like you have your own anti-Silver Griffins being formed."

"It's funny you should put it that way because they would agree. Old family lines like that love the pomp and circumstance. A crest of some sort, secret handshake. There's probably even a golden wand somewhere out there that only special members get to wave around. They're exhausting."

Leira gave a crooked smile. "You're more fun than you let on, aren't you?"

"When the world's not practicing magic as a group I can be a real hoot!"

"Why did you want me to know about this new twist to the whole dark magic thing?"

Lacey leaned forward on her arms, talking in a hushed voice. "Because of the power that you possess and because you stand outside of all the groups."

"I work for the Feds."

Lacey grimaced. "For now. Things change and that's a job. Being an SG is a lifetime commitment. We love a little pageantry too. There's a whole ceremony with candles and you get a new wand. Better than becoming an Eagle Scout." She gave Leira a wink. "I find the humor where I can, even in the middle of turning beautiful animals into misshapen Lego projects. I'd like to stay in contact with you because either way, your help will become invaluable to easing the transition as the gates open and the levels of magic increase on Earth. It will become tempting for so many to start using magic all the time. Most of that will be ours to take care of, and we will. But some..."

"Sounds like a good idea. I'm always open to listening." Leira lifted the backpack. "Now about this lamp."

CHAPTER ELEVEN

Lacey Trader took Leira out the opposite door from where she'd entered and down a long hallway to a short flight of stairs that led her up to the surface of the Chicago Water Tower. The shiny black purse was swinging from her wrist.

It felt good to be above ground again and seeing natural light but it didn't last long. They passed by the small theater that acted as cover for the building and the box office with posters on either side for the new play, *The Potted Potter* and a friendly owl in glasses and a maroon school jacket. *All seven Harry Potter books in 70 hilarious minutes*, it read.

Fake news. Magic is real, people. Leira picked up her pace to catch up with Lacey.

Lacey kept walking, leading them down another flight of stairs to the front of a large vault.

A Wizard sat in a wooden chair to the side of the vault, chewing on a pencil as he worked at the crossword puzzle in the day's paper.

"You're not cheating now, are you Foley?" Lacey smiled at him as she pulled out her wand. "Expandoria." The great tumblers visible in the enormous door turned slowly, gears shifting and turning, pushing against other gears as the door opened a wedge but not quite far enough to get inside.

"Not yet but the day is young."

"What's your record this week?"

"I've only had to use my wand a couple of times so far, but you know they get harder as the week goes on."

"So you tell me." Lacey held out her fir wand as a stream of gold energy poured out of the top forming into large, barbed hook at the end that hooked itself to the door. "Expandoria Infintinia!" Lacey pulled back on her wand as the door swung open letting out a low, long creak.

Leira watched the three-foot thick door open in awe, her eyes wide. "I have to admit that is cool. Will it do that for me? No... okay."

Lacey looked back at Leira, one eyebrow arched and walked into the cavernous room without answering her. She had no intention of telling the PDF agent the area had been converted to a repository of lesser artifacts that could maim or kill on a smaller scale. It was a sworn secret among Silver Griffins and even fewer knew where to find its replacement.

Lacey waved her wand through the air, as the lights came on overhead, row after row after row.

"No shit..." Leira walked next to Lacey onto the landing that led to a flight of stairs and looked out over the Silver Griffins vault that stretched up two stories. "That has to be the length of two football fields!"

"Three is more accurate." Lacey said it like a proud parent, despite knowing its diminished size. It was still impressive. "And there's another floor beneath this one of more dangerous items that stay locked away from everyone but the top level of Silver Griffins."

"What does more dangerous mean?"

"Handling them incorrectly, even by a Witch like myself can turn you into dust or let loose a plague or mess with time."

"Okay, asked and answered. Where is this baby going?" Leira set down her backpack and unzipped it, pulling out the lamp and unfolding the cloth. The brass shone in the light. "You just want to rub it and make a wish."

"Last thing you want to do. A lot of artifacts are set up to respond like that. You'd be surprised. I don't want to find out the hard way that there's something trapped that we free inside the vault to wreak havoc."

Leira held the lamp away from her body by the handle. "Where are you storing it?"

"Follow me." Lacey went down the stairs and took a path down the third row, making a left at the L's and stopping in front of a row of plastic bins. "These used to all be metal or wooden, some velvet-lined, but plastic lasts longer and is just as easy to enchant. We haven't transferred everything to them, but we will over time." *Into the new vault someday.*

"All good info to know."

A witch passed out of the archives, turning sideways to get by Leira and gave Lacey a knowing look as she passed. "You think this is just fun background, but you have the ability to do some of these things too. You just perform magic differently. You don't need a host like a wand. You are the host." Lacey put out her hands for the lamp as Leira handed it over. "My, this one has quite a buzz to it. Feels like old magic, too. Way before my time. I wonder how far back it goes."

Leira glanced at the bin next to where the lamp was going and read the label, "Golden Lariat."

"That was used by an Elf in the mid-1800s in the wild, wild Western territories to rob banks and stop trains."

"Elves gone wild. You don't think of them as thieves. Why steal when you can create what you want?"

"For some there is never enough and for others it's about power and for others it's exclusivity. For the old families it's all three mixed with dark magic."

They walked back toward the front of the vault as Leira tried to read as many labels as possible in passing. Gold doubloons, an innocent looking salt and pepper shaker set that looked like a dog and cat, a broken umbrella. "Not broken." Lacey pointed at it as she sped by. "Part of its charm. Looks useless and should be thrown out but those ribs are enchanted and will wrap themselves around their prey. Messy business."

"Not getting why that's useful."

They got to the platform and Lacey turned and looked back over the vast collection. "Not all of these artifacts started out with bad intentions. Something happened to most of them. Something as innocent as a lightning strike or someone mishandled it. I've even seen a case or two where the energy that was poured into an artifact didn't mix well together and things went badly awry. Oh yes, energy has its own personality."

Leira looked at the vast room. "And the Silver Griffins protect all of this."

"Our sworn and solemn duty from one generation to the next. But we've only been doing this a few hundred years and have already amassed all this. We've never had to deal with protecting the vault *and* the gates opening." Lacey took Leira by the hands, the purse dangling off her arm, and looked her in the eyes. "We are going to need help. I can't tell you what or when, but I can feel it in my bones. Come on, let's get you started on your journey home. You'll be in your own bed tonight!"

"Modern transportation..." said Leira as she followed Lacey out of the vault.

"Not really. It's almost as old as the vault!"

"Wait here," said Lacey. "I need to check on something." The same witch was waiting for Lacey by her office door.

"Of course," said Leira, still taking in every detail. *Every agency has their secrets.*

Lacey stepped just inside, smiling at Leira. "What is it Roseanne? Has something happened to the dragon?"

"No, some of our agents caught poachers in the act. The animals are safe, but no one is sure what to do with the bad element."

Lacey did her best to hide her surprise. She could see Leira tilt her head, looking at her more closely. "Turn them over to General Anderson. We don't have any jurisdiction with humans."

"There's a wrinkle," said Roseanne. "They're not human,

like we suspected. They were all magicals and they're refusing to speak despite our best efforts."

Lacey pulled the purse closer. "That is an interesting twist. Send them all to Trevilsom Prison and let them sit for a while. Someone will crack."

"We got to them just ahead of the Gardener. I don't think they would have lasted if he got to them first."

"Well done. How is the dragon in our care?"

Roseanne whispered a spell, illuminating a picture in her cupped hands. The dragon was curled in a ball, sleeping under a stand of trees, the whirring and clicking slowed. "Adapting but lonely."

"We may need to remedy that. I have to go. My guest is waiting."

"Why didn't you tell her about the new vault?" asked Roseanne, looking up at Leira. "I thought we needed the help."

"It's always a tricky thing to balance assistance with secrecy. It's better this way for now. We can always seek more help later, but we can't take it back once the knowledge is out there."

CHAPTER TWELVE

Wolfstan Humphrey walked into Charlie Monaghan's office in a foul mood. The supply chain of animals had been disrupted and some comic book misfit had vandalized one of his cars right under his nose. The opposition was growing too comfortable.

Worst of all, he still didn't have the old plans to complete an updated version of the Fleeker CAT scan. His lip curled into a satisfied sneer. *Maybe there's something I can do about that one.*

Charlie got up from his desk and waited for Wolfstan to take a seat. The CEO of Axiom was dressed in his favorite blue power suit and a red tie, his smile firmly in place. But internally he was tired and foggy. He couldn't shake the feeling that important details were getting away from him.

"Wolfstan, glad you could make it." He put out his hand just as a wave of nausea threatened to overcome him. *Not now, not in front of him.* Sweat was forming on his upper lip. He grit his teeth, pressing his toes down inside his shoes and took in a deep breath, smelling the perfumed air in his office. *Stay present. Keep your wits about you.*

Wolfstan went to shake Charlie's hand. An odd human custom. But just as he gripped the man's hand he saw the darkness roll through Charlie's eyes, filling the sockets. He hesitated, almost pulling his hand back. *Dark magic has a hold of him.* But Wolfstan did what he always did in the face of something ominous and powerful. He jumped in and grasped Charlie's hand, squeezing tight. *I can use him.* "Charlie, I think we got off on the wrong foot. Let's start again. I could use some help with my supply chain..."

"He is blowing up my fucking phone!" Louie slammed it down on the counter. He had only had the phone for a short time, since he was convinced of the necessity of throwing in with the PDF. General Anderson wanted him connected to the rest of the team and when he balked there was mention of parting ways.

"Great!" Louie had said, relieved it was so easy to ditch them.

"And I'll let the Silver Griffins know where they can pick you up."

Louie had let out a sigh and taken the phone.

He was staying in a condo on the East side of Austin, provided to him by the U.S. government, but had yet to figure out how to get around besides walking or hitching a ride. They had even given him a debit card that was to be used for living expenses only, but Louie had plans to see a little of the night life. For now, though it was enough to get to know the basics of living in Austin, Texas.

The HEB grocery store overwhelmed him on his first two tries, but he came up with a strategy and shopped only two aisles at a time. Then he would come back later to try two more. One night he had gluten free pizza from the frozen aisle set aside for people with allergies and topped it off with a rice bagel and sunflower butter. He despaired of the human race and their idea of food after tasting that until he finally made it down to the snack aisle.

The phone buzzed, inching its way across the dark marble countertop.

"Never should have given that creepy bastard my number. Hell, he remembers it better than I do." The phone vibrated again as another text came through.

Charlie wasn't letting things go.

Louie had tried putting a charm on the phone but quickly learned that Lois and Patsy had beaten him to it. The phone had its own kind of magical block that prevented Louie from changing anything more than the ring tones. He was stuck. The GPS around his ankle and the one in the phone made sure his handlers always knew where he was and if the phone was near him.

It stopped buzzing only long enough to start up again, shaking till it fell off the counter and hit the carpet below.

"Okay, dude, you can do this. You can get this maniac off your back. Hell, you've faced down worse things than a pissed off human being with a little money. That octopus monster, whatever it was... that was worse. There's a few Kilomeas that I'd run from every time. That Witch you dated last year for a hot minute was pretty scary. Woooo...." A shiver went down his back. "Let's get to it."

He leaned over and picked up the phone, scrolling through the messages. "Sensing a theme here. Pissed off, angry, on fire, ready to kill... Oh look, a small amount of polite. A respite from the swearing. Nice touch. More swearing. Wow, dude. That one is uncalled for and I'm pretty sure I can't do that to myself even with magic. If I could, I wouldn't get anything done during the day."

There was another theme to the messages that Louie quickly picked up on and was relieved to see that Charlie Monaghan had at least one thing he cared about more than getting even. "He really is jonesing for that ore."

Louie put the phone down, not sure what to do next. He looked down at the GPS on his ankle and thought better of it but then the phone buzzed again. "Fuck it, I'm going. Over, back... only be gone a little while."

He went and dug in his satchel till he found the small case with different sized metal picks in it and carefully chose one. They were artifacts once owned by a Wizard who had lived in London during the Victorian era and was fond of breaking into empty houses in the more posh sections. He had poured magic into the tools so he wouldn't get caught waving a wand at anyone's door. Better to be called a thief than a heretic in those days. They were one of Louie's prized possessions and had gotten him out of more than one tight place.

"Don't let me down now!"

There was a spell on the ankle bracelet to keep him from pulling it off, but Louie only saw that as an inconvenience and a challenge. "Not the first time someone has tried to nail me down. Once... literally." He shook his head, remembering the pub on the edge of the Dark Forest near the ocean. "Shot nails out of his mouth like bullets..." He worked the tip of the pick into the lock on the bracelet, working it around till he felt a click. *That's just the start.* "The trick is to relax and let the pick do the work." He took in a deep breath and let it out slowly, focusing his energy on the pick. It moved his hand, guiding it to turn a smidge to the right and bear down, turning back to the left. "I knew it!" He pulled the pick out gently, raising his arms in victory as the ankle bracelet fell away, rolling onto the carpet.

He pulled out his wand and opened a portal to Oriceran, turning back for a moment to grab his sword before quickly climbing through to the other side. "Time's a wastin'. Got to get that guy off my back." He felt his muscles relax as he smelled the familiar scents of the flowers in the forest and looked up at the two moons starting to show in the sky. "Maybe I won't go back at all," he said, with a sigh. He moved quickly along the ground, listening for the sound of any magical creatures that walked on two feet.

It wasn't long before he found his way to his small cabin and made his way inside. There was a note stuck to the table with a knife.

'Gnomes are still pissed off at you. Don't go scavenging near the base of the mountains just yet. Might take another week or two. Minding the store for you and taking my usual cut. Ronnie'

Louie let out a snort. "Miss that little dude. Usual cut." He snorted again and shrugged. "Better than losing my spot." He went into the only other room in the cabin and dug through an old wooden chest, pulling out bits and pieces of broken artifacts and a dirty tunic, an old pair of boots that had a hole in the bottom of one of them. There in the bottom was his only other real treasure besides the sword on his back. It was a piece of Oriceran ore the size of his fist and worth more than he could spend in a year, maybe two. He was saving it for his retirement.

He picked it up, holding the heavy ball in his hands, feeling the rough edges against his skin. "Hell, in my profession, what's the likelihood I'll get to retirement. Long way off anyway. I could find two more treasures by then, maybe more." He grabbed an old shirt and smelled it, his head whipping back from the stench. He threw it into a far corner and dug for another, carefully taking a sniff. "Much better." He wrapped up the ore and put it into his satchel, throwing it over his back next to the sword as he headed out of the cabin, shutting the door. He waved his wand to hide the small dwelling from view. "Might be a hovel, but it's my hovel."

He hurried deeper into the forest to find a better place to open a portal and see who might already be looking for him.

Peyton stumbled down to the four lane road that ran alongside the state park just as a battered white truck with wide side mirrors came barreling down the road. Metallica was blaring out the open window, the sound reverberating off the hillside. The altered Light Elf startled at the sight of something moving that fast and lashed out, bending a mirror back against the cab.

"Damn hippies!" The driver leaned on his horn, only angering Peyton more. The rising emotions fueled the erratic energy jumping around Peyton's body in an electric grid, rolling out along the ground in widening circles.

The driver watched in amazement in his rear view mirror, pressing his foot down on the accelerator but as the blue wave of sizzling light crept closer the truck sputtered and locked up, slowing to a stop. "Oh shit, come on, come on, come on." The man jiggled the keys trying to get it to start but nothing was working as he reached for his phone, hurriedly dialing nine-one-one.

"Hello? This is Aubrey Fellowes. I'm driving on McKinney and there's some... some... man and he's lit up like a Christmas tree! What? Yes, I can be reached at this number. No, he's not on fire." Aubrey turned halfway around in the seat and looked back. "Listen, I think he's being electrocuted. I don't see a downed line but..."

Aubrey slowly lowered his phone, his mouth hanging open.

Peyton was swinging his fists at the unstable magic, his panic building inside of the blue light till it tore open again creating an unstable portal to an old Austin power station near Ladybird Lake. He fell backward into the hole, the energy still searching for a stabilizer, pulling him along as he landed among the weeds and rusted beer cans. The magic continued on its path, pushing out even further, creating waves along the top of the lake, upending kayakers and paddle boats. The sand along the bottom of the lake stirred, the water turning a muddy brown and fish popping up to the surface.

Aubrey got out of his truck, his phone clutched in his hand and walked toward the hole ripped in the air. "How is that possible?" He looked through to the lake, the breath caught in his throat.

"Hello? Hello? Are you still there?" The operator's tinny voice kept repeating itself. Aubrey got closer to the portal, reaching out his hand just as an arm came out from the dark edges, clawing at his shirt to grab ahold of him and attempt to pull him into the world in between. He let out a strangled cry and pulled back, gravity helping him as his shirt ripped and he stumbled backward staying upright. He was still staring at the rip in the air, his hand over his mouth, unable to take his eyes off it. Peyton was on his knees, holding his head and the waves were picking up on the lake just as the portal snapped shut with a loud *crack*.

"What the fuck just happened?" A nearby revving pulled his attention away. "Huh?" His truck was suddenly starting, the keys still dangling from the ignition. He shook his head, backpedaling away from where the portal had been, lifting the phone up to his ear as he ran. "I think you'd better get to the old Seaholm Power Plant. Shit is getting real. Trust me, something's not right, lady. I gotta go," he said, hanging up and sliding the phone into his pocket as he got back in his truck. "I gotta get the hell away from here."

CHAPTER THIRTEEN

Lacey Trader walked Leira back to the old rail car, number four-four-one, touching each one of the numbers on the side of the rail car again, to see them light up and sparkle.

"Any chance this thing can take me to Austin, Texas instead of D.C.?"

"I told you we'd get you home to your own bed tonight. I like to keep my promises whenever possible." She smiled and put out her hand for Leira to shake and Leira noticed the tattoo of two interlocking circles on the inside of her wrist.

Leira climbed up into the car as the engines came on, steam blowing out the back as the gaslights lit on the inside. "That's mostly for show. The children love it," said Lacey.

Lacey waited till it started to pull away, waving and smiling. Leira turned around, peering out the back of the car as a Wizard caught up with Lacey and gave her a message as her smile quickly faded. Leira watched her waste no time and raise her wand in the direction of the car.

She watched in amazement as a shower of sparkling bubbles passed over the entire car, making the inside glow for just a minute.

"Wonder what that was about..."

Lacey and the Wizard were just small specks when the train finally gained full speed, rushing down the track. Leira turned around and settled into the comfortable seat, glad to be headed home. The train took turns, and twists into different tunnels. At one point, Leira was certain it neatly turned one hundred and eighty degrees on a large turntable and headed down a different tunnel that appeared out of nowhere, traveling in a different direction.

There was nothing for her to do but sit back and relax and enjoy the ride.

Thirty minutes later the rail car slowed as the wheels spun more slowly and steam again pushed out the back. Leira stepped out and looked around at the darkened station, wondering where she was... exactly.

A wooden sign over the closed snack bar read, Tanci-taro. "Oh, come on. This can't be right."

"Oh good, you're here! I wasn't sure what to do if you didn't show. That big rail car showed up, but I didn't see you anywhere at first." Felix Hagan was standing in the shadows at the bottom of the staircase doing his best not to touch anything.

"Where the hell are we? Feels like I'm Alice in Wonderland and a giant rabbit with a pocket watch is going to hop by any minute now."

"Tell me about it. Turns out my heart can take strenuous exercise down a dozen flights of stairs at a moment's notice. Who knew? They flew me out here and I was met by a couple of guys in dark suits who told me to take the stairs and don't touch anything. Something about humans and this stuff being like a giant bug zapper for us. Whew, I am sweating through my shoes. There is not a dry spot on me!"

"Hagan, you still haven't exactly told me what we're doing here. Or where we are for that matter. Focus. I take it there's a mission. Must be a big one." Leira leaned back and looked up at the ceiling. Above them was a mural of men and women dancing together, painted in bright colors stretching the length of the car. "These places are amazing!" She looked back at Hagan. "You can tell me while we climb. Start with where we are."

"Okay, but we're going at my pace or I'm shouting ahead to you with as much air as I have left. Be prepared to use your magic to try and pick up my wheezing voice."

Leira gave him a dead fish look and stepped aside. "I'll even let you lead."

"That's gotta be killing you. How many flights before you give up and run ahead, do you think? Let's bet on it. You're a nice person, so I give you five entire flights and then it's see you later, Hagan."

Leira let out a laugh. "I'd stay at least close enough to make sure you were still moving. I don't want to have to report back to Rose that you're missing in action."

Hagan started up the stairs more vigorously than Leira expected. "You have to be kidding me! You're holding out on me. Hagan, you've been working out!"

"Rose makes me. Don't get too excited. We're climbing a

skyscraper's worth of stairs. Somewhere near the top I expect to see visions and start making deals with them to get me out of here by any means necessary."

"If I promise to buy you doughnuts for the next month will that help?"

"Won't hurt..." Hagan took in a deep breath and kept climbing, turning at the first platform and pulling off a small tab of blue painter's tape. "Left my version of breadcrumbs on the way down to make sure I didn't venture into bogeyman land. It's a maze. I know it looks like stairs but it's really a maze. Stairs go off in different directions and wait till we get further up when they seem to curl back around. I'm telling you, it was blowing my mind. Like being high without any help from outside sources. Okay, okay. We're in Tancitaro, in the western Mexican state of Michoacán. Or as we think of it in Austin, the avocado capital. I'm really hoping they have some killer guacamole somewhere up there."

"Okay, now I have a vague idea of where we are. I crossed a border into another country. Weird."

"Yeah, I'm guessing no one checks passports down here. The general sent us here as fast as possible because he got reliable information that we are close to the site where the animal experiments are taking place. Most of them at least."

Leira grabbed Hagan by the arm, suddenly energized and excited. "No way! How could we get that lucky?"

"You can thank the reliable source. Patsy and Lois said it was routed through your friend, Perrom. He's been on the case ever since you saw the sanctuary outside of Austin. Like a dog with a bone. They took a page out of this world's way of doing things and put trackers on all the animals." Hagan and Leira got to another level that split into four different directions. Hagan nodded his head and pulled off another piece of tape, just as a low howl came out of the darkness from one of the other staircases. "If that doesn't make the hair stand up on the back of your neck..."

Leira looked into the darkness wondering what was down here with them. *Is it coming this way?* "Let's keep moving."

"Good idea. There's enough of a battle already waiting for us. Why get in a small skirmish ahead of time?" Lonely sounding howls erupted from the opposite direction as if they were answering the first call. Hagan stopped in his tracks, listening as Leira pulled in enough magic to send out a stream of energy. "I don't think we're entirely alone down here." The symbols on her arms glowed in the semi-darkness.

"I gathered that much information." Hagan pulled out his handkerchief from his back pocket and wiped his face. "Not all that sweat is from climbing these stairs."

"Yeah, I gathered that much, too. It's okay. You have your gun. I have these guns..." Leira flexed her arms, smiling at her partner. She was taking the stairs easily, holding her back straight as she climbed, turning to look in both directions, keeping a watchful eye. "Did we get any details?"

"We're being met by the Mexican version of the PDF and they're going to help us raid the place but there's not much time. Apparently, they move around a lot and by move, I mean entire countries. They can't trace it back to its source yet, but we have our suspicions."

"Axiom Corporation, I presume." Leira shook her head. "Something is not right there, and I mean beyond the obvious."

Hagan fell silent as they climbed toward the next landing. He ripped off another piece of tape and they climbed again, landing after landing, getting closer to the top.

Twinkling lights caught Leira's attention and she glanced to the right. "Look at that! Reminds me of the stop in Washington, DC but they're here, in the middle of the air."

Floating in the air, halfway between the bottom and top were the constellations. Another composite of Oriceran and Earth's heavens twinkling in the darkness beyond the stairs they were standing on, following the path of another set of stairs.

"Makes me wonder what's in that direction," Leira said, wistfully. "So much to explore down here. Would take years! To think that by morning these staircases will be teeming with magical beings all headed someplace."

"I hear that the homeless of the human variety live under the New York City subway in forgotten tunnels. What's to say that there isn't such a thing as homeless magical beings we've never even heard of roaming down here?"

"I'd say that's a safe bet. Probably why we keep getting warned to stick to our own path. What's the goal of this mission, exactly? Did General Anderson spell it out?"

"Cripple the operation as much as possible and rescue as many animals as possible. The animals are going to one of the Gardener of the Dark Forest's sanctuaries. That's the deal that was made. No wiggle room."

"What would we do with them, anyway? Patsy and Lois showed me pictures of what's been done to them. Someone should pay for that kind of freak show and the animals should be taken care of away from prying eyes or more misery." Hagan stopped a moment to take a breath, shutting his eyes for a moment to try and get rid of the image. "Hard to unsee something like that. Takes a cold heart to think that's a worthwhile experiment."

Leira stopped next to him and patiently waited. She remembered her first reaction in the Dark Forest. She ran her fingers along the bracelet. "We'll get our chance to do something about it, but we'd better keep going. There's still a few flights to go and there's a clock on the whole thing."

"Right! What an interesting life, Berens. One minute I'm trying to figure out who shot a guy in his own house with the doors all still locked, thinking that's a pretty good mystery. The next I'm doing my best not to think about what's howling in the bowels of the earth and does it have wings or fangs or breathe fire."

"That's an active imagination there, Hagan. Maybe it's a wild troll."

Hagan's eyes widened and he looked at Leira, startled. "Is that possible? Is there some kind of version that's a were-troll?"

"You're too gullible, Hagan. Okay, you were right. I'm taking off ahead of you and doing some scouting. Not to worry. I'm keeping my eye on you at the same time. Stay alert and yell to me if there's trouble. I'll run back down the stairs."

"One more howl or a loud growl and I'll be right behind you."

Leira took off up the stairs, taking them two at a time, letting a small amount of magic flow through her, enhancing her ability to sense what was around her. She could feel the presence of other magical beings not too far away. She recognized the magical trails left behind by Elves and Gnomes and Witches and Wizards. Some of them were even recent, too recent to be from when the substations were open. There were other trails that she'd never seen before and their energy was stronger, more chaotic. Sparks sputtered off the trails as if they couldn't be contained and blended in and out with some of the others.

Near the top of the stairs Leira felt the air grow warm and clammy. She found a metal door similar to the one she had passed through in Washington and opened it, cautiously peering out to see what was on the other side.

"Senora?" A dark-haired man with a thick moustache, dressed in dark blue fatigues doffed his baseball cap and gave a small bow with his head, putting the hat back in place. "We've been waiting for you. Is your partner still with you?" Where a gun normally would have been holstered the Wizard had a grey wand made from the Ahuehuete tree, the national tree of Mexico.

"He's right behind me. Are you the backup?"

The man smiled, the creases deepening around his eyes as he stepped back. "No ma'am, I am just one of many." He looked to the right and Leira followed his gaze, looking into the distance at a fleet of SUVs parked in a dirt parking lot, their engines quietly idling as they waited patiently for her and Hagan to arrive.

Leira's eyebrows shot up, wrinkling her forehead. "It's an armada. Are those all magical beings?"

"Every last one. Your partner will be the only true human being on this mission. He must be quite a warrior!"

Leira counted the number of magicals she could see standing by their vehicles and saw a few more sitting inside the cars. Thirty of them all ready to go. She looked back at the Wizard standing next to her. "You know, he is... He really is."

"I'm sorry. I forgot to introduce myself. My name is Jorge Estevez, a member of Mexico's Paranormal Division. You must be Leira Berens. You are legendary to us here."

Hagan came up the last stairs and out the door, bending over for a moment, resting his hands on his knees. "That workout will last me for a good month or two. That was intense. Do you know I heard birds near the top? Can that be true?"

Jorge ducked his chin, smiling as he looked away. "Yes sir, there are many birds living in there. There's an entire ecosystem built inside of there that stretches for miles and comes to rest at a kemana on the far side of town. You must be Agent Felix Hagan." Jorge held out his hand, gripping Hagan's and giving it a vigorous shake, a broad smile across his face. "Another legend. A human being investigating magic. You are very brave, sir. Very brave."

Hagan was surprised at the greeting but managed a smile and finally stood up straight, his hands on his hips.

Leira gave him a crooked smile. *About time others noticed.*

"Come on, let's roll," said Hagan. "Time to kick some Dr. Evil ass."

"Yes!" Jorge punched the air with his fist. They followed

him to the caravan and got into an SUV in the back seat. Grim-faced agents all quietly piled into their cars as Jorge got in the front seat along with another agent and they started down the dusty road. Their car quickly fell into line in the middle of the pack and Leira watched out the window at the passing landscape, wondering about the battle that surely lay ahead.

Harkin doubled back toward the mountain range hunting for signs of Peyton. He found a wide swath of trampled underbrush and saw the residue of blue magic splaying off in every direction. *Not normal.* He crouched down, his eyes glowing and watched the broken and fading entrails splinter everywhere. "It has to be Peyton." He stood back up again and followed the strongest trail as he heard the Gardener riding up from the west.

The Wood Elf was astride the enormous lion bounding up a trail that was barely visible, stopping just short of Harkin. "You found the pieces of magic. It has to be him," said the Gardener, resting a hand on the antlers.

"How can you be sure? His magic has changed so much." Harkin put his hand against the blue pieces of magic and felt the frustrated sputter and sudden surge.

"You know it's him. You can feel the magic is broken. I can tell you about every magical who's set foot in the Dark Forest just by reading the trail they left behind. You know what this one tells me? Nothing. That's how I'm sure. But it ends at the Gnome's lair."

"Did they get to him first?"

The Gardener sat back on the lion, the black vines in his hair slowly turning green again. "No, they ran out of the caves shouting at me about the gruesome Light Elf who fell into a portal to Earth." The Gardener scowled and crossed his arms over his chest. "They swear they saw a tear in the portal to the world in between. The trapped souls almost took him." He let out a frustrated sigh. "That would have been an even worse fate. We are done, Harkin." He bit off the words as a snake wound its way through his hair. "You are going to go retrieve him from Earth."

"That's a big world. How do you suggest I find him?"

"Start with Turner Underwood in Austin, Texas. The Fixer will hear the cries of a tortured magical, even a broken one. He can help ease the way with Correk, too. You are at the center of all of this, Harkin. You have to go."

Harkin grimaced and watched as a red fox with black ears sensed the trails of diseased magic nearby and drew back, running quickly in the other direction. "I may have waited too long... for any of it to be put right."

"There's only one way to find out. Go and put it right the best you can."

CHAPTER FOURTEEN

"They're in a series of warehouses out by the Lopez avocado fields. That's some of the oldest fields in Tancitaro," said Jorge. "We think they've been paying off the family that own the fields to use their old facilities and to look the other way as they come and go with large trailers full of exotic animals. We owe a debt of gratitude to your sources or we wouldn't have put all the pieces together. It's a well-run operation despite all the activity and from the outside the trucks looked like they were shipping avocados in and out and not animals."

"Terrible business," muttered the other agent, shaking his head.

"Let's get this done," said Leira.

They drove for miles down back roads past vast avocado groves and small houses that abutted the roads here and there. Occasionally someone looked out of one of the houses and saw the passing flotilla of large black vehicles and quickly let go of their curtain, ducking back inside, not wanting to get involved.

They arrived at the edge of a large estate with an arch over the road made of iron in the shape of an avocado tree. On one side the metal was twisted into the words, *Since 1935* and on the other side, *Lopez Farm*. "This is where we get out and go on foot. The facilities are about a mile into the estate. Chances are they may already know something is happening but if we spread out, we may still have a better chance of stopping them from leaving or destroying everything."

Leira and Hagan piled out of the car with everyone else and stood at the edge of the groves.

"We will head up the middle of the grove. Ready?" Jorge held out his wand. "Ligero..." A bright, narrow light shone from the end of his wand, lighting the way as they moved quickly through the trees. Everyone kept up as they got closer to their destination. There were low lights off the sides of the windowless buildings but nothing to suggest there was any activity going on in the middle of the night. Lopez checked his radio, turning it off and signaled with his wand, sending out a stream of energy from it that connected to the next wand, and then the next wand, connecting the group.

"Go to positions!" Jorge's words traveled down the thread of the magical connection, erupting into sound at each stop. The group moved in, running quickly across the open ground, wands at the ready, their faces set and determined. Hagan drew his pistol as Leira pulled in the energy under her feet, her arms and neck glowing from the symbols. The stone inside the bracelet turning to liquid as it spun in a whirl in its setting.

The first squad got to the building and opened fire with

their wands to open the large doors, but the magical pulses bounced back, pinging against the metal, sounding like small stones being hurled by children. Another squadron joined them, adding their magic but it added nothing as the pulse blew back, shining in the Wizards and Witches faces and shaking the avocado tress behind them. There was a steady thud as ripened avocados hit the ground and rolled away from the wave of magic.

Leira stepped up with the third squad as they crossed the circuit with streams of magic, but nothing was being accomplished.

Leira dug her heels into the ground and focused. "Go get 'em," whispered Hagan, a scowl on his face. "I'll be right beside you. Let's get those bastards."

Set an intention. Open the doors.

A wide swath of magic poured up Leira's legs and out of the center of her trunk, her arms and hands pointed at the door, her face set in a dangerous scowl. She was in no mood to be turned away.

Open the doors. It felt like there was shouting inside of her head. *Open the motherfucking doors!* There was a roar inside of her now.

The energy lifted her forward onto her toes, threatening to pull her off her feet. She flexed her legs, focusing as the bracelet rattled against her skin, forcing her heels back down as the magic rose, testing the artifact on her arm. The door bowed toward her, pulled by the magic, still not giving in as Leira held her position and the others continued to add their powers to hers.

A boom erupted, so loud it was only heard in hindsight. The wave of magic pulsing over them, passing over their heads and knocking some to the ground, leaving them breathless. Hagan crouched down behind Leira as the magic flowed past them and he looked up to see a green shimmering light filling the night sky. "Wow," he said in awe as his bones ached from the pressure of the wave.

The doors finally snapped in two, swirling over their heads and flying into the groves, shearing off the tops of trees before landing in a loud bang. "It's all true!" Jorge stared at Leira, his mouth open in amazement.

"Focus!" barked Hagan, making himself stand upright despite the pain he felt from the force.

"Adelante!" yelled someone in the front and everyone steadily progressed forward, their wands out with the magical lines crossing into one stream that was pointed inside the opening to the building, searching out streams of darker magic.

Leira ran forward, her arms shaking from the strain of the magic pulsing through her, barely kept at bay by the artifact on her arm. They ran inside and found large sheets of plastic hanging from the ceiling to keep different surgical areas sanitary. Cows were lowing, pulling against chains around their ankles, their heads arched up and back and their eyes wide.

Leira felt their pain drifting through her. *There's that connection again. What is happening to me?* The stone in the bracelet briefly turned colors, settling back into amber.

Hagan stopped for a moment on the threshold as everyone rushed past him, taking in the scene in front of him. Each of the animals had a different part of their internal organs missing, replaced by moving parts that were visible beneath a thin membrane. Some had mechanical legs and one near the front looked as if his entire head had been surgically removed and reattached onto an artificial neck. On the backside of each cow was a brand of an F with streaks behind it as if it were in motion. Hagan swallowed hard as bile rose in his throat and anger filled his entire being. "Never in all my years."

He rushed forward, his gun pointed, searching for any of the scientists or corporate handlers who were in charge. *Human beings are behind this. For once, bullets will work just fine.*

No one was tending to the animals even though there were surgical trays beside the cows located in the back of the warehouse. The group got to the connecting building that formed the bottom of a T shape, turning the corner and running down the long building.

"There they are!" Men in white lab coats were running toward a door at the far end, glancing back over their shoulders. The door was wide open, and others were just escaping into it just as wands came up and pointed in their direction.

"Not all of them are humans."

"A glamour must have hidden them from view." Leira whipped her head around as a trail of dark, silvery magic whooshed past her in a fast-moving stream headed in another direction. "The Wizard," she hissed. She recognized the trail and was tempted to turn toward it, hesitating. *Work with the group. Stay on the mission. Be a part of the team.* Turner's words from her lessons were playing in her mind.

She ran forward with the agents toward the door, keeping an eye on Hagan who was resolute and determined to be at the head of the pack, his gun drawn. Leira's hesitation had put her at the back and she looked down to read the quickly moving symbols, flipping over on her arms.

"What?" The warning came just in time.

She spun around with her arms out and the magic rapidly pulsing through her. It was ramped up as far as the artifact would allow aimed straight at the dark Wizard coming out of a swirl of Dark Mist. He laughed, his voice coming out in a high pitch and raised his hands, dark energy pouring out of him. He had become one with the mist from the world in between. Leira's stream of gold and green energy slammed against the Dark Mist's and they pushed against each other. The pain was blinding, and tears came to her eyes as she gritted her teeth and stood her ground.

She heard Turner's voice in her head again as she felt herself weakening and the Dark Mist's energy grew closer to her. Jackson's words echoed in her head, leaving an ache in her heart.

Dad...Mom... Nana... help me. The thought was fleeting for just a moment, but it was enough. Magic poured in from both directions joining hers. Leira immediately recognized the signatures of Jackson's magic, along with Eireka and Mara. Tears poured down her face as she felt them alongside her. The mist still kept coming, pushing harder against the stream of light as Leira felt herself being pulled toward the world in between and the grasp of the Dark Mist. "No!" she yelled through clenched teeth.

The Wizard's eyes were completely black as he slowly walked toward Leira, leering at her.

She felt someone next to her and looked over to see Hagan aiming his gun at the Wizard, one hand on Leira's shoulder. "I can ground you. Trust me," he shouted. "Do it!"

Leira looked at Hagan as he gave her a hard nod. "It will pull you in too."

"Then we will fight our way back out. Do it!"

Leira shook her arm till the bracelet dropped off, hitting the dusty floor. The whirl inside the setting immediately slowed down and returned to a stationery stone. Hagan gripped her shoulder tighter, digging his fingers into her skin as Leira took a deep breath and let go of the magic. A bright light filled the warehouse, lighting it from one end to the other as the energy poured through Leira unfettered, filling every inch of her. A feeling of bliss overtook her, and the pain and worries left her as the energy slammed into the Dark Mist, pounding it back.

It's working... She was staying just to the edge of this side of the veil between the light and the darkness. Hagan was keeping her grounded.

The familial strings of magic peeled off her, unable to keep up and split apart, fracturing into smaller bits of light.

The Wizard growled, throwing back his head in pain and frustration, his silver hair glistening under the lights. He turned his attention to Hagan, veering away from Leira just slightly, aiming a pulse of energy straight at Hagan's chest.

Leira felt a moment of panic inside the bliss as the magic smashed into Hagan, the sound of his ribs creaking as some of them cracked. He hung on for as long as he could, his gun falling from his grasp as he fell backward, his grip loosening on Leira's shoulder just enough till he let go. His head hit the floor with a thwack and his eyes closed as he lay crumpled on the ground.

Leira felt the split inside of her being as she tried to pull away and tend to Hagan, but the light was set loose and sought out the darkness, pushing against it. She felt herself getting swept up into it even as she looked to her side, trying to find a way out.

A shower of sparks erupted in the center of the streams as a portal opened and a sword emerged cutting into the energy, followed by Louie yelling in an ancient language. The sword was moving swiftly, cutting through the stream, interrupting the flow. He could hear the ancient spells in his head and felt the push to say them as quickly as possible, shouting them out one after the other.

The Dark Mist swirled around the Wizard, rising to the roof and spreading out to the sides, sensing another strong presence of light, attracted to the energy flowing through Louie. The Wizard opened his arms wide, the darkness pouring through him as the Dark Mist came close enough to swirl around Louie's feet.

"Noohra Asmata Ginzia Almayya Harasha." Louie yelled the words over and over again as the spells from the first Wizards to walk the Earth came to him through the sword pushing back the Dark Mist.

Leira was lifting off her feet even as she reached out trying to grasp Hagan's hand. *Not again. Not again. Correk... I need you.*

Louie yelled the words again, slicing the sword through the air and bringing it down through the Dark Mist. "Noohra Asmata Ginzia Almayya Harasha! Hshuka Htam!" The mist was being strangled, turning to wisps of smoke, retreating quickly along the ground, absorbing into the Wizard who was being pulled backward. He was spinning like a top as he screamed into the void, disappearing with a sharp bang leaving a stillness in the room. Leira felt a ringing in her ears as she felt herself being gently pulled apart. *There's no pain.* She glanced back toward Hagan, wanting to reach for him as the light tugged at her harder.

Louie raised the sword over his head, neatly putting it back into its sheath on his back in one clean motion, as he slid on his knees toward Leira. He hurriedly picked up the bracelet, pushing his way through the force of the energy surrounding her and put the bracelet onto her wrist, pulling her close and hugging her to him, grounding the energy through his body.

"You're part human," Leira whispered in surprise in his ear as the energy whipped backward, slamming into them, throwing them to the ground. The wind was knocked out of Leira as she looked to her side, Hagan's face inches from hers. "Felix..."

She shoved Louie off her and rolled over, gasping for air as she grabbed Hagan's wrist, checking for a pulse. "Help the others," she yelled at Louie. The sounds of fighting could be heard through the open door. "Go! Go! I'll be alright. They need you."

Louie looked around at where he was standing and saw the tortured animals, a look of horror coming over his face as he ran for the door, pulling out his sword.

Leira kneeled by Hagan's side, trying to find a faint pulse, placing one hand on his chest. "There it is, there it is." A pulse beat against her fingers, barely there as she blinked back tears, wiping her face on her arm. "You would be so pissed off if you knew I was crying over you."

She bit her bottom lip, her face determined and placed her other hand across his broken ribs. "Please..." she whispered, her throat aching, setting an intention with one word. "Please."

Light grew around her hands, warming them as it passed from her hands into Hagan, seeking out the destruction and setting the bones, healing the jagged tears inside of him. Leira shut her eyes and let the energy flow evenly through her.

"Rose, I'm home..."

She opened her eyes to see Hagan trying to lift his head, confused.

"Lay back, lay back. You've been injured. We're in Mexico closing down Frankenstein's reboot."

"That black smoke. The whack job..." Hagan tried again to lift his head.

"It's okay. The world in between sucked it all back in again... for now. We're good. The cavalry showed up and is helping them roust the enemy. You lay still."

Cheers erupted from the down the hall and behind the door. Leira looked up to see Jorge emerge, leading the scientists with their hands tied behind their backs in ropes of gold light with sharp thorns digging into their skin. There was a burn mark down Jorge's cheek and his face was swollen on that side, but he was smiling, waving to the others to head for the cars.

"Is everyone okay?" He handed off the prisoner to another agent and looked down at Hagan, concerned. "Do we need an ambulance?"

"Probably," said Leira.

"No," growled Hagan. "I think I'm in one piece but how's that possible? I heard a loud crunch when I went down." He gave a gentle shake to his head. "I was trying to ground you. Wait... what happened? How did you come back?"

"There's your answer."

Louie came out of the door, his sword back in its sheath, marching happily behind the last of the prisoners. A few well-chosen artifacts were safely tucked in the rucksack on his back.

"Louie meet Felix Hagan, a legend among magical beings."

Louie knelt down and took Hagan's hand, helping him up to a sitting position.

"That was pretty boss what you did, standing up to the Dark Mist like that. Not a lot of Oricerans would do that."

The blood rushed to Hagan's head and he closed his eyes for a moment, waiting for it to pass. "Berens is my partner. It comes with the job description."

Leira smiled as she patted Louie hard on the shoulder. "How did you know to show up in the nick of time? That was like a miracle."

"Jackson called me and told me to get my ass over here. He used our safe word from back in the day when we were scavenging together. I never heard him use it in all the days we were out in the field. It was reserved for when things were beyond going south, and conditions were not favorable to survival."

"What's the safe word?" asked Hagan as Louie helped him slowly to his feet, holding on to him to make sure he was steady.

"Shit storm."

Leira gave a crooked smile. "Jackson called you with magic?"

"No, he used a phone. Come on, that's ridiculous. Magic has its limits. This isn't Disneyland. We don't just yell into the wind and it travels across country. He had my digits. Fortunately, I was back on this world. Don't ask. I had a moment of personal reckoning. Jackson yelled *shit storm* into the phone and a bunch of coordinates, and I dropped the phone and took off. Here we are."

"You didn't ask a single question. Thank you, man." Hagan coughed hard, the bruising on his ribs making him wince. "I'm okay. Not broken, I can live with this."

"You don't ask questions in those moments. You just go. Rule number one is you show up when your friends ask for help."

"Yeah, that's a good rule." *Thanks Dad.* "Come on, let's get going. These animals will have to be transported across the border. That's going to take some doing."

"That's our concern."

Leira didn't hear the Gardener of the Dark Forest arrive, riding on his lion, the great antlers stretching out to either side. Perrom was standing by his side, the irises of his eyes moving in different directions taking in everything.

"Friend of yours?" asked Hagan.

"You're real..." Louie smiled, his eyes wide.

"Hagan, this is the Gardener of the Dark Forest. A myth to most Oricerans but very real. He is the protector of so many plants and animals and birds... on two different worlds. And this is Perrom, Correk's best friend."

"We're here to manage moving the animals. We'll take care of this part of the operation," groused the Gardener. He was doing his best to hold back his anger at what he was seeing. The lion let out a low rumble, pacing slowly back and forth.

"Head home and we can talk later," said Perrom. "Tell Correk I'll see him soon."

CHAPTER FIFTEEN

Hagan sat on the banks of the lake, dipping his fishing rod into the water. The troll sat next to him with a smaller pole, lazily moving it back and forth. He was wearing his small black cowboy hat and red boots, chewing on a blade of grass. From a distance to people in passing sailboats it looked like an older man had dressed up his hamster. Not so strange in Austin that it would make people take more than a second look just to be sure.

A pink box of doughnuts sat between them.

The troll looked up at Hagan and let out a trill. "Everything okay?"

"You can stop checking on me, little guy. I'm doing okay. We're just fishing. I'm not going to get into trouble just sitting here. No magic." He waggled his hands as the troll blew a raspberry in his direction.

A black crappie jumped through the air in the distance as the troll stood up excited. "We'll be eating good tonight!" He let out a whoop and tossed his cowboy hat in the air.

"I tell you, Yumfuck, this whole magic thing might be a

younger man's game. I'm pretty sure I was kaput this last time. Not sure how I managed to pull through. I think I saw Rose telling me everything would be okay and to just let go." A shudder passed through Hagan. "When I got home, I had to tell Rose some of what happened, but I left out some key details." He looked sheepish and shrugged. "Well, I did for a good hour at least. She wheedled it out of me with pie and one of her classic looks. It was the one where she sits across from me and looks patiently at me till I crack. The woman is a mastermind at getting me to tell her the truth!"

"You are a necessary part of keeping the peace, Agent Hagan, but maybe it's not right by Leira's side," squeaked the troll. "You're my buddy. I'm going to need you to stick around this world for a little longer before you take off for some other dimension."

Hagan chuckled. "What is it I can do for you, little buddy, besides pick up the tab?"

"Tell me more about your kind. You know, I see you as the most magical creatures of all."

"No kidding!" Hagan was surprised as he looked down at the tiny troll. He gave a tug to his line but there was nothing there. "Slow day."

"Good fishing."

"I suppose, if you want to chitchat more than you want to eat."

"It'll all work out. Always does." The troll rubbed his face with his paw, sliding his hat back on his head to catch the warmth of the sun. "The natives on this planet have a remarkable capacity to come together and work as one large, fluid movement. Have you noticed? It's in your DNA to cooperate, not compete. You have to go against your natural instincts to take up arms against each other."

"We're pretty good at that, if you haven't noticed. If we weren't, I'd own a hardware store in Dripping Springs and spend most of my time explaining the virtue of different drill bits."

"Your kind spends way too much time talking about the ones who went south. They're the minority but they eat up a lot of attention and scare the crap out of the rest of you." The troll held up his paw. "I get it. One bad one can do a lot of damage. But when even a small number of human beings come together to work for the good, strange things happen. Others see it and want to join in, and offer what they have, even when they have so little. They can even see it on TV and want to join in!"

"These days, the millennials would see it on the internet, pretty sure. Social media, remember? Got us in a lot of hot water for a fleeting moment there. Funny how that all went away."

The troll gave Hagan the side eye, his mind working. "Tell me more about the social media. Mara says it can do anything."

"You're gonna have to go to somebody else for the lowdown. I can tell you more about what people are like in the flesh." Hagan reached into the box and pulled out a cruller. He bit into the soft dough, letting out a deep and contented sigh as he felt a twinge from the bruising along his ribs. "Son of a bitch," he whispered, his mouth full of doughnut. He tore off a piece and put it in Yumfuck's lap.

Yumfuck leaned over and gave it a good lick, nibbling around the edges.

"Never seen you savor anything before. You're in a mood." Hagan's line gave a hard tug and a jerk and he sat up, reeling in his line but by the time it got to him all that was left was a piece of the curly tailed grub from the end of the hook. "Today's your day, fish." Hagan put another grub on the hook and stood up to cast the line, gently pressing his thumb against the reel as he sat down.

"I've been thinking of a career change." The troll took off his hat and rested it in his lap. His green hair shone in the sunlight.

"Didn't know you had a career besides sticking close to Leira and eating."

"All trolls have jobs if they're not bonded to somebody. Getting bonded is usually our way of retiring but I live with Leira. My old career was the study of plants on Oriceran. I helped take care of the royal gardens."

"You don't say... will wonders never cease. How come you spend so much time acting like you're a new sponge just taking in the world?"

"First of all," said the troll, holding up one claw. "I am new to Earth and second, your kind talks more when they think the listener doesn't understand. You learn a lot. But Mara had my number from the start. Figures. She was born on Oriceran."

"That's an interesting bit of news."

"Would be to Leira and Eireka too. I don't think she's shared much about her childhood with them. Let them find out about me and Mara in their own good time."

"So what's the career change? Baker? TV host?"

"Crime fighter." The troll lowered his voice as far as it would go. "I am Batfuck..." he growled.

"Might need to refine the name a little. Maybe not." Hagan smiled, raising an eyebrow. "A little caped crusader? Makes it easier to know what to get you for your birthday."

"Utility belt!" Yumfuck cackled.

"When is your birthday?"

"We celebrate being alive every day. It seems strange to wait. There are hundreds in my village and every time I see one of them, we hug like it's our birthday. Woot! Woot!" The troll raised his paws over his head.

"Good to know. I'll put one tiny utility belt on my shopping list. Have to ponder what kind of tools you'd need. I can probably get Rose to whip up a cape and mask." Hagan shook his head. "What a weird life."

"Two sizes, please. Large and small."

"Right, good point. Need a mask when you're eight feet tall so people don't recognize you." Hagan bit down on his doughnut and licked his fingers before he picked up his thermos, pouring out a cup of coffee. "Just promise me you'll be careful. I won't try and tell you not to do it, mostly because you won't listen and you'll do it anyway."

"And you'll keep my secret."

"Well, that goes without saying. What kind of a Commissioner Gordon would I be if I busted your secret identity? It's just between you and me, little buddy. Do your best to not make me regret that."

"Deal."

"Given any thought to what kinds of cases you're going to take on or will this be for general cries for help?"

"Batman has no limits."

"Yeah, that was a great movie. Saw it a few times myself." Hagan winked at the troll. "No details yet, I take it."

"I haven't gotten that far. Still thinking it over." The troll leaned back on one elbow, tugging at his pole but nothing was biting.

"Solid plan. If you get anything tricky will you do me a favor and run it by me first? I'd sleep better at night if you did. Think of it as a favor to me."

"I will go you one more and give you my digits." Yumfuck dug around in the creel Hagan brought with them and pulled out his phone, handing it up to Hagan.

"You got some muscle on you there, Yumfuck. I get tired of holding my phone in my big mitt and you lift that thing up like it's nothing. You may make a better crime fighter than I give you credit. Is it scary that I'm a little excited about this new venture?"

The troll held up his paw, curling under his claws for a fist bump. Hagan held up his fist, bouncing it against the troll's fist and opening his fingers, waggling them.

"That'll be our secret handshake for your new venture."

"We'll need a bat signal, too."

"That one might be trickier, but I'll give it some thought. Hey, you got a live one!"

The troll's fishing line started pulling and tugging. He pulled back hard as his boot slipped in the dirt. He held on tight to his pole while the fish made a run, pulling the lightweight troll along the shore. Yumfuck skidded along, going face first into the lake, plowing behind the fish, his hands still tightly around the pole.

He pulled on the pole just enough to get himself into a sitting position and put out his heels, pulling himself to a standing position, waterskiing behind the fish, zigzagging around the lake.

"Steer him this way!" Hagan waved his arms over his head. "Hang on, I'm getting some video of this for Rose. She will never believe this one without a little proof."

Hagan held up his phone as the troll held up one arm, then pointed a leg out behind, smiling and showing all his tiny teeth.

"Yeehaw!" yelled Yumfuck, waving at a passing boat as he rode over the wave created in their wake.

The fish slowed near shore and Hagan picked up the long net, scooping the wet troll out of the water as he pulled the line behind him. Eventually the fish emerged.

"I think that sucker is bigger than you!"

Hagan put down the net to pick up the troll in one hand and hold up the fish from the line on the other.

"I was right. The fish is bigger. That's a winner. Good job, little buddy. This will make some good eating."

"Let it go. It fought valiantly. We can stop for tacos."

Hagan set the troll on the ground so he could shake out his fur and worked the hook out of the fish's gills, throwing him back. "I like where you're going with this. Let's pack it in and we can head toward home. Not allowed to report to work for a few more days but I might stop by and see what's up. Just check in."

The troll gave him a look.

"That's pretty good. You almost look like Leira when she does that to me. Much like you, I can be a little stubborn so just go with it. Come on, let's roll. You might want to work on that name a little while you're at it."

The troll let out a cackle. "I'll think about it."

CHAPTER SIXTEEN

"Wait, this is it?" Mara wrinkled her forehead, sizing up the greying ramshackle cottage with peeling paint that was standing in front of her. "This is a lounge? Where's the circus theme? I'm underwhelmed." To the left was a strip mall with a nail salon, a Wag the Bag and a hardware store with a large parking lot. Mara glanced over there and back at the cottage. "Jack, you own a bar. You should know what a lounge looks like."

Jack let out a hoot of laughter, clapping his hands together. "It's amazing, right?" He spun in a circle, his arms out wide. "Nothing to see here, folks. Move it along, right? It works beautifully."

Toni smiled and pulled out her wand, waving it in the shape of a door. "Apparet porta," she said. Sparks formed, cutting through the air and leaving a rectangular space large enough for them to walk through.

Mara's eyes widened and she smiled, looking through the new opening at the long, low slung building inside.

"Oh, now that's a neat trick. Just when you think you've seen everything."

"Go on in," said Toni. "Hurry, the spell doesn't last long, and we don't need any lookey-loos."

Mara went through the magical door and stopped short, her hands on her hips, taking in the blue vertical stripes along the top of the building and the different life-sized paintings of fire eaters, acrobats, and clowns along the bottom. In the middle in large letters was a painted sign that read, Carousel Lounge. "Wow, Cousin Petie has it bad for the circus."

Jack walked forward, passing through the shimmering ward and ignoring Toni's cut-out door. "Yeah, you don't really need the spell to open it, but we wanted to give you a little show."

"It was Jack's idea," said Toni, chuckling. "He loves doing that one."

"You still need to know the spell to get through. That's all Cousin Petie. Come on, let's go find your refugees."

Jack held open the door, giving Mara a slight bow as she entered. Inside was a mix of Austin honky tonk mixed with small town circus with a curved drop ceiling made of yellowing square vinyl tiles. The blue vertical stripes were repeated inside and below them were posters of bands who had appeared on the small stage in the back. Red and blue pom poms were hanging from short strings near the front of the stage and metal tables and chairs crowded the middle. A heavyset bartender in a blue work shirt and red suspenders wearing a black top hat stood behind the bar that ran along the wall closest to them. It was covered in red vinyl with a black and white checkerboard floor underneath. Just to the left of it were heavy red velvet curtains.

"There is a lot going on here. Decorating by yard sale," said Mara. "Everyone in here is a magical?"

"One hundred percent and on top of that it's invitation only."

"How do you get invited?"

"If you're a refugee and not too much of a dick that's an automatic in. Otherwise, you have to know someone," said Jack, tapping his chest. "Like the owner of the Jackalope. I'm a trusted advisor."

"Whatever you need to tell yourself, Jack." Toni waved to a witch leaning over a beer and a shot of bourbon. "Hey Sally, nice to see you again."

The bartender took a long look at Mara and leaned his large belly over the top of the bar, yelling, "Cousin Petie we have a new one!" He gave a salute to Mara and went back to loading beer bottles into a metal cooler.

The velvet curtains parted abruptly sending up dust motes as a lanky wizard with dark hair slicked back to show a prominent widow's peak on his forehead and sporting a waxed moustache came sweeping into the room. He was wearing a threadbare tuxedo jacket with long tails and brass buttons over a high collared white shirt and stiff cuffs with faded blue jeans.

"Welcome to the greatest show on earth," said Cousin Petie, with flourish, clicking his black hightop sneakers together. "I hear we have a new initiate." His deep baritone rang out.

"You would have made a great barker."

"Why thank you. Wait, I know you." He narrowed his eyes and ran his finger along the curve of his waxed moustache. "You're Mara Berens!" His face lit up and he opened his arms wide, turning to face the few customers sitting in there in the middle of a weekday. "This is Mara Berens! She's legendary!" He ticked the reasons off on his fingers. "Started the underground portal, escaped the world in between..."

"We helped," interrupted Jack, earning a frown and a head shake from Toni.

"Thank you, but I'm really here to see Cari," said Mara, holding up her hand to show Cari's height.

Cousin Petie started to say something else but gave a nod instead and did a two finger whistle, exposing the shiny elbows of the jacket. "It's safe to come out. It's your rescuer," he sang out.

"Mara!" Cari came bursting out from behind the red curtains, bounding across the tile floor and into Mara's arms. Travi was not far behind.

"Cari, and Travi! You made it." Mara squeezed the girl tight, feeling a release of pressure from her chest. "What happened on Enchanted Rock? Are Lincoln, Weezer and Harry okay?"

Cari bounced on her toes, her long dark hair swinging along her back, words spilling out of her. "We were waiting for our next pickup and these bad guys showed up straight out of a portal. But before they could do anything an old Light Elf appeared and blew them away! He aimed his cane at them and this silver bird on top of it came to life, flying right at them. You should have seen how fast he opened a portal. I was there and then I was here before I could say anything, even let out a scream!" Cari was breathing hard, her eyes wide.

"Turner Underwood, a perfect description."

Travi wrapped her arms around her daughter from the back and smiled. "It was very exciting. I've heard tales of the Fixer, but I never expected to meet him."

"Just like that..." Cari snapped her fingers. "We were here." Her voice came out in a high pitched squeak.

"The gnomes?"

"The gnomes! The brothers!" said Travi. "They're fine. They were picked up by relatives and have already moved on to Toledo, Ohio. No one should be able to find them there. But we'll be staying here with Cousin Petie for a while."

"Who was clever enough to infiltrate the underground to cause so much trouble?"

Cousin Petie interrupted, his deep voice booming across the bar. "Troublesome, really. An Elf going on about who he lost in the Great War and no one has ever found their remains. He was after revenge with no end to it."

"A descendant from the other side of Rhazdon's war. It's terrible how that war keeps generating new trouble," said Mara. "Did he get away?"

"He slipped through a portal of his own, but Turner Underwood will find him and then we can start our new lives." Travi pressed her lips together, her eyes shining. "Peace is all we've ever wanted."

Mara took her hand, squeezing it. "And you'll have it. We'll make sure of it."

Leira walked up the long grassy pasture toward the dense forest in the middle of the sanctuary just outside of Austin. She was there to test out a theory. She came up to the crest of a hill and thought she saw something moving at the edge of the forest.

Perrom... good.

She waved her arm over her head as he emerged from the forest, the squares on his skin flipping back to their natural resting state of honey brown skin. He stood there, patiently waiting for her to walk the last mile. She was in no hurry this time to get there.

The battle to rescue the animals and shut down the operation took a toll on her, if only temporary. She wanted to enjoy the quiet solitude and listen to the sound of the Texas wind blowing across the grass, the sun warming her face. *Hagan signed on for this work long before you were his partner. He gets to decide his fate, not you.*

Leira had been having this argument with herself since she got Hagan home, safe and sound. *You would never let anyone tell you what you could or couldn't do.* "Give him the same respect." She stopped and shook out her hands, breathing in the warm air deeply. She smiled and started back up the hill. "Better enjoy the calm moments while I have them. Start adding up the gratitude. Come on, Berens. Remember where you were just a little while ago? Mom in a psych ward, Nana missing in action? Now you're a magical badass and you met your father. Bonus, he's not the dick you thought he was all these years."

Perrom called out to her in the field. "That's a peculiar thing that people like to do here. I could hear you arguing with yourself halfway up the hill." Perrom tapped his pointed ear. "Exceptional hearing. These points are like antennae."

Leira ran the rest of the way, her legs responding easily. Running was still one of her favorite things. "Using magic to do it doesn't hurt, either."

"No, it doesn't. Shall we go?"

"Thank you for meeting me here." Leira followed Perrom deeper into the sanctuary.

"You said it was important and involved the animals, and you're a friend of Correk's." He looked over his shoulder at Leira. "I can see that he trusts you." He glanced back again. "You fight like a great warrior."

"Warrior... never thought of it like that. Where I come from, they call it doing your job."

Perrom laughed, surprising Leira. "That sounds like a version of something Correk would say. I can tell there's Elven blood in you." He looked back again. "Jasper blood."

"Correk told you?" A tall vine growing around a tree with large white trumpet-shaped blossoms turned toward Leira's voice. The blossom closest to her head blew out a fine powder that she breathed in before she could stop herself. The rest landed on her face, sinking into her skin. "That can't be good."

"It's harmless. You'll see colors when you hear music, but the effects are temporary. I'll show you." Perrom reverted to the language he used on Oriceran singing the words as Leira watched the colors splash into the air, all around her, filling the space, twirling together and fading away. "See what I mean?"

Leira sang out a note to see what happened, watching the colors take different shapes. "Mary had a little lamb, little lamb..." Red, orange and blue colors floated in front of her, taking the shape of the nearby trees, eventually fading.

Perrom looked back at her, amused at her singing. "Children on Oriceran seek out those vines. They bloom in early spring and the singing goes on till summer."

"The karaoke of the plant world. I wonder if it's ever heard Journey."

Her reverie was broken by the sound of a deep lowing from the distance. An orange blob vibrated in front of her face as the lowing died down.

"The animals..." She touched the top of her bracelet and felt it warm against her skin, giving off a low vibration.

Perrom was watching her closely, his irises moving back and forth. "Correk didn't tell me anything. He wouldn't break your confidence. You can feel the animals, can't you." He tapped his chest hard. "It's inside of you... a connection to their life force through the artifacts."

"It's more complicated than that. It's something about the combination."

Leira looked up expectantly, stepping over a low root, only to realize it was a snake that slithered over the tip of her other foot and into the underbrush. She kept moving, keeping just behind Perrom, reminded there were still a lot of creatures in the sanctuary she knew nothing about and had never seen before. The trees rustled overhead, shaking.

"You know about the connection. Can you tell me more about how it works?" she asked.

"No, but the Gardener of the Dark Forest may be able to. He knows a lot of old teachings he learned from the Gnomes a very long time ago. They started training him when he was still under a hundred years old and just a teenager living in the woods on his own."

"Training him?"

Perrom lifted a branch out of the way, holding it for Leira as they passed under an old weeping willow.

"Taking care of him is probably more accurate." Perrom let out a low whistle and a black cloud of bees erupted from a bush in front of them, hovering for a moment. He let out another whistle and pointed to the west as the bees followed his command, flying in a narrowed buzzing formation. "It's where he met my mother, the Dryad. She lives inside the trees. They made an interesting pair."

"I suppose a lot of parents do. Looks like you've learned a few things too."

"My father made sure of it. If you know your way around, these sanctuaries are paradise. If you don't, they become very dangerous, very quickly, which I suppose is the point. Come on, we can keep going now. Their sting takes weeks to get over. The Gardener was abandoned in the woods when he was a young child. He survived on his own for a while and that's back when the woods were actually dangerous. It's why he has such an affinity for everything in it. It's also what made him such a great conversationalist." He gave a tired smile.

"Parents are an interesting breed. Not sure I'd be that good at being one. I keep getting tangled up with dark mists and in fireball fights. Would make it hard to convince anyone to go on a play date with my kid."

"Elven parents would understand." Perrom put a finger to his lips and slowed down, making no noise as he walked. They entered a glade where the rescued cows were grazing, chewing on cud as the machinery inside of them quietly whirred, turning cogs and wheels while some stood on artificial limbs.

"Never ceases to horrify and cause a kink in my brain," whispered Leira. "They're not in pain anymore. I can feel it."

"No, my father did something. I saw him working with herbs and a few other ingredients, but he wouldn't tell me exactly what he was using. Not that I expected him to. He whispered a spell into it, and it took flight, mixing with the air, calming them all down instantly. Perrom stood at the edge of the herd, talking calmly in a low voice. "They're still skittish especially around anything that resembles a human being."

"They trust you." Leira pressed her hand against the scar on her belly. The stone in the center of the ring was swirling and changing color to a pale blue and green. She looked at it more closely. "It's like a magical mood ring. It's reading the energy of the field."

"The field... and you. I have heard stories about Jasper Elves being able to tap into the light of other beings and connect with them, but I thought those were fairytales made up by overactive imaginations. What does it feel like?"

Leira took Perrom's hand in hers and held it tightly, creating a bond. The scales along his arm flipped over to match her skin, flipping back. "Let me show you." She walked slowly toward one of the cows and put out her hand. The cow looked up, agitated, swinging its large head, its eyes wide. "It's okay, it's okay," Leira whispered. *Far from okay but that's the best I've got.* "Sweet girl." She gently touched the back of the cow, running her hand along the fur, stopping just short of where the opaque covering was over the machinery. She steeled herself to look directly at what the humans had done as the connection between herself and the animal grew stronger. Leira closed her eyes and felt herself being pulled into the moment, letting go of any worries about what might happen next, or memories of the battle that was still so fresh.

Leira felt Perrom's arm shake and opened her eyes to see him taking on the look and feel of the fur that was still visible on the cow, sadness passing across his face. She gently let go of his hand to break the current as his scales returned to their warm brown resting state.

Her hand brushed along the cow, making contact with the rim of the artifact holding the machinery together. Her body began to shake violently and the stone within the bracelet spun in a black whirl. Perrom tried to reach out to her but Leira shoved him away, protecting him.

A current of pure, dark magic was passing through her.

The symbols on her arms blazed in a bronze color, spinning in circles, impossible to read. But Leira could feel what the energy was doing from the inside out. Where it had been, what it wanted, what it had been doing. There was a connection to all the darkness that spread out far and wide.

Her body continued to shake, the scar on her belly burning as it gave off a glow, visible through her shirt. It felt as if her entire body was vibrating and there was no way to stop. Her shoulders ached as her teeth rattled and she had to use all of her muscles to keep herself upright.

She wanted to keep the contact going... there was something new in the darkness she had to see. It was telling her something.

Talk to me. Show me where you've been.

Her own light swirled around the darkness, listening to Leira's intent, guiding her deeper. *The two sides are working together.* It felt like she was shaking from somewhere deep inside. *Let me see. Let me see all of it.* She gritted her teeth even harder, stopping the chattering, bracing herself for what it might show her.

Rolling hills, large mansions, horses running alongside a fence. What is this?

The darkness and the light pulled her along, intertwining, speeding along the ground, seeping into the large house at the end of the road and swirling into the rooms.

Wizards and witches. I can feel it. It's a meeting. I can't tell if this is the present or the past or the future. I can't tell.

The combined energy didn't answer, rolling onward, into other rooms as the light changed from day to night and back again. Leira felt a wave of nausea rise over her and she bent over the side, throwing up on the ground, her hand still on the edge of the artifact.

The black and silver and blue and gold stripes of the energy glowed from within as Leira found herself inside of another large house and the energy spilled down stone stairs into a basement, past rows of wine bottles stacked to the ceiling and under a large wooden door into a locked chamber, pushing back into a long tunnel far below the house.

Where is this? A shudder passed through her as she felt the darkness surge through her. At the far end of the tunnel there was something chained to the wall, wailing and thrashing. A low rumble followed by an angry roar echoed off the paved, curved tunnel.

The energy found its destination at last, swirling around the six-foot tall beast that stood on two legs, covered in fur, its fangs hanging over its lips. Tall horns protruded out the top of its head. *They've made a fucking minotaur...*

The beast sensed the presence of magic and thrashed in the air, swiping at it with its long claws. Its bloodshot eyes were enraged as it opened its mouth and roared again, a blue flame of magic surrounding its entire body. *A magical fucking minotaur. Why?*

Perrom watched in horror as he put two fingers in his mouth and let out a loud, sharp whistle. He moved his fingers, changing the pitch, letting out a second sound.

A wizard and witch were approaching down the tunnel carrying lit torches. Leira could feel the magic trying to pull away as she stared at the beast and noticed a change. Something was happening to the beast. He cried out in pain as he twisted his head around, the thick fur disappearing from his hide and his jaw restructured itself. Leira could feel her heart pounding even inside of the energy. *It's a man...*

He glanced up and seemed to be able to see through the magic, his dark brown eyes making eye contact with her.

The light suddenly changed course, skimming along the ground, yanking Leira forward and jumping to another location. *What are you showing me? Are these connected?*

The energy rolled on, crossing over roadways and traveling up a well-manicured entrance past beds of curated flowers that spelled out Fleeker, rushing onward to the front of a large corporate building. Leira felt the darkness rolling out to greet her energy, coiling around it. *Is this the source?* The darkness brushed against Leira, creeping up her arm, getting to know her better.

The light sensed Leira was in danger and let go of the darkness, shoving Leira backward as she caught the last glimpse of a Witch placing a blanket over the naked body of a man chained to a wall. As her hand came off the artifact attached to the cow she felt the darkness pull away from her, whipping out of her body and slithering into a void, disappearing into the distance. The images faded as Leira returned to her body.

She crumpled to her knees next to the cow, still shaking as she put her hands on the ground, trying to steady herself. She spit on the ground, trying to get the taste of ashes out of her mouth, absorbing what she had seen. *The old line families, they're gathering. That's what I saw.* Her head was spinning as she pieced it all together. *Lacey Trader was right. Those fuckers are not happy campers and they made their own build-a-monster to do something about it. But what was that building? There's still a piece that doesn't fit.* "I need to find Correk."

"What the hell just happened?"

"Not entirely sure but part one, I think, is the old families just doubled down on the humans and have come up with a plot of their own that is making all of this look short-sighted and tame. I need to go."

"And part two?"

"I don't know yet. It may be even worse."

"You got what you needed?" Perrom set off down the path the way they came, directing Leira out of the dense part of the forest.

"I got far more than I bargained for, as usual."

CHAPTER SEVENTEEN

Don ran around the car and opened the door for Eireka, waiting patiently till she was out before he shut it behind her. He held out his arm as she put her hand in the crook of his elbow and they walked together into Foreign and Domestic, the hot new restaurant on the north side of Austin in an old skate shop.

Don was dressed in the best of the two suits he owned. The navy blue one that showed off his eyes and the elbows weren't too worn out yet. The only other suit he owned was black and he kept in his closet for funerals or when he went to the bank for a loan. Tonight was a blue suit occasion.

He looked at Eireka as she carefully stepped up the stairs in her sling-back heels, marveling at how he had gotten a second chance with someone that beautiful. He loved the way her hair had a wave right near the top of her forehead that made it fall against the side of her face. Or the way her ass swayed from side to side whenever she walked, like all the parts were taking their time and knew just what they were doing.

But it's her eyes. She glanced up at him and gave him an easy smile. *It's her eyes. You can see how kind she is just by looking in her eyes. She's tougher than I am but is so slow to anger. Even after all she's been through, she gives everyone the benefit of the doubt.* She leaned in and rested her cheek against his shoulder for just a moment and he felt a surge of excitement run through him. I am the luckiest son of a bitch who ever walked this planet or that other one everyone keeps talking about.

"Here let me get that." He stepped forward and opened the door to the restaurant, his coat jacket swaying from the small book he had tucked in it for later. That was one of the secrets he knew about Eireka that most people didn't get to know. She loved poetry.

Giving her the book would get him one of those looks he craved. The look he wanted over and over again. Surprise that someone had seen that far into her and understood. He wanted to see that look again.

On their third date since finding each other again they had sat inside of a Starbucks near the UT campus and talked for hours as people came and went all around them. Don kept getting up to go buy something every time the manager gave him a look, just so he could keep looking across the table at Eireka.

"Poetry is what helped me hang in there," she had said so earnestly. She leaned forward in her chair, her elbows resting on the table and whispered conspiratorially to him. "It's my guilty pleasure. Lucille Clifton or Naomi Shihab Nye. Nye wrote, 'The river is famous to the fish. The loud voice is famous to silence, which knew it would inherit the earth before anybody said so...'" She ducked her chin down, vulnerable and blushing. He wanted to reach out and take her hand in his rough, calloused one, let her know he was all in, right then and there but he knew he had to wait. *Third date... show a little patience. Don't be a dick, rule number one.*

"That's from her poem, Famous. I used to repeat it to myself all the time in the middle of the night when there was no one else there and it was hours till morning. It's a funny thing that the place they send people who can't keep it together is set up in a way that it's the very place that may unwind them the rest of the way. You don't have to be out of your mind going in to lose your way while you're in there. Thank goodness I could dream of Leira."

That's the other thing about her. She loves people so easily. She doesn't couch it in anything, make you bargain for it. She doesn't even wait to see if it'll be returned like it's not even the point. Like she's fine if you don't. I'm not even sure I could figure out how to do that. Well, do it for anyone but her.

"All those years when I thought I had lost you, I wondered what I could have done differently. The thought of you made me feel equal measures of joy and sadness in opposite directions and all at once," he had said.

She looked up at him surprised with that look like he had seen something inside of her she had been holding onto for fifteen years, not sure what to do with it. Her eyes had shined with tears and she was the one who reached out and grabbed his hand, rubbing her fingers against his palm. He could feel his pulse pounding in his ears and held as still as possible, not wanting her to stop the simple gesture.

She looks at me like I'm ten feet tall and could take on giants and when I'm with her that's how I feel. Like anything is possible just because she believes enough for both of us. We could do anything together or nothing at all and everything would be alright.

He could feel the excitement bubbling up in him again as they waited to be led to their table. He had called and explained very carefully to the maitre'd that he needed a table off by itself, not too close to the front or the back. Out of the path of fast-moving waiters. *You can do this. Don't be a bonehead twice in a lifetime.* He found himself wishing he could live to be a hundred and beyond, a new thought. Just so he could look at Eireka Berens across a table each one of those extra days.

They sat down at one of the glossy wooden tables in the center of the room, pulled apart from the others nearby. "Thank you," said Eireka as she settled into the white metal chair, taking the menu from the waiter. "I'll give you a few moments to look at the menu. Would you like anything to drink?"

"Champagne," Don blurted out, pointing at Eireka and himself. "For the two of us."

Eireka gave him another one of those easy smiles, dimples showing in her cheeks. "Going all out."

"I wanted to take you somewhere nice." He was second guessing himself. No white tablecloths. *Maybe this wasn't the right place.*

"I love it." Eireka looked around, the light reflecting in her green eyes. *She's happy. Okay, we're good.*

The waiter gave Don a conspiratorial wink as he passed by him. Don glanced around the restaurant and saw the bartender glancing over, a smile on his face and the wait-ress waiting by the tables in the corner smiled harder when she saw Don look in her direction. *This entire place is happy for us.* He looked at Eireka and couldn't wait any longer. *I will screw this up if I have to wait. Let it all start now. Let me find out now if it's possible to be this happy and get it all.*

"She will know I love her now, the world will know my love for her! A man risked his life to write the words," he said, haltingly, repeating the words he had memorized in the shower and while working underneath a car and when waiting at a traffic light. Eireka lifted her chin, startled, her mouth open just slightly in wonder and amazement. That look came over her face and he almost lost his place, worried for just a moment he would ruin the moment, but then the words came back to him again. *Thank God for all that practice.*

He kept going, breathlessly, afraid to take in air till he got to the end, finally gulping it in, looking into her eyes. *Those eyes, the way she looks at me.*

She waited till she was sure he was done and pressed her hands to her face. "Thomas Lux. His poem, *I Love You Sweetheart.*" She reached out and grabbed his hand with both of hers, squeezing tight. "The most wonderful way to say you love me. The best... I love you too. What a wonderful gift!"

He felt the blood rush to his head and a million thoughts scatter through his mind, each one wanting to be said. *Stick to the plan.* He reached in his coat pocket and pulled out the book he found in a second-hand bookshop. An old book of poetry with long forgotten poems. It was perfect.

He put it slowly down on the table and slid it across to her knowing she would open it carefully. Take her time and turn each page. Even without knowing it, she would play her part beautifully.

She gave a shy smile as she read the cover, moving her lips without making a sound. She opened and turned to the first page and saw that different letters were carefully cut out of the page. A giggle escaped her and she ran her finger over the tiny holes, piecing the word together.

She loves puzzles. That's another secret very few know about Eireka Berens, but I know.

"Will..." she said, saying it slowly, turning the page. There was nothing cut out and she looked up confused but Don sat there patiently, not saying a thing. He knew she would figure it out, keep going and be all the more delighted that she discovered it on her own. He could wait. He'd waited this long. *Fifteen years.*

She kept turning and finally got to another page that had the small, carefully executed cut outs and she ran her finger over them, parsing out what letter was missing. "You..." she said, delighted. She turned the pages a little faster this time, still careful not to miss the next clue. There it was.

Her finger pressed down as she worked out the first letters. "M...a...r..." She looked up in surprise, a smile spreading across her face. "Marry..." she whispered, as she suddenly dropped the book where it lay and reached across the table grabbing Don's face with both of her hands, her fingers spread wide, kissing him hard against the lips. She was leaning halfway across the table, her eyes wide open, laughing as she kissed him again.

Those eyes. I could look at them forever.

She sat back in her chair, her face flushed, not saying a word. Waiting to see what would happen next.

He reached over and opened the book, turning the pages toward the back to show her where he had cut out a hole just big enough for a small velvet box. He took it out and opened it, as it made a soft click. The ring glittered in the lights as he said in a strong voice, louder than he intended, "Will you marry me, Eireka Berens?" He thought his heart would break from joy.

"Yes, yes I will..." She held out her shaking hand as he slipped on the ring and the restaurant exploded with clapping and laughter and shouts of "Congratulations!"

The waiter brought over two glasses of champagne and set them on the table as Don knelt by Eireka's side and she leaned down to kiss him, taking his face in her hands again. "A thousand times yes," she whispered close to his face.

Worth all the waiting. I hope I live to be a hundred just so I can look into those eyes.

"I love you too," she said again.

In this moment, I have everything.

CHAPTER EIGHTEEN

The troll stood on the edge of the couch, leaning toward the TV. He was wearing an old washcloth tied around his neck as a cape and was punching his paws in the air. Correk was looking back and forth between Yumfuck and *The Dark Knight Rises* on the television.

"This is a new phase." He looked back toward the kitchen and the bedroom but didn't hear a sound. "Have you seen your larger half around here? We keep missing each other."

Yumfuck shrugged and growled at the TV. "I am Batfuck," he said in a low voice.

"That's wrong from several angles."

The troll let out a cackle and blew a raspberry at Correk while farting out the other end.

Correk stood in one fluid motion, avoiding the colorful gas that floated toward the ceiling. "Aloha. That's the entire picture right there. Quite clear why trolls live outside. More space for gases to dissipate." He sat back down on the far side of the room in the red velvet chair, looking around the small guest house. *My time here is almost up. Maybe it's even past due.* "Did I tell you I saw a baby gargoyle today in middle America?"

The troll turned and made an O with his mouth, feigning surprise. He leaped across the cushion, and down to the floor, bounding over with his arms outstretched, pulling himself up onto a nearby side table and leaping out, neatly landing on Correk's knee. The washcloth flapping behind him. "Well I grew up in Gotham and I turned out alright."

Correk kept on talking, ignoring the tiny caped crusader's impersonation. "Yes, it's true. My first time in the field as a Fixer. Not sure if I'm a Fixer in training or just a Light Elf along for the ride. A Witch actually thought she could hide a gargoyle in suburbia." He shook his head.

The troll eyed him suspiciously but said nothing.

"For some reason I thought this role would be a little more complicated. We transported a small gargoyle through a portal and then went home."

"You need a cape and a mask too."

"I don't think things have gotten to that level yet, but I'll keep you in the loop. Things have grown quiet. I'm wondering where my father is."

"You've accepted the idea that he's alive. I've been waiting for this moment. You had to get here in your own time."

Correk got up and put the troll back on the couch, going back to the red chair. "What do I do with that information? The assignment is officially over and I could leave…" The words hung in the air.

The troll rolled back onto the couch, laughing. He

stood back up and cheered at the TV before letting out a sigh and sitting back down. "You could always go back to Oriceran."

Correk looked around the room again, not saying anything.

"You don't want to leave her." Yumfuck threw the idea out there, his eyes glued on the television as he watched Batman sit on the edge of a tall building overlooking the city. It was giving him ideas.

"What? Don't want to leave who?"

The troll blew a raspberry. "It's not like you to wonder what to do next. You get an assignment, you go. Light Elves are not known for their introspection. You don't want to leave her."

"Full sentences, nice. It's about time." He sat back, unwilling to say it out loud. *I don't want to leave her.* He shook his head. *No, that can't be.* "That can't be right. She's equal parts annoying and courageous. Half the time I'm wondering how to get us out of some near disaster."

"Maybe in the very beginning but things changed. You almost died, Leira got her entire family back. You fought side by side. You took a road trip together. Things went boom. It's like you've been doing the action hero's version of dating all along."

Correk opened his mouth to argue again when the door burst open and Leira came barreling inside, almost dropping her purse on top of him.

"You're here! Just the person I was looking for. I need to talk to you." Leira held her purse in both hands, looking around the room, wondering what to do with it. She walked into her bedroom and threw it on the bed and came back, pacing in the center of the room.

The troll leaned to the left as she passed by so he could get a better view of the television and leaned to the right when she passed back the other way.

Leira stopped and looked down at him and looked over at Correk. "Is that supposed to be a cape?"

"I am Batfuck," growled the troll.

Leira let out a tense laugh. "Yeah, you are." She couldn't shake what she had seen and started pacing again, trying to figure out where to start. "It feels like I haven't seen you in a week instead of just a day. Packed a lot in while you were off being the Fixer. You must have a lot to tell me too."

"Ha!" Yumfuck snorted without looking away from the movie.

"You go first."

Need to ease him into this shit show. "There's a lot. I'll give you the highlights because there's a big boom at the end. I saw Lacey Trader and she gave me a personal tour of *the* vault. We shut down that operation in Mexico and rescued all the animals that were there. Not all of it went exactly as planned." She was talking fast, gliding over the details. *Save the part about taking off the bracelet for later.* "Louie showed up out of nowhere with some kind of magic sword to save the day. Jackson sent him."

Correk sat slowly back in the chair, listening to what she was saying. *He had missed all of it.* "Did the bracelet do its job?"

Fuck... Leira might not tell Correk everything but she wouldn't lie to him. "Mostly. Took it off because I had to." She waved her hands around, talking quickly as the bracelet slid on her wrist. "Got the bracelet back on and won't be taking it off again anytime soon. Not a smart idea. But that's not even the part I wanted to tell you."

"Wait, what?" He slid forward to the edge of the seat but Leira was on a roll and kept talking.

"I went to the sanctuary to see Perrom and get some answers." She brushed her dark bangs off her forehead. "Fuck, I'm not explaining this well."

"You're doing fine." *I don't want to leave her... but it's time to go look for Harkin.* He put his hands together in front of his chest, lacing his fingers together.

She stopped right in front of the television. "Hey!" barked the troll. "Move it or lose it!"

Leira arched an eyebrow at him and took a step to the side.

"He believes he's watching an instructional video. Like job training," said Correk.

"For what, moody posing in a rubber costume?"

"You saw Perrom?" He was helping her get back on track, watching her move, realizing she was turning to him because she trusted him. *We have all changed when we weren't looking.*

"Yes, I saw Perrom," she said, pointing at him. "I went to the sanctuary to get answers to something. This bracelet is pulling in energy of a different kind, or maybe it's me. I keep feeling this connection whenever I'm close to the modified animals."

"Is that what we're calling it now?"

"Have to call that nightmare something. Perrom took me to where the rescued animals were being held and I felt it again. A connection!"

"You don't normally get this excited."

Can't jump to the end of this story. He'll never hear the rest of what I'm saying, if I do. "I touched the artifact connected to one of the animals. It was almost by accident and when I did, I felt a surge of dark magic pour through me, almost as large as the light source. I could even hear the sound in my ears like it was real."

Correk sat forward, tensing his muscles. "It was real. You don't see electricity, but you know it's there. Darkness passed through you. Are you alright?"

He's focused on me. Not going to be the point in about two minutes. Leira's eyes widened as she put up her hands. "The light joined the darkness, modulating it. The two joined together like one stream for just a few minutes. Might have been longer. Inside the stream time doesn't seem relevant. I saw things. A large estate somewhere, two of them, I think. There were Witches and Wizards gathering. I think it was the old families who still practice dark magic. Lacey said they're pissed off about human beings messing in their territory and turns out they're surprisingly proactive and really well organized. An anti-Silver Griffins. The magic showed me that down in some kind of basement from another era there was a... can't think of a better word than beast. Fur, fangs, stood upright and really angry, pulling at the chain around its ankle. I think it's living in one of the old homes." *Reel out the rest of the story.*

"Like an eight-foot troll kind of beast?"

Leira looked back at the five-inch troll who smiled up at her, showing all his tiny sharp teeth.

"No, more gruesome but maybe that's because I know Yumfuck is on my side."

"How do you know what the beast is for?"

"That's why I was looking for you. I couldn't tell if that was past or present. Time bent back on itself. But he was wearing around his neck an old talisman with an infinity symbol on it."

Correk felt a chill move through him. "Old dark magic. Rhazdon's old symbol. It must have been a powerful artifact filled with dark magic."

"Yes, that's the dark stream that ran through me like I was a conduit for it. I became a human wand. It was ancient from before the gates opened the last time. Inside of the magic I knew what they were planning to do with him. They're building their own army of monsters to hold back the humans." Leira gripped Correk by the shoulders, her eyes widening from wonder at the horror she had seen and felt. "Right before the magic ripped me back and split apart, I saw something. There was this name. Fleeker. I could feel the strength of the magic and..." She hesitated. *Could it be true?* "It was stronger than Rhazdon."

Yumfuck looked up from the movie, standing up and flexing his little muscles.

Leira squeezed Correk's shoulders, feeling the full measure of what dark magic could do in the wrong hands. "It changes everything, and we have to stop it before they can do it again. The beast... it shifted. I saw the beast become a man. Fuck." Leira took in a deep breath, nausea coming over her as she remembered the vision. "They're using people against themselves turning them into fucking beasts."

"That's not possible." There was an edge to Correk's

voice, and his expression turned to stone. "That goes beyond my father's research."

"Apparently it is because I saw it and I felt it." Leira swallowed hard.

"Excuse me," squeaked the troll.

"In a minute, Yumfuck. They've unlocked the worst kind of magic. Rhazdon must have stolen it from the Gnomes' vault when she broke into it. The balance of power may be shifting."

"Lacey called it. The old families are afraid that power could tilt away from them and they're ready to go there in order to keep it or gain more. They're afraid of what the humans might figure out on their own and they've found a way to scare them back into their cages."

The troll bound across the couch and tugged at Correk's tunic. "I think…"

Correk put out his hand and lifted the troll. "That won't work. People will bring out a bigger weapon and start a war. Hunt the magical community if they have to. Human beings don't take well to someone hunting them."

"That still doesn't explain the animals and all the gears and parts. How does that add up?" Leira pounded her chest. "But I can feel the connection. The two are somehow tied together."

"My father's research is involved." Correk shook his head. "We will need reinforcements."

"I knew you'd understand. We need to tell Turner Underwood and come up with a plan."

"Don't you mean tell General Anderson?"

"No, not yet. I can't tell him exactly where I saw the house or how many houses and I got the very real impression there's already more than one prototype. More than one beast, and not all the same. They're doing their own experimenting but with even darker intentions, if you can believe that. I keep thinking of a piece of advice Lois gave me early on that human beings have their limits when it comes to our kind. If he knew that humans were part of the experimentation all our roles become different. He would feel compelled to tell others. Dark forces like Axiom would actually work with the government to stop it. We don't know how Fleeker is tied to any of this. That could work against us too. Everything would become jumbled. I'd prefer not to get to chaos just yet, if I can help it. But I need your help if we're going to rein this in before it gets any further."

The troll leaned over and grabbed a lock of Correk's hair, yanking on it. "You'll want to hear this. Batfuck was out on patrol..." Correk grimaced and pulled the troll off his shoulder handing him off to Leira.

"Turner Underwood went out for the night," said Leira, settling the troll on her shoulder.

"I am Batfuck," he said, waving his paws.

"He wouldn't tell me any more than that, but he'll be back soon. Till then, we can spread the word among the kemanas. The old families are no friends of other Oricerans living on this world. They will run through the underground cities creating havoc if it helps them with their mission. And the beings who live underground can act as our lookouts, letting us know if they see things."

"All over the world."

"That's the idea. This will take some organization and planning."

"We need to find Turner and come up with a plan. If we don't stop them this will make the prophets right but not in the way they expected. The gates will open to mayhem." Leira took out her buzzing phone and looked down. "It's my mother again. She keeps calling but not leaving a message. We should probably get over there. Who knows what else has blown up?"

"I do. I've been to Fleeker. It's the missing puzzle piece. Batfuck knows all."

Leira plucked the troll off her shoulder and held him up in her palm. "What have you been up to?"

"Crime fighting," squeaked the troll, smiling broadly and showing his sharp, tiny teeth. "And I've been to Fleeker."

Leira gave the troll a crooked smile and kissed the top of his furry head. "Okay that was a rash mistake. You taste like dirt and Cheetos. Tell us everything."

CHAPTER NINETEEN

Turner Underwood was traveling to a kemana located under Paris. The entrance was near the Eiffel Tower that stood over the kemana like a giant iron antenna. It was built by the local magical community in the late 19th century and over the decades that followed different groups filled it with their own little bits of magic as a way to leave something of themselves behind in Paris. He went to the patisserie just down the street and waved to the owner who gave him a begrudging grunt and a nod as he passed through to the back, picking up a hard roll still warm from the oven as he went by.

He got to the old kitchen where there were ovens lining one of the walls. Most of them had been modernized but there was still one tall oven with a black iron front that had been in use for just over a hundred years and was said to put out the best baguettes. Turner pocketed the roll as his eyes glowed briefly and he whispered an ancient spell given only to the most trusted of magical customers. An old Norse spell from thousands of years ago.

"Hniga dyrr soemiligr landi."

The front of the oven creaked and easily opened, hinged like a door, revealing a staircase behind it that descended into the Earth. There were lanterns lit near the top to guide the way as Turner knocked his cane against each step and the oven closed behind him.

The bakers standing around in the kitchen wearing grey aprons covered in flour barely noticed except to look up and see if it might be a friend. Magicals had been using the shop since the tower was erected and the shop was built as an entrance. An older, redheaded baker with a cigarette firmly clenched in his teeth smiled as he saw who it was and went back to pounding out the dough, rolling it over as he blew a perfect O into the air.

Turner walked steadily down the stairs, placing the cane on the step below and stepping down, one after the other. The descent was a mile into the ground alongside a dazzling yellow crystal. Many believed it was what gave Parisians so many inspired ideas about art and fashion and literature. Turner knew he was getting close when the lanterns gave way to the natural light given off by the pieces of the rock buried into the wall every few feet. It gave everything a warm, golden glow.

Leira and Correk had caught up with him just as he was coming home from his date, singing a bit of the song he had heard earlier that night at Cheer Up Charlie's on Red River not too far from downtown Austin. He had seen their grim faces, waiting patiently, leaning against the green Mustang and knew there was trouble.

He frowned, tapping his cane hard against the next step, remembering what Leira had told him. "They've crossed a line!" he shouted to no one in particular. His words echoed off the walls and floated out into the opening that was getting closer.

"There has always been an unwritten rule for the benefit of all of us! You leave humans out of it!" Anger plowed up through his chest making it hard for him to concentrate or to breathe deeply. For thousands of years purveyors of magic had agreed to the rule, despite whether they dabbled in the light or the darkness. "We can blow each other up, torture each other, concoct whatever horrible spells we want to, but no one touches the native population!" He bellowed, his chin quivering with anger, shaking his fists. He shuddered, thinking about what someone may be plotting with the artifacts and gears and humans.

Only once before had anyone thought to menace the natives of the planet. The Atlanteans and their arrogance had spilled over and they meddled in local affairs, manipulating people. It didn't end well and the Atlanteans fled, went underground or were wiped off the map. Their kingdom was destroyed and sunk to the bottom of the cold ocean floor, eventually forgotten by time.

Turner collected himself, pausing on a step as he took a deep breath, held it and let it out, remembering his morning meditations by the lake. He pressed down his purple tie, making sure the pearl tie clip was still firmly in place, and steadied his homburg, waiting till he was calm enough to walk through the crowds without being noticed. "Let's do this."

He took the last steps and wandered into the French street scene that closely resembled what was going on upstairs, but down here with Kilomeas and Gnomes and Elves sitting at outdoor cafes, smoking little cigarettes and drinking endless cups of dark coffee arguing about the state of affairs. A pixie flitted by, close to Turner's head on her way to the cheese shop. Two smaller pixies floated by in her wake, following right behind her.

The aroma floated out of the open door from the shop and caught Turner off guard making him instantly relax. He made a mental note to stop in there before returning to the topside. This city always did that to him, above or below ground. He could lose himself here for days and look at art or listen to people argue passionately about whether or not graphic novels were really novels or if coffee was better than wine.

"It's not all happening today. There's still time," he muttered to himself.

"Flowers?" An older gnome held up purple lilies wrapped in green wax paper, her other hand stretched out. Turner pulled out a small gold coin and placed it in the center of her palm, taking the flowers. *This is better. I won't arrive completely empty handed when I share the dire news.*

He passed down the street, marveling at the parts of the Eiffel Tower that were below ground and most never got to see as he passed around to the left and took a side street that quickly turned into three-story walk ups that were renovated in recent years. The Willens that had lived in them for generations sold them for gold coins and were happy to move further down the street to let the Elves move in and redo everything. "Circle of commerce," muttered Turner looking up at a red brick building with a black door where an Elven father could be seen through the window lifting his small son in the air, making him laugh. "Might as well be the circle of life."

A Willen in a worn printed silk black jacket hurried past him, the sound of metal clinking together from deep within the folds of his skin as he scurried down the road. Turner made a point to keep his distance, not wanting to lose his wallet without even knowing it. The Willen tipped his beret in Turner's direction and he returned the salutation, putting his other hand inside his coat to see if his belongings were still there, just to be sure. "Such clever creatures."

He traveled even further into the older section, tapping his cane against the ancient pavers that still lined the roads in that part of the underground city. They had held up remarkably well even after hundreds of years. Pieces of the crystal were set into tall streetlamps, lighting the way with the same golden light, giving the illusion of early evening.

He turned down a narrow road between two houses, coming to a wrought iron gate, concealed by overgrown wisteria vines that were threatening to swallow it. Purple blossoms hung heavy over the top, hiding the latch. He lifted the vines and slipped underneath, raising the old latch and started up the path that would lead him into a lonely part of the underground city.

The old mystic who lived at the top of the road would know someone was coming long before they got there, and she would prepare for their visit. She never received many visitors and knew long in advance who was coming and often had visions of what they wanted to tell her. It no longer surprised him when she told him what he needed to know before he had a chance to lay out his problem.

Over the years he had made fewer visits, consumed by his work as the Fixer. He looked down at the date on his watch, calculating how long it had been since his last visit. "Too long since I've made the journey." At some point he would have to bring Correk here and make the introductions for him to this woman. "That should blow his fucking mind all the way back to Oriceran." Turner Underwood chuckled despite the gravity of what brought him to this door.

He walked up the few worn wooden steps and got to the large carved door that portrayed mermaids swimming up to the edge of the large pane in the middle. He leaned to the right and turned the brass key on the side of the door, letting out a loud, tinny ring. He stood back and patiently waited, watching the old woman shuffle toward the door through the large pane in the center. Her hair was long and silver even when he was a young Elf and was first introduced to her back when he served as an apprentice to the last Fixer almost eight hundred years ago. It was a different world.

She opened the heavy door easily, despite her age of thousands of years and smiled brightly, her teeth worn down to nubs and her face a sea of wrinkles. "You've come for a visit!" Turner once again gazed upon the face of Tess the seer, the prophet of Oriceran. "So many revere you and believe you're long dead, lost to history. Looking rather good for a dead woman!" It was their old greeting that always got a laugh from Tess.

"Somehow, the mailman still finds me."

She reached out with her hands to feel his face, her milky blue eyes staring straight ahead. He felt her cold, bony fingers trace his forehead and swoop down his long nose, running lightly across his cheek bones.

"It's more than a social call." Turner waited till she was satisfied that she knew how he was doing and had taken his energetic pulse through her fingertips. He took her hand, placing the purple lilies in her hands. She put her face in the center of them feeling the soft petals against her cheek. "What a wonderful surprise!"

She stepped back so he could come into her house. It was where she had settled and lived since the last time the gates closed between the two worlds. Almost 25,800 years ago when she was just a small girl.

The human spark inside of her DNA was transmuted by the magic from Oriceran in a way no one had ever seen before or since, pouring images into her mind of events that were to take place in the distant future. Something magic could never do and made people fear her as well as draw closer, wanting to hear more. But what gave her inner vision also took her sight, leaving her blind. The gift also took her privacy. She retreated from the clamor of both worlds and sought refuge tucked in a corner of an underground city.

Turner was a lot more brash when he was younger and asked her endless questions that had nothing to do with anything and she had entertained them all with patience. "Why is your house so bare?" he had asked

"You get knickknacks for your walls and your side tables so you can admire them with your eyes. I'm afraid all that is lost on me. Not to worry. I have a very colorful life in here." She had patiently tapped the side of her head. "I see in full color with light and sound. It's quite a show!"

He smiled at the memory, looking around and realizing the house was just as plainly decorated with nothing hanging on the walls, no mementos anywhere, as the last time he had been there.

Turner followed Tess back to the parlor that was just off the kitchen. Both of them were older now. He took his familiar seat at the table on an old metal chair with a padded vinyl seat. "I'm going to get you a few magnets for your refrigerator. Something with scratch 'n sniff so there's something in it for you."

Tess laughed easily and leaned against her counter. "Now that's something I would enjoy. I can name the smells myself and then the next time you come, you can tell me if I was right." Tess moved quickly around her kitchen, putting the flowers in a clear glass vase with water, making them hot tea and putting cookies on a small plate. "It can be so damp in the spring here, even underground. Seems to just seep through the layers."

Turner knew better than to rush her and waited for the ritual to be over. She came back into the parlor carrying a tray, setting it down on the small table.

He took the mug that was offered to him as Tess settled into her seat, breathing in the smell of chamomile. She had worn away the edges of his impatience over the years, teaching him there was never a reason to rush headlong into anything.

"There is always a space between the reaction and the response." Tess turned her face toward Turner expectantly. He looked at the deep lines in her face. Her long silver hair was pulled back in a simple silver clasp.

"I suppose you're right." He took a sip of the tea, feeling like he was the student again.

Tess let out a short laugh. "You're a poor liar, Turner Underwood. Why bother? Tell me this, do you believe the world has ended while you've been sitting here with me?"

"No, I don't but if I'm going to tell the truth..."

Tess let out a loud whoop of laughter. "Lie if you care to the seer, it won't change the story I see."

Turner felt himself relax like he always did when he came to see her. "I've never been this fearful of anything in all my years as a Fixer. The darkest magic has been set loose and there is the potential for great harm from so many directions right now. I'm not sure where to start and I'm not sure how much time I have to fix it."

"Ah, I see your problem. You have swum out into the deep waters where you cannot swim without help. Unfamiliar territory. The Fixer will have to ask for help from others and still you will not be sure of success."

"That is not unusual. It's the consequences this time if I make a wrong move and there appear to be a lot of potential wrong moves with consequences that could darken the world."

The seer blew into her tea, making images appear, rising out of the steam. Her eyes looked like they were following them, her brows knit together. The steam figures took on a life of their own, changing into two dancers, then two dogs and finally two birds, rising toward the ceiling and disappearing into thin air. "There were shifters in this world before. Hell, there's some who live in the shadows now." She made a face, wrinkling her nose, remembering unpleasantness from the past. "Once it's in a bloodline you can't get it out, but they quickly learn to hide."

"So, you know what's happened."

Tess covered her face with her hands, focused on the images inside of her mind. "I know some of it. I have been having troubling dreams of human beings twisting into great beasts, roaring at their captors. And the torture of beasts of all kinds, held together by mechanical bits and pieces. I cannot see how it will end if that's what you needed. That is being kept from me." She tapped her finger on the table hard. "The old families have been planning for longer than you realize. They fear the revelations of Oriceran. I suppose that's my part of this current trouble. I told them more than they needed to know and then gave them plenty of time to brood about it. Thousands of years. It's the gates opening that people fear even if it means magic will return to this world. The families can count how many years there are till the gates start to open just like everyone else. There is only one more generation before we will all feel the effects. Slow at first but things will gradually change. Still, there is something else, inter-twined with them... or someone. I'm afraid the dark fami-lies have taken on more than they realize. That may be the real danger."

Tess sat back and rested her hands on the table. Turner watched the veins in her hands and wrists color a deep navy blue and come to life, pulsing, standing out against her pale skin. The color spread up her body like a tree growing roots till her entire body was crisscrossed with the living web of darkened blood lines. It made her milky blue eyes stand out all the more amid the busy pattern of her skin.

Turner wanted to ask her if it was painful but held his tongue. He sipped his tea, waiting for Tess to speak.

"Human beings and their technology are a new wrinkle the old Wizarding families did not expect and they hate not having control even more than you. They are making assumptions that will not serve them well. Like the belief that shifters are new to this world or that the ones who do exist do not gather in packs, much like the old families." Her voice came out in a high-pitched squeak. "It's in their nature to travel with an alpha who guides them and that will be no different with the ones who have started out as human and been changed by an ancient ritual and powerful artifacts. The pack will sense their presence and even seek them out. It's not even the first time this has been accomplished." Tess sipped her tea, preparing to choose her words carefully. "They are playing with very old magic that originated from the world in between, brought into Oriceran by a being who was only darkness. That magic was banned centuries ago for good reasons and is even dangerous to contain in a vault."

Turner blanched, making himself breathe steadily to hide his reaction from Tess. *Rhazdon stole some of that magic out of the vault.*

"Unexpected consequences occur when magic is bent to our will."

"Is that why you can't see the ending to all this?"

"I believe I have told you this more than once, Fixer. We are not in the grasp of fate. What would be the point if everything could be known as if it was already decided?

What I see are possibilities if we stay on the path we've chosen. But human beings are wonderful creatures who embrace their choices and even celebrate them at the beginning of every new year."

"The ones who are torturing animals are not so wonderful."

"No, greed and power have overtaken them, and they may pose the bigger threat. Do not lose sight of that thread and follow it to its end. For now, I will leave you with a warning and a hope. You are right to fear what the old families are up to and to try and stop them before they can really get started. An army of shifters to do their bidding is only the beginning of their plans and could create a new class of beings that want their own power. Squash the families before they get a taste of victory and the world learns of their plans. Find yourself a warrior who can fight them in the dark corners where the world is not watching. Someone clever at putting together the clues they will surely leave behind. Heed this warning. Stop them soon." Her voice shook as she pressed her hands flat against the table. "Then follow who is helping them and do not assume you know the answers before they appear."

"That will have me staring out over my fucking lake later this evening with a couple shots of rye. What's the good news? Please tell me that wasn't the good news."

The seer gave a patient smile, but her face was strained. "Darkness approaches that could spread like a virus. The good news is you have an unexpected ally that will seek you out. Don't be quick to judge. You want to turn them away, even banish them. That would be a grave mistake. You will need them just as much as they will need something from you. Give it freely." Tess smiled, pressing her hand to her chest as she lifted her chin. "The female energy is strong with you. A good sign. Both of your saviors are female. Interesting. Both cannot be contained. You will know them both when you lay eyes on them next." Tess started to rise, signaling it was time for him to go. "You have what you need, even if you don't see it yet."

Turner lifted his cane, pressing it against the floor as he rose. "You're talking about Leira Berens, aren't you? That's one of them."

"Look at you, the puzzle is already halfway solved. Seek her out and use her abilities. She will be uniquely qualified to stop this new menace. You will see. Maybe even the second one." Tess smiled. "The human spark contains so many gifts."

"Why not give me both names?"

"I learned a long time ago not to overplay my hand with the cosmos. I'm not to tell so much it interferes with what's coming. I can only guide and then the rest is up to you. Now go, but don't take so long to visit me again." She grabbed his face with both her hands and kissed his cheek, tenderly as if she were kissing her own child, sitting back down in the chair and letting Turner Underwood see himself out for the long walk back to the streets of Paris. He would make a point to pause and buy some cheese to go with the roll still in his pocket. *This may be a longer war than I anticipated. Better to enjoy this moment now. Then I will find Leira Berens.*

CHAPTER TWENTY

Correk and Leira walked across the large open area of Zilker Park to where Eireka and Mara were sitting on a blanket, quietly looking out over the city. The anticipation was making Leira tense and she wanted to run across the grass to her mother, get it over with and start dealing with whatever had gone wrong, but Correk held her back. "We will deal with whatever it is, like we always do. Together."

Leira got to the edge of the blanket and stopped, her hands on her hips. "Hi Mom, Nana, we're here."

"I can see that moment of Zen was wasted on you," whispered Correk. He sat down on the blanket and gave a tug to Leira's pant leg, forcing her to finally sit down. "I've never been here before. It's a beautiful park."

Mara pointed in the direction of Barton Springs. "There's a swimming pool nearby filled with water from natural springs. When it gets hotter we'll have to go there. Sneak the troll in for a dip."

Leira kept watching her mother, waiting for the news,

still wired from everything else she had learned in the past few days. The troll was nestled in her pocket, curled up in a pair of silky underwear snoring softly. There were too many people around to let him out in the open.

First, I want some answers. "You were blowing up my phone all day and now you're not saying anything. And you want us to meet you out in public, which means you want us to keep the magic in our holsters." Leira narrowed her eyes, studying her mother. *Can't be the psych hospital. No way I'll let that happen again.* "Is someone bothering you?"

"Stop being a detective for five minutes and just be my daughter. Relax, it's okay."

Correk saw the look that passed between Eireka and Mara and noticed Eireka's hand was tucked under her leg. *This is good news.* He felt himself relax and sat back, resting on his hands, only making Leira more suspicious.

She looked at her grandmother, tilting her head to the side. "You're being weirder than normal, too. Did you bring somebody else over from Oriceran? Some *thing* else? An entire village of refugees? Spill it, it's already been a super-califragilisticexpialidocious kind of week."

"I get it, kid. Good news is not exactly in your wheel-house. Let's see if we can change that a little. Go on, show her." Mara hugged her daughter and sat back, giving Eireka a little space.

Eireka slowly pulled out her left hand, holding it out with her fingers spread wide, the ring shining in the late afternoon light.

It took Leira a moment to catch up with what was happening. *This is good news? This is good news!*

She leaned across the blanket to get a better look at the

ring and leaned back, her mouth open wide but no words coming out. She looked at Correk and back at her mother, doing her best to switch gears. Every thought in her mind slipped away and instead for a moment all she could do was chatter like a delighted child. "You and Don? Well, of course you and Don. Are you happy? That's a really nice ring. Don is a great guy."

Correk placed his hand on Leira's knee. "Breathe," he said, demonstrating for her, an amused smile on his face. "There's no crime here for you to solve. I think this is the part where you just get to be happy."

Leira looked momentarily confused as she stayed motionless, resting on her knees looking around. *I have almost lost each one of you... Some of you for years. Some of you in some deep shit holes. But we're all okay and here together... with good news. What is happening?* Her eyes shined with tears as she started to laugh, slowly at first until the laughter took her over and she couldn't stop. She reached out and hugged her mother, enveloping her in her arms and holding on tight.

"Give me some of that," said Mara, as Leira let go of Eireka and wrapped her arms around her grandmother, the scent of lilacs filling her nose and the laughter continuing to erupt out of her. She let go and went to sit back. "Oh, what the hell," she said, giggles escaping her as she wrapped her arms around Correk, holding him tight.

"Oh, okay, we're doing this." Correk put his arms around Leira, feeling the muscles in her back and the soft skin of her cheek against his. He smiled before he could stop himself and looked up to see Mara, a smile on her face and her eyebrows raised, wrinkling her forehead.

He let go just as Leira turned away, lunging back at her mother, taking her hand and moving it around in the light to see the ring from different angles. Mara kept looking at Correk and he glanced up at her, doing his best to remind her he was a Light Elf.

Not buying it, she mouthed. He rolled his eyes and looked away.

"When's the wedding? There'll be a wedding, right? Do I get to be in it? We can do it at Estelle's! No... okay, you have someplace else in mind? So, potluck is out." She sucked in her bottom lip, thinking of the possibilities.

The troll let out a soft trill in his sleep, rolling over in Leira's pocket and kicking his legs.

"Slow your roll, granddaughter or you'll get the bends. You have to ease yourself into being this happy. Could give you a really good charley horse if you're not careful." Mara gave her a nudge and a crooked smile.

"We haven't set a date or a place yet, but of course you're in the wedding." Eireka smiled in surprise as Leira hugged her again, finally sitting back, still holding on to her mother's hand. "You all are if you want to be. We want something simple, we know that and we want to include everyone who's important to us. It'll be a celebration of everything we've come through as well as a wedding."

"And there will be cake."

"Yes, of course. Three tiers. Maybe even a candy bar in your honor, Correk. Jars of candy you can sample."

"Or a snack table..."

"Again, your wedding, not ours. We should celebrate. Go for pizza at the usual place or do that potluck! Let everybody celebrate with us. Of course, this is your news. You should pick! Where's Don? Shouldn't he be here?"

"It's like there's a string in her back that someone keeps pulling," said Correk.

"Don and I thought it would be nice to have a dinner at his place this time. He wants to show off his nest, which is where we'll be living."

"My segue to launch into my news." Mara cleared her throat. "Don't give me that look, Leira. It's not the other shoe dropping. You can hold on to this bit of happiness. It's real, it's wonderful and it's lasting. But I've been back in this world for long enough now and my roommate is moving out soon. It's time I got on with my life as well."

"Good for you, Mara," said Correk.

"Take a page out of the same book, my dear."

"What's that about? Correk has things to do. He's the new Fixer. You're projecting, Nana."

"Yes, that must be it. Well, in my search, I went to Oriceran to seek out the wisdom of some old friends and get some ideas."

Not Oriceran. Leira held her breath, preparing herself to be happy for her grandmother. Let her lead her own life.

"And that all led me back to this side of the veil. There are a growing number on Oriceran who want to prepare this world for the gates opening and they want to start with the younger generations of Oricerans who live here on Earth. They're looking for land on the East coast and putting together all the details but... they think I'd make a good headmistress... and I agree with them." Mara pressed her lips together, waiting... anxious to hear what they'd say.

"Yeah, they want you! You're staying here!" Leira lunged

across the blanket again, swinging her coat pocket, disturbing the troll, who poked his head out to see what was happening. He pulled out the red underwear behind himself and leaped across the divide landing in Correk's lap. Correk held open his pocket and stuffed the underwear inside, keeping it open till the troll climbed inside and resettled himself, curling back into a ball.

"Yumfuck will have to get used to happy Leira as well." *For however long the coming battles let you be happy. May it stretch out for at least a little while.* "Congratulations, Mara. You are the perfect combination of nurturing and badass to keep an entire school of hormonal children who can set things on fire with just their hands, in line." Correk gave her a nod of approval as everyone else looked momentarily surprised and concerned, stealing glances at each other.

Leira was the first to break into a wide grin and let out a whoop of laughter. "He has a point. You managed to raise me through my teenage years, and I turned out okay." Leira gave Correk a preemptive pinch on his wrist.

He swatted her away. "And you hang with the troll and didn't end up online or get pulled into one of his ideas."

"Although, you got him to do a few of your card readings and you survived the world in between for four years and resettled countless magical refugees."

"Nothing I can put on a resume..."

"Well, unless you're dealing with folks from Earth, then it all counts and it spells out badassery in big, bold letters."

This time Correk pinched Leira and arched an eyebrow at her, playfully rolling his hands together as if he was about to form a fireball.

"You can practice now, on these two." Eireka let out a laugh, holding up her ring to admire it again.

"Yeah, suddenly this blanket is getting crowded," Mara whispered to her daughter. Eireka was surprised but looked at the two of them.

"You should really look up once in a while," said Mara.

Leira let a small seedling of energy sweep through her as she touched Correk's arm, sending a jolt through him.

"You are too competitive for your own good," he said, forming a pea-sized fireball and tossing it at her. "Got you last."

"I suppose I shouldn't be surprised that this would be my daughter's style of flirting," Eireka whispered back.

"Or that she wouldn't even know she is flirting. Classic Leira. On the hunt for a killer, she misses nothing. Tall, blonde and hunky hanging around well after the mission is over, hovering in fact. Can't see a thing," Mara said in a low voice, as Eireka reached out and rested her hand heavily on Leira's knee.

Leira looked up to see her mother's arched eyebrow and lips pressed thin and let out a laugh, settling back. "I'm almost twenty-six years old and hunt bad guys, but one good look from Mom... Not sure you can ground me." She leaned closer to Correk and whispered, "This is not over. Sleep with one eye open, Elf."

"Okay, I brought the booze so we could do a toast out here." Mara dug out a plastic pitcher filled with champagne and orange juice. "Figured this looked a little classier than a bottle in the middle of the park. She handed out the plastic flute glasses and poured everyone a glass.

"Mom, you do the first toast and then Nana."

Eireka held up her glass. "To all the Berens women past, present and future. May we always know better times, but at the least will always stand by each other's side... No matter what comes. And to the friends, and lovers who stand with us. Cheers to all of us as our family grows to include one more."

"Here, here..." Correk clinked his glass against the others and took a sip.

"Okay, Nana... your turn. No pressure but that was a good one. Don't fuck it up."

Mara laughed easily. "Our old joke when you were in high school. Nice reminder. Okay..." Mara shook out her hand, buying a little time as she gathered her thoughts. "Here goes... May we linger just long enough at the good-byes to cherish and be grateful for what we've had and for what we still hold in our hearts, and may we just as swiftly turn to look toward the future at all the possibilities that still lay ahead. And wherever we land, may we always be of service to ourselves and others and find ourselves in good company as we trudge this road together."

"Aw, you did it, Nana. That was perfect." Leira lifted her glass along with the others, as she wondered what changes the future held and how many of them would have her looking back with gratitude. *There are shifters in the world.* A shiver passed down her spine as she took another sip.

CHAPTER TWENTY-ONE

Leira slept fitfully that night, tossing and turning as she dreamed of the beast chained to the wall. She woke with a start and looked at the clock next to her bed. *Four a.m.* The guest house was quiet, and she could hear Correk rolling over in his sleep in the living room. *Not even sure that was a dream.* "It seemed so real." She sat up in bed and swung her legs over the side, standing up and stretching her back. "Water would be good." She smacked her lips together and scratched her head just as her phone began to buzz on her nightstand.

She looked down already knowing it was General Anderson. He was the only person who called at all hours.

"Hello, sir. Must not be good news."

"It's not the best. There's a cache of artifacts up for grabs and there's not much time. They're in a tricky location, 2.4 miles under water in the North Atlantic. Closest land is Newfoundland. They're in the hull of an old shipwreck from the last century. I've sent you the coordinates and there's a plane waiting to take you to the coast and fly you out by helicopter. News of more treasure to be found on the shipwreck is about to break on social media but we've been able to keep out the parts about anything magical, so far. We need to get there ahead of the run of the mill scavengers this time. There could be people on site who know nothing about an artifacts race and just want the adventure or to get rich. We'll be sending out extra crew for that reason. Alan Cohen and his team are accompanying you. Meet at the government hanger in one hour or less for takeoff."

"Do we know what the artifact looks like?"

"It's a crown in the shape of silver vines. There may be more. I trust you'll be able to tell the difference. Patsy and Lois will be on call if you need any online assistance. That's all."

Leira heard a click before she could answer him. Moments later the coordinates appeared on her phone. 41°43.5'N 49°56.8.'

A crown made of vines. I wonder...

She changed quickly, brushing her teeth and doing her best to get the piece of her hair sticking straight up to lie back down again. She slipped into her running shoes and leather jacket and crept into the living room, gently shaking Correk till he opened his eyes. "What's happened? Are you alright?" He sat up, rubbing his eyes, swinging his legs to the floor.

"I'm okay. Everyone we know is okay. I'm headed out on a mission, but I have a question for you. We're going in search of an artifact that's a crown in the shape of silver vines." Leira let that sink in...

Correk stopped rubbing his eyes and looked at Leira.

"You think it might be from the Light Elves' royal court. It's possible. Where was it found?"

Leira held up her phone to show him the coordinates and he repeated the numbers, his eyes glowing as the lines of a map appeared between his hands. "Turner showed me how to do this."

Leira gave him a crooked smile in the darkness of the living room. "Pretty cool."

Correk moved his hands around, shifting the map while a small orange ball remained steady over the coordinates. "Something about this seems familiar. Did the general say the name of the ship that sank?"

"No, and I don't have a lot of time before I hit the road. Did the royal court lose anyone in the last two hundred years in a sinking?"

"There was a princess who was a cousin to the King and Queen. Her name was Sophia, and she liked traveling to this world to play among the humans in high society back in the 1900s. New York City was one of her favorite places or Vienna. I used to listen to her stories of salons that held court with painters and writers. She said it was like being in the Light Elves court but with far less formality. I think she found the Queen and King a little stiff."

"Go figure."

"I was enthralled by her tales of dancing in great ball-rooms or riding on the new steam engines."

"I can relate to that last part. Sometimes I forget how old you are."

"It was frowned upon to use portals like that but she had a strong will."

"That strong will did not end well for her."

"Or more than fifteen hundred others as I recall, and more than a handful were magical beings. It has to be hers and if it is that means that crown holds magic from generations of Light Elves. I should go with you."

"You can come to the hangar with me, but I can't guarantee they'll let you on the plane. Or you can trust me to bring it back and you continue your lessons as the Fixer with Turner Underwood." Leira put her hand on Correk's shoulder. "It'll be okay. We have to get used to this. You're going to get called out even more often than I do but we'll be able to come back and tell each other all the wonders we saw that day, or what creepy thing tried to slime us."

"If the crown is there, there should be a necklace nearby that holds just as much power. Every royal has one, some more powerful than others. They should both be returned to Oriceran."

"I will pass along that message with no guarantees. But at least I can stop it from falling into the wrong hands and becoming part of something macabre. That would be a gruesome twist to the tale of Princess Sophia. Go back to sleep if you can. I hope to be home by dinner. Will you be around?"

"I never know what the days hold, these days. You'll need a warmer jacket. The North Atlantic is never warm this time of year."

Leira went to the hall closet and dug around in the crate in the back for a knit cap and a pair of gloves and stuffed them into her backpack. She stopped at the door and turned back for a moment. "What was the name of the ship Princess Sophia was on?"

"The Titanic. Have you heard of it?"

CHAPTER TWENTY-TWO

Leira pulled up in the green Mustang to the government hangar. "The Titanic... Kind of a big detail for the general to leave out. Have I heard of it? I'm the king of the fucking world... I've heard of it." She got out and slung her backpack over her shoulder, shutting the car door as she took an assessment of the situation.

There were a lot of people milling about in the hangar, getting the plane ready or checking with the helicopter that would be waiting for them on the other end in Newfoundland. Alan Cohen was in jeans and a green puffy coat and heavy boots, wearing a knit hat standing near the wing of the plane next to four other agents who were all bundled up for the cold.

"They have to be sweating their balls off waiting to leave Austin. Every last one of them must be a Boy Scout. Already prepared."

Alan spotted Leira and gave her a wave, breaking into a smile that he quickly dropped as the other agents looked at him.

"Yeah, that's not awkward..." muttered Leira as she walked into the light just outside the open hangar. She joined the PDF agents as Alan introduced her to everyone. "You remember Mark and Gail? This is Agent Grundy and Agent Watkins, both experts at operating the small submarine that can get us to the ocean floor. This is Agent Leira Berens, our own form of special ops who will be handling the artifact once we find it."

The two agents gave Leira a curt nod but made no movement to shake her hand. Leira was getting used to it. *Nobody wants kooties.* Some of them were afraid of what might happen and stories of the black mist trying to slurp up agents had made the rounds and even grown a few new details. Alan noticed, scowling but moved everyone toward the plane. "We should get moving. We're on a tight schedule to get in and out before any media planes circle over the area and catch us poking around. We have to be done by midday. No later. Those are the estimates of when we might have company."

The flight on the plane was too noisy for casual conversation and everyone kept to themselves reading a book or playing music. Leira shut her eyes and got a little more sleep, resting her head against the jump seat. They landed and were quickly escorted off as the sun was rising, running for the waiting helicopter, its blades already spinning. The helicopter landed on a Navy ship not far from the coordinates and left not too long after depositing its passengers.

Leira watched it go. "We are leaving this ship tonight, right?"

"That's correct. We want to attract as little attention as

possible while we're out here. They'll be back by noon and we'll make an assessment of the mission at that time."

The other agents were already heading inside to get warm and wait for further instructions. Leira stayed outside a little longer to get away from the cold shoulders and to look out over the ocean.

"Sorry about the other agents' behavior." Alan came and stood next to her.

"Not your responsibility to make them play nice."

"It kind of is but I have to pick my battles. I think they're afraid you could turn them into some small woodland creature if they piss you off."

"That hasn't come up yet. I think that's a more advanced lesson. How accurate is this information? I mean, what makes anyone think there's any kind of artifact down there? I thought everything that could be taken from the Titanic was already in a museum somewhere."

"We did too but we may have been wrong. There's been stories all along about the Titanic being haunted, but everyone chalked that up to the ship and what happened. Then we got this video." Alan held out his phone and showed Leira a video of the ocean floor near the rusting hulk of the Titanic, encrusted by shells and other sea life.

"I don't see anything out of the ordinary."

"Keep watching."

A larger fish passed by the screen, stirring up the sand along the bottom as a purple glow started to emanate from the ocean floor. A school of mackerel that had been swimming in large formation scattered in all directions as if someone had lit a bomb in the center of them. The video went closer and pointed down in the direction of the glow and there on the bottom, sticking up out of the sand was an old, rotting metal chest. Inside the chest a crown was partially visible. Silver in the shape of vines.

"Whoa..." Leira looked closer as bubbles emerged from the chest. "Air bubbles from the bottom up."

"We got this video before it hit social media but we're not entirely confident there weren't copies made. We need to remove that artifact first and get it safely locked away."

"When do we get our Cousteau on and head for the bottom?"

"They're getting set up now. Only three of us can go down there. You, myself and Agent Grundy. Agent Watkins will remain on the ship, controlling aspects of the retrieval, along with Mark and Gail."

"Did they come along to just look pretty?"

"General Anderson is worried about this artifact. I think they're our backups if something happens to us." Alan smirked as he gave a shrug. "We're all expendable moving parts in one big machine. Even you and me."

"Then let's get this going. My first underwater sea adventure. I can check this off the bucket list and move on to other things."

"Like what? I can't imagine what's left for you to try."

"Like skiing. I've never been skiing."

Alan laughed. "So things of the more normal variety."

"They're sorely lacking from my life skills. I can tuck a few in, in between dark magic and hot artifacts that come with submarine rides."

"Maybe take up ballroom dancing or learn how to sing karaoke."

"Oh, I already get after the karaoke. I know how to sing some Bon Jovi."

"That I would love to see. After you. They're setting up on the starboard side."

"Look at you using the fancy lingo. You learned that on the flight here, didn't you?" Leira followed him around the ship to where the submarine hung in its metal harness.

"There's a chance I studied up on a few technical terms so I wouldn't look completely lost in front of the rest of the crew."

"You really were a Boy Scout, weren't you? Go on, admit it. I called this one right."

A Navy Lieutenant met them by the submarine. "Good morning sir, good morning ma'am. Get in any bathroom breaks you may need for the next few hours because there will not be any more chances for peeing by yourself till you are back off the vehicle. No? Everyone good? Excellent. Then let's get you loaded and get this bad boy underway. You are to follow the instructions of Agent Grundy at all times. He is specifically trained to run the submarine and, in an emergency situation, will know exactly what to do. No second guessing him, no winging it. You will be more than two miles beneath us, so there's no room for hot-shotting it. Are we in agreement on all that I've said to you? Great, let's get this show on the road."

CHAPTER TWENTY-THREE

L eira sat in a chair bolted to the floor with a clear view of the round window and the sea life floating by as they slowly descended to the ocean floor, the pressure in the cabin remaining stable and the same as the surface. Leira leaned forward in her chair, careful not to interfere with Agent Grundy or to touch anything on the panel in front of her as she gazed in wonder at the school of haddock swimming by, the distinctive black stripe down their back with the black thumbprint just above their fin.

Agent Grundy leaned over the microphone. "Descending to 0.289659." A scratchy, "Confirmed" came over the speakers. "Continue."

They were sitting in tight quarters, Alan Cohen right behind Leira, looking out a smaller porthole, his side facing her back. Agent Grundy was just inches to Leira's left, ignoring her as he worked to maneuver the submarine to the ship wreckage.

A squid swam by, its eight tentacles pushing back and forth in perfect rhythm. The squid swam above the submarine and out of view, just as quickly reappearing, closer to Leira's window, attaching itself to the pressurized glass.

"Not to be concerned," said Agent Grundy. "He'll leave as soon as we descend a little further and when he figures out there's nothing to eat here."

The squid rode with them a little further, finally letting go, shooting a cloud of black ink in its wake, obscuring the view from the window.

"That'll clear in a minute," said Grundy, in the same detached voice.

"Fun guy," whispered Alan.

"I think fun is not allowed in his job description."

"Not if you want this to go smoothly." Grundy looked over at them. "Small quarters. Can hear every last word. Not afraid of your powers either, Agent Berens. Don't like having untrained civilians on my vessel, even if you do work for the same company as I do."

Leira gave him a crooked smile. "Now that I can respect. Can they hear every word we're saying on the ship?"

"Only if I press this button." Grundy leaned forward and pressed the button, saying into the microphone, "Descending to 1.72617." The response came quickly. "Confirmed."

The high pitched, rumbling sound of a blue whale could be heard through the walls of the submarine. Leira's eyes widened as she listened to the long, low call. Grundy glanced over at her. "That whale is probably miles from here. They're the loudest animal on Earth at 188 decibels, louder than a jet plane."

"I'm liking you more and more, Grundy." A school of

rabbit fish swam by followed by a Greenland shark who was gaining on them.

"I get that a lot. You have to warm up to me."

"Don't you mean that the other way around." Alan looked out the portal, listening to the sound of the whale as they descended further and the light faded in the water to inky darkness.

"No, I don't."

Leira smiled and looked out the front portal. The lights on the mini-submarine illuminated a few feet ahead of them as they came in view of the hulk of the Titanic.

"Son of a..." Leira's voice came out in a hush and she leaned forward trying to get a better view. Her eyes glowed and the symbols lit up on her arms involuntarily as she let the energy easily flow through her.

Grundy kept looking over at Leira, watching the symbols change as he pressed the button and said, "We are at destination."

"Confirmed."

"We're going to blow air out over the site where we believe the artifact to be to see if we can stimulate it again." Grundy pushed different buttons on the panel, shifting the submarine as it turned, making a wide half-circle. "Ready to begin," he said into the microphone.

"Confirmed."

Leira looked out the window as the sand was stirred up, blocking the view of the lights, the sand glittering as it swirled in front of them.

Through the middle of the sandstorm a purple glow emerged, widening out in rays.

"We have contact," said Grundy, letting go of the button.

"Now what?"

"Now we retrieve it and head back to the surface. Pretty mundane stuff as far as being on the ocean floor is concerned. Most interesting part is that it glows."

"And that this is the Titanic."

"Sure... I suppose. I've seen more interesting wrecks. There's an entire graveyard off the coast of New York from U boats stopping merchant marine ships during World War II. Now, those are interesting."

Leira looked back at Alan and smiled. "To each his own wreck."

"Okay, we're lining up with the retrieval arm. You can watch it on that screen right there."

A padded mechanical arm encased in foam rubber went slowly toward the old metal locker on the ocean floor.

"That purple glow makes it easier to spot the thing. One easy day at the office. Not sure why they made you guys fly all this way. We could have returned your piece to you."

"We're Plan B..." Leira felt the submarine shift slightly to port side. "Is that supposed to happen."

"No," said Grundy, curtly as he maneuvered the arm. The vessel shifted again to the port side, dipping. "Something's wrong with the mechanical arm. It seems to be caught on something. That's not possible. I haven't gotten it even close to the wreckage yet."

Leira looked at the screen but all she could see was sand swirling around and the arm pulling downward, jostling the submarine. "Wait..." She narrowed her eyes, looking closer at the screen just as something darted in front of the window. She turned her head in time to see a large green fish tail disappear from view, swatting the window. She looked back at the screen to see if she could make anything out. I could swear I saw a hand. *It's not possible. Must be a long forgotten doll. Has to be.*

Agent Grundy was pushing different levers, holding down a button becoming more and more concerned. "We're not moving. We're stuck on the bottom."

"That's not good."

Grundy leaned into the microphone and said as calmly as he could, "We are involuntarily stationery, presently."

"Shorthand for fuck, we're trapped, I take it. I think this may be where I hopefully come in handy."

The submarine suddenly jerked downward and rocked to the side. Leira held on to the arms of her chair as Grundy fell against the far wall, banging his head. He crawled back into the chair, a small trickle of blood on his forehead and a slight panic on his face. "We are being manipulated toward the ocean floor." He let go of the button and kept pushing levers, looking up at the screen.

"He can't just say, we're fucked, can he? I give him credit for not panicking." Leira saw a swirl of something large swim just out of reach of the lights just in front of the sub.

"They train that into them. I think this is the part where we ignore instructions and interfere anyway. Do whatever you can do."

Leira looked at Alan and gave him a nod. *Breathe Leira, keep your head. You can do this. Same world, just with a little water. You've been underground further than this and that's this week. You've walked on other worlds. Just a bunch of water. Breathe and set an intention.*

Leira took a deep breath, shutting her eyes to get the image of water all around out of her mind. *Set us free, help us to get the artifact.* She felt the energy coming in through her feet, cool and wide, in a rush of power as it funneled straight through her and out of the ship. She felt herself gliding out, into the water with it, letting herself be pulled along. It was easier to see into the darkness outside of the ship with the glitter from the magic helping her.

The energy swirled around the mechanical arm, spinning down to the bottom, latching on to what was tugging at it, upending the vessel.

Leira gasped from inside the submarine.

"What is it?" Alan got out of his chair and stood over her, wondering what he should do as the symbols flashed along her arms.

"Mermaids..."

"What's that she said? I know I took a pretty good knock on the head, but I could swear she just said, mermaids."

Leira could see what was interfering with the retrieval. Two mermaids, both with long brown tentacles on top of their head were angrily pulling at the mechanical arm. The magic swirled around their waists, causing them to loosen their grip as they looked down at the glittering trail. One of them let go, swimming up toward the sub and around to the window as Leira's eyes popped open and she found herself looking face to face with it.

Leira got out of her chair and pressed her hand against the thick window, her eyes still aglow and smiled in amazement. She looked down at her arms and read the symbols, not recognizing all of them but just enough as she looked at the thin tentacles floating on top of the mermaid's head. There was the same symbol she had seen in the basement of the old family estate. "Now we know what became of at least some of the Atlanteans from so long ago. They learned how to shift into mermaids."

Grundy stopped pushing levers and stared, open-mouthed out of the window, not moving at all. Alan came and stood next to Leira, watching the mermaid. She saw Alan and growled, baring her teeth as Leira felt the energy pulse outward, seeking the crown. The mermaid shook her head, leaving the window and swam toward the chest.

Leira let the magic pull her out again and watched the mermaids hold onto the crown as the light from her energy swirled all around them. One of the mermaids formed her mouth into an O, blowing bubbles through the water, clutching the crown. She let out a plaintive cry that sounded like a scaled down version of the blue whale, modulating her pitch.

The other mermaid reached into the chest and retrieved a gold braided chain with a crystal hanging from the end of it. She clutched the necklace, spinning in a circle, throwing up sand, trying to get out of the magic that held her back, but it wasn't working. She was held to the bottom.

The necklace. Leira took a deep breath, returning to her body and looked down at the symbols on her arm, noticing the stone in the bracelet was blue and green. *All is well. Then what's going on?* "Oriceran..." The symbols on her arms said, Oriceran.

The mermaid let go of the necklace and swam back to the window putting her other hand against the glass and Leira saw it. The symbol of the two interlocking circles tattooed on her wrist, but this version had two fish tales. *Agents for the*

Silver Griffins. They're retrieving the artifacts for them. Allies. Lacey Trader knows more about what's happening than she let on.

Leira let the magic subside within her and felt it fading away in the water, flowing backward through her and dissipating. The mermaid looked to her right and saw the swirl of energy break apart and pulled her hand from the window, giving Leira a thumbs up as she swam back to the locker.

"Did that mermaid just signal you?" Grundy looked from Leira to the screen where he could see the mermaids lifting up the entire box and swimming away. The submarine rocked back to position and Grundy pushed more levers, signaling the surface. "Someone else has retrieved the artifacts."

"Someone else?" came the answer. "Can you repeat?"

Grundy looked at Leira and Alan as he began the ascent to the ship. "You can explain this one when we get up there. I'm not saying anything. I love my career and I'd prefer not to have crazy or mermaid written anywhere in my file." He leaned over the microphone and pushed the button. "Ascending. Will give further details topside."

They sat in silence till they got to the top and were retrieved by the ship. Leira got out of the mini-submarine first, blinking against the sunlight. She stepped down onto the ship and faced the Lieutenant, waiting for Alan and Grundy to get safely on the deck.

"Another magical force was already there and took the artifacts with them. I recognized the symbol and I know where it was taken. I'll let the general know."

"Another magical force..." The words seemed to sink in

for the Lieutenant and leave him speechless. Grundy looked down at his shoes as Alan looked the Lieutenant straight in the eye but didn't say anything.

"Is everyone alright?"

Grundy looked up. "Yes sir..." ignoring the goose egg on his head. "The vessel should be fine as well. I'll..."

"You'll put it in the report. Very well." The Lieutenant looked back and forth at each of them. "The helicopter should be here shortly. Make sure you're on it." He walked away without another word, contemplating a new world order that included magical forces.

The helicopter arrived and all of them got on board, Mark and Gail peppering Alan with questions that he ignored. He sat back in his chair and shut his eyes, at least pretending to be asleep. No one asked Leira anything. She leaned over to Grundy. "You should get your head looked at when we get back. Just to be safe."

"That was supposed to be a routine mission," was all Grundy said as Leira sat back, flying the rest of the way in silence. The plane ride wasn't much different.

When they at last got back to the hangar in Austin, Texas the general was waiting for them, smiling.

Leira got to him first, ahead of the others. "Someone else got there first."

"I'm well aware. Just grateful it wasn't some damn corporation or a foreign government."

"You knew about the... the mermaids?"

"I had reports on it, no evidence. Lois and Patsy reached out to confirm they were working with the Silver Griffins. And I'm told that they're not exactly mermaids. They shift between human and something that swims in the sea. Strange world, don't you agree?"

Leira nodded her head not saying anything. Mer-shifters... *I wonder if I can get anything out of Lois.*

The general waited till everyone was out of the plane and standing in front of him.

"Job well done. I know it didn't turn out exactly as planned but that's a constant in what we do. We got in and out quietly without attracting media attention and no bad operatives got ahold of some very powerful items. I'll say it again," he said, smiling. "Job well done." The general turned and went to his waiting car, not staying for any formal goodbyes. He gave one last wave as he slipped into his car.

"World just gets weirder and weirder," said Grundy, watching them drive off.

"Especially with magic in it," said Mark, glancing at Leira.

"Take out the stick, asshole," said Grundy. "She's alright in my book."

Alan put his hand in the small of Leira's back, guiding her away from everyone else. "About that dinner. Tomorrow night? As long as the world doesn't blow up. We can keep it simple and just get burgers or something."

"Sure, why not. As long as the world doesn't blow up."

CHAPTER TWENTY-FOUR

L eira drove back to the guest house, parking right in front of Estelle's and went through the gate, anxious to get home.

"Leira!" went up the cheer from the regulars who were all lined up at the bar. Estelle swatted Craig with the bar towel that had been over her shoulder as he tried to pour his own beer, leaning over the bar. Cassidy and Mitzi were holding out their feet, comparing new shoes.

Leira smiled and waved but kept going, walking into her home and dropping her backpack onto the red velvet chair and shutting the door behind her with a soft click. She leaned against the door, glad to be back on dry land and in a place that was familiar. *That was a little beyond even my freaky meter. Fucking mermaid shifters. I have only seen a small piece of the wonders of this world.*

There were voices drifting back to her from the kitchen and she realized she wasn't home alone. She took a deep breath and let it out, walking slowly into the kitchen and found Correk and Jackson sitting opposite each other at the table. Correk rose up from his seat when he saw Leira and went around the table, brushing his hand against her shoulder. "I'll let you two talk. I'm going to go have a beer at the bar with the regulars. Mike and Scott claim they have thought up a new drinking game that will amaze me. Something about drinking every time Estelle blows a smoke ring."

"Sounds like a good excuse to drink." Leira went around the table and sat down across from her father and waved to Correk as he went out the door. Leira could hear a sudden chorus of "Correk" shouted across the patio.

"I hear there may be t-shirts," said Jackson, a smile drifting across his face.

"Oh, then it must be a real game. I'm sure Estelle is sponsoring it. You doing okay? I take it you heard the big news."

"What, that Mara is going to head up a school and be allowed near children? Yeah, what's that about?" He tried a smile again, but it just wasn't holding.

Leira waited him out, keeping quiet. *Hagan's rule. Don't talk first.*

"I'm happy for your mother, I swear. If there's anyone in this world who deserves to have a good life, it has to be Eireka Berens. You run a very close second."

Leira reached across the table and took her father's hand. "Still, it can't be easy. I know we just met..." They both laughed easily. "...but since we're related, I feel like I can meddle in your business."

"You get that from your grandmother... on your mother's side in case I wasn't clear."

Leira laughed again. "That's another thing. I don't know anything about your family. My family, I guess, on your side. There's so much I have to learn. But...Jackson... Dad... you need to get a life."

Now it was Jackson's turn to laugh. "I don't stay holed up in that cabin as much as Turner Underwood likes to tell people. Although, I do like my alone time." He held up his hands. "I do see your point. I could try a little harder to be sociable. After all, I'm a family man now." He smiled, the creases deepening around his eyes. "Still sounds so weird. I suppose it will for a good while. I'm a father of a grown woman."

Leira gave him a crooked smile. "Maybe you can buy me a beer sometime and introduce me to your friends."

"I think you already met him. His name is Louie. Okay, okay, I can work on that too. I'm pretty fond of that Gnome Louie hangs around with. I think his name is Ronnie. That'll count as two. I can build from there." Jackson grinned as he leaned over the table. "Tell me the truth, is this Don guy good enough for your mother? I asked Correk but he wouldn't tell me. He said he'd rather eat a fireball than talk to me about any Berens women."

Leira got up and went to get two glasses, opening a Dr. Pepper and splitting it between her glass and the one for Jackson. She slid his glass across the table to him and he took a sip. "Two moons, this planet knows how to do a few things right."

"He's a very good guy. I've known him since I was little. He always stood by Mom, even when others were calling her crazy. She was the one who pushed him away to protect him."

"I suppose we all make mistakes trying to do the right thing." He took Leira's hand and held it. "I want you to know something. I forgive Mara for what she did all those years ago. It needs to be that way, no matter why she did it or what happened because she lied. I can't get any of those years back, but I can make the most of what I've got and in Elf years it still adds up to a hell of a lot. Call it my first big act as a father. I won't put you in the middle of a family feud, so that means I'm letting it go."

"I get that from you."

Jackson tried to get out what he wanted to say next, but the words caught in his throat. "I should be getting back to my cabin. Ronnie's probably tired of feeding my dog and the furry mutt needs me anyway. I've been neglecting my business and scavengers are happy to hone in on your territory when your back is turned."

"It's okay, Dad. I'll be here. Is there a way to call between worlds?"

Jackson leaned back and laughed. "I'm pretty sure that hasn't come up yet. But I'll make sure messages get to you and I'll visit at least once a month until I get on your nerves and you tell me to go home. You can even come and stay with me. I'll give you the bed. The dog would love to meet you. We don't get a lot of visitors, as you might imagine."

"I'll bring a housewarming present."

"There you go... I could use anything." He smiled again, looking at his daughter. *I would do anything for her.*

"When I hear about anybody traveling to Oriceran I'll make sure to give them a letter for you. They can take it to the post office and let the pigeons deliver it."

"You've learned a lot about the world you come from and in such a short amount of time."

"Kind of a necessary crash course. There are still volumes I need to learn. Every day lately it gets pointed out to me how little I know of the world right in front of me. I can't imagine how much more I could learn about Oriceran. Did you know that Earth has beings living underground and there's an entire railway down there? Running all the time!"

"I've heard stories. Tales make their way back to us on Oriceran, especially about the magic community here. It can be hard to tell what's real and what's not, but I know there's a lot more than human beings realize. It's kind of funny how they go about their business every day with this assumption that they've discovered pretty much every-thing there is to know about their world and it really adds up to what could fit in a thimble."

Should I tell him? "I saw something the other day. The magic took me on a wild ride, and I found myself on an estate somewhere here on Earth." She hesitated, not sure how to finish.

Jackson softened his expression, resting his elbows on the table. "You can tell me anything, for the rest of your life. I'm your Dad."

"This isn't your typical father daughter kind of conversation."

"We aren't your typical father and daughter, so we're good. Tell me. Maybe your old man can shed some light on it. Scavengers are good at hearing things others don't mean to tell."

"I found myself in an old basement. I swear if I didn't know better, I'd have called it a dungeon. The whole cliché. Stone walls, beast at the other end, chained to a wall. That was bad enough. I thought they had created some kind of Frankenstein of their own like the bionic animals. He even had a pendant around his neck with the infinity symbol on it."

Jackson's expression hardened and he curled his hands into fists. Leira kept going, seeing the images in her mind.

"But before I could see more a Witch and Wizard approached and the magic saw fit to yank me out of there."

"That's good," he said, heatedly. "The energy will protect you even against your own curiosity. It's part of being a Jasper. The light is always on your side."

"Even if it wants to keep me forever." Leira shook her head. "Just as I was about to get swept back across the veil and into my own body, I saw a few things. The beast became a man and I swear, I've thought about it ever since I saw it. He knew I was there and was asking for help. I can't shake the feeling."

"But you have no idea where this was?"

"Other than on Earth, no. Somewhere green where the trees grow tall but that's not much to go on. Did you know that it was possible to create a shifter?"

"That's not new magic. It's some of the oldest kind and always filled with darkness. Light has no need to twist magic like that. Shifters have been rumored to exist for thousands of years, but no one will talk about them. They're the pariahs of the magic world."

"Is there a reason for that beyond the usual ignorance?"

"I suppose it's because of what they were created from. They were made at least partially from unrestrained darkness. It didn't pass through them like practitioners, and even that has its consequences. The darkness becomes a part of them, reconfiguring their very essence and making it unstable. It's why they can shift. There's a belief that the darkness overrules any other impulses and eventually a shifter would turn on you in some pretty gruesome ways. If the old Wizarding families are playing around with that shit, they should be prepared to watch their own herds be thinned when a shifter or two gets loose and takes off their heads."

"If humans find out that the old families are picking them for their experiments then a new kind of hell will be unleashed as well. Thousands of years ago when they were doing this, I'm betting it was probably pretty easy to use the native population and get away with it. That won't be the case this time."

"That does add an entirely new dimension to it. I will keep an eye out for you from Oriceran and see what I can find out. See if anyone knows anything about a new population of shifters, but it won't be easy. Oricerans don't even like talking about them. It's our form of a bogeyman and plenty of people have superstitions about shifters."

"I saw some beautiful ones today, miles under the sea. They looked like mermaids but with tentacles for hair and they were part of the Silver Griffins. Like an underwater division. They were friendly, in a way. Didn't seem to care for humans much."

Jackson sat back in his chair, his eyes widening. "Wow...

they may hold a piece of your puzzle for you." Jackson shook his head. "I don't know, it's a lot. Sea shifters and they work for the Silver Griffins. Mermaids are common on Oriceran, but this is not the same thing. Not at all. Keep me in the loop and I'll do what I can. You have my word."

"I can't shake the feeling that the shifters are just the start of something."

"The bionic animals…"

"Yes, the animals." Leira's mind drifted to the sweep of magic curling around the Fleeker sign. *Too close by… and why?*

"That is an entirely new horror, but I will keep an ear to the ground for you."

"When are you thinking of taking off for Oriceran."

"Tomorrow seems like a good day to go. There's not much reason for me to hang around here anymore except to annoy Turner Underwood. A worthwhile reason but maybe it's time to go home and see the dog. I'll be back though, I'm your dad."

"How about Thanksgiving?"

"Have no idea what that is, but sure. I'll come on your birthday too. When is your birthday?"

Leira laughed and said, "It's coming up soon, you haven't missed it this year. It's May 15th."

"The 15th of every May, I'll be here, and I'll bring a present. Imagine what a scavenger can come up with." He gave Leira a wink. "Some pretty good shit out there, just lying around in Oriceran caves."

"Nothing stolen. I'm going to have to insist on that one."

"That's a deal. No presents that were stolen. Now, in my world, if you leave something lying around for longer than a few years, it's free to whoever finds it. You're just going to have to accept that rule."

"Deal... Dad?"

"Yeah, Leira."

"I'm glad Mara dragged you across the veil."

"Yeah, me too, kid. Me too."

CHAPTER TWENTY-FIVE

Leira spent the rest of the day filling out the reports for the general and went to bed exhausted. The next day she saw her father off as he opened a portal in her living room and found herself missing him as soon as the portal closed. "Don't get weird, Berens. You just met him and he'll be back. You're a federal agent. We don't boohoo. Need to focus on figuring out where that estate is located and gather more information. That's a better use of my time."

She tried to reach Lois but for once, Lois was nowhere to be found. "She's probably off with Earl," said Patsy over Facetime. "I'll tell her you're looking for her. Maybe the general knows. He can always reach her. You want me to ring him for you?"

"No... no... it's not that urgent. Let's keep this call just between us, but if you happen to see Lois, ask her to call me."

"Will do," said Patsy, filling her mouth with green peanut M&Ms. Leira studied her face as she signed off, looking for any telltale sign that Patsy was lying to her, but it was hard to tell. Patsy was always a little nervous. *Something's not right. My spidey senses are on high alert.*

None of the magical community were out at Enchanted Rock or at the Jackalope. It was as if everyone had gone underground. "I wonder if they've heard something. If they have, it was apparently bad news."

Leira finally headed home, remembering she had agreed to go to dinner with Alan Cohen and thought a shower was a pretty good idea.

Now, here she sat in the red velvet chair by the door, waiting. "I don't see why I can't meet him out there."

Eireka and Mara sat on the couch facing her as Correk leaned in the doorway to the kitchen. They had all gathered to see her off. Leira glared at Correk for telling her mother, who told her grandmother.

"I also don't see why my going on a date became a kind of team sport. Why are you all here?"

"Because this happens so rarely, dear and Elves don't live forever. I probably only have a good eight hundred years left in me. Who knows when this will happen again? It's like refusing to go outside and look at Haley's comet. Who does that?" Mara gave her a smile and a wink.

"Despite what my mother said, we're here to support you and take pictures." Eireka pulled out her phone and held it up, taking a picture. "Oh, that's a good one. I can put it on my Facebook page. Do you think Alan would let me get a good one of the two of you?"

"This isn't prom, Mom, and yes, I know you missed my actual prom, but you're not sucking me in with the psych hospital story tonight."

Eireka smiled, suppressing a laugh. "We have come a long way. I figured that one would wear off, but I was hoping it would take longer."

"Oooh, she's testy. Must be nervous. Have we done a background check on this young man?" Mara leaned forward, resting her elbows on her knees.

"No, but the Feds have. We're good, you can stand down."

"I will never understand Berens women," muttered Correk, taking in Leira in a dress. *She's beautiful. How did I not see that before?* "I don't think I've ever seen you in a dress. No, wait, there was that ball in Chicago when we were trying to catch a killer and get back the necklace. This would be the second time and it's not job related. It's not job related, is it?"

"No, we're not going over a case. Fuck, I hope he's smart enough not to bring up work."

"Might want to chill on the swearing," said Mara.

"This is me. He might as well fucking get used to it or this is a one and done."

"Are you taking the troll with you? Where is Yumfuck anyway?"

"On one of his walkabouts. He'll be back when he's back." Leira smoothed out her dress, picking off a piece of invisible lint.

"Probably out fighting crime." *Leira's going on a date... with someone else.*

"Funny, not funny. Look, there will be no chaperones on this date. I am capable of protecting anything that needs protecting."

Mara noticed Correk shifting in the door. *Interesting,*

but not surprising. How these two clever people cannot see... ah well, time will tell...

There was a soft knock at the door and Leira jumped up to open it, ready to sprint out the door before her mother could ask for a group selfie.

Alan was standing there in a sports coat and slacks, his hair neatly tucked back. In his hand was a small nosegay of pink roses. "Hello...these are for you." He smiled nervously, holding out the flowers. "I wasn't sure what to bring you and the woman at the florist shop said you'd love them. She was adamant that all women do. I questioned her as thoroughly as possible and found no holes in her story." He smiled, the dimples in his cheeks showing as Leira took the flowers and held them up to her nose, breathing in the sweet scent of roses.

"You will find out as the night goes on, I'm better at tracking felons than small talk." He looked down at his shoes for a moment, still smiling. "I'm hoping rigorous honesty will help me out when I say something particularly stupid."

Leira held the door open only a few inches, doing her best to lean down and grab her purse without letting go of the door. She could see a few of the regulars leaning over from their bar stools, trying to get a better look. Estelle shot Craig and Michael with the seltzer spray from behind the bar, ending their prying. "Act like you were born with some common sense," said Estelle, throwing them a bar towel to wipe up the spill.

"Aren't you going to invite him in?" Mara called out in a sing-song voice as Leira rolled her eyes. *Of course it's Nana busting me.*

Alan's eyebrows shot up, wrinkling his forehead. "Oh, is your family... are they inside?" He put a foot on the threshold, forcing Leira to open the door wider.

"Why yes, the gang's all here. Most of them anyway. Why don't you come in?" Leira held out her arm, ushering him in as she whispered, "Sorry..."

He looked at her, smiling, as he took a look around, nodding, holding out his hand. "Hi, I'm Alan Cohen, nice to meet you."

Eireka and Mara stood up, grinning broadly as Eireka ignored his hand and grabbed Alan in a hug. Mara waited and took her turn, stepping back to get a better look at him. *Not bad. Better move fast, Correk. This one might be a keeper.*

"Correk, nice to see you again." The two nodded at each other with a low grunt, causing Mara to roll her eyes. Eireka raised her phone, waving at Alan to get closer to Leira.

"Okay, let me get a few pictures. Humor me. Oh, you got flowers! Perfect. Hold up the flowers in front so we can see them in the picture. Leira, don't make that face. It's not your best. Smile and say whiskey! Wait, one more. Do you want to change poses? Oh, that's good, Alan. Come on, Leira, we could have been done by now. Boy, you two look good together. See, I got a few good ones."

"Okay, thank you, Mom. We're going to go now. Don't wait up because you'll be back at your own place. Correk, please let the troll know I'm out and tuck him in for me."

"What if Correk has plans? He might have met someone." Mara smiled mischievously, looking back and forth between Leira and Correk.

Leira startled and stumbled over her words. "Oh, right... Have you... I mean, did you? You don't have to..."

"Shoot her and put her out of her misery," said Mara.

Eireka laughed as Correk shrugged, his face warming. "I'll be here and can let in the troll."

"What?" Mara shrugged as Correk scowled at her.

"Okay, enough waterboarding for one night. We're leaving and not looking back, no matter what." Leira grabbed Alan by the arm and pulled him out of the guest house as a cheer of "Leira!" rose up from the bar, followed by another spray of seltzer.

Leira looked over to see several people spitting and wiping their eyes as Estelle raised her hand and gave a wave, a thin trail of smoke winding its way toward her red beehive.

Correk went to shut the door and watched Leira walking out the gate, still holding onto Alan's arm. A wave of anger ran through his chest. *No, that's not possible. I don't feel that way about Leira. Not her.*

Mara leaned close enough to whisper in his ear. "You can be a blind fucking moron sometimes, Elf man. There's still time, but you better man up and do something soon or forever hold your fucking peace."

"Berens women," he muttered, as he shut the door, wondering when the pair would head for their own home. *Soon, please with all that is good and right in the world, let it be soon.* And what to do about Leira. *Damn.*

"Let's play Truth or Dare! Correk, you're going to go first."

"Fuck me..."

"Pick truth... we have questions."

CHAPTER TWENTY-SIX

Hagan sat in bed with Rose watching the news, holding her hand. His favorite part of the day. *Whenever I'm with Rose.* He looked over at her and smiled. She was wearing her reading glasses, looking down at a book, occasionally looking up at the television. It was her usual way of watching the news. With her other hand she was holding the book steady, keeping a finger where she was reading, doing her best not to lose her place. It took her forever to finish a book, but she loved buying them, leaving a revolving stack by her bed.

"Rose? You have a minute?"

"Always for you," she said, looking at him over her glasses. "What's on your mind, Big Guy? Ooh, did you get the seed order sent? It's time to put in our vegetable garden if we're going to do that this year."

"Yes, order was sent last week. It's already on its way to us. I have a work thing I need to reason out and we both know you're the real brains of this operation."

Rose let out a chuckle, lifting his hand up to her mouth and kissing his wrist gently. "Smart man."

"Why we have thirty-five years tucked under our belts." He hesitated, pressing his lips together, blowing out a breath. Rose took off her glasses and shifted so she could see him better.

"Sounds like this is gonna be a good one. Are you asking for help or forgiveness? You know you'll get either one."

"Help, please." He thought for a moment about the doughnuts he had hidden in the trunk of his car where they'd stay cool overnight before he headed to work but decided to let that go. *No need for verbal diarrhea.* "I'm thinking about hanging back a little more on these missions. Helping out from the office more. They're getting more complicated and, well..."

The image of trying to get off that warehouse floor, and with help, flashed in his mind. "This might be a younger man's game to face off with a sample platter of bogeymen. Something new pops up every day and they seem to always bring something no one's ever heard of before."

Rose patted his hand. "You don't need to convince me, dear. I know how tough you are, as tough as they come. It takes a strong man to know when it's time to stand down, at least part of the way. It's not a sign of courage to put yourself or your partner at risk just to prove something."

"I knew you'd understand. I just hope Leira doesn't think I'm abandoning her out there." Hagan grimaced, looking up at the news. Another week with no rain.

"Leira Berens doesn't operate that way. The woman is loyal to a fault and can see what people are really made of, inside. It's what has made her such a good detective. She will not only understand, she'll probably buy you those doughnuts you love so much and are currently hiding from me." Rose gave Hagan a sidelong glance, her lips pursed. "You know, you might share one or two with me once in a while. You're not fooling anybody with all your shenanigans, hiding them everywhere."

Hagan sat up straighter and put down the remote. "Consider it done!" He threw back the covers and swung his legs over the side of the bed, sliding his feet into his slippers. "Turns out, I might have a few handy I can share right now."

"Uh huh, thought you might. Sounds perfect right about now. Just one or two, you know. We don't need to finish off the box all at once."

Hagan headed for the stairs. "Of course not, dear." Maybe just bring in a few. Not necessary to bring in the whole box.

CHAPTER TWENTY-SEVEN

Perrom waited by the edge of the Dark Forest, easily blending in with the trees behind him, waiting for the right moment. Ossonia was due to walk by on the main road at any minute on her way to the post office. It was part of her usual routine and she was fond of schedules, precision, everything in its proper place. Perrom knew because he had been watching her from afar... for years, wishing her well, hoping things could be different.

The scales along his arms flipped over expectantly, changing with the movement of the branches behind him, keeping him hidden. The irises of his eyes scanned the horizon looking for the familiar figure walking determinedly down the road.

There she is... Perrom felt his heart beat faster and stepped out from the background, not wanting to startle her. "Ossonia..." He called out, raising his arm as his skin settled back to the warm honey brown.

Ossonia stopped on the road, turning to see who was calling her, her forehead wrinkled. She put her hand over her eyes to block the sunlight and held her satchel closer to her chest. "Perrom, hello!"

He crossed the distance between them, practicing the words in his head that he wanted to say. "Mind if I walk with you?"

"Not at all. Makes the journey fly by with good company. Have you heard from Correk?" Ossonia saw Perrom's face darken. "It's okay, I'm only asking about an old friend. I've let him go," she said, softly. "It's time to get on with things." She squeezed his arm. "You don't have to answer that. We both know he's happy where he is and is doing well."

The words Perrom wanted to say flew out of his head and he scrambled to come up with something to replace them. *All these years of waiting and I can't think of anything to say?* He swallowed hard and blurted out the first thing that came to mind. "Will you go to the Two Moons ball with me? As my date, will you go?" He held his breath, ready to disappear back into the forest if Ossonia said no, never to bother her again.

Ossonia stopped walking, surprised and looked at Perrom, saying nothing at first. Slowly a smile spread across her face and she clutched the satchel tighter. "Yes... yes, I will go with you. What a perfect idea!"

The irises in Perrom's eyes all focused on Ossonia's face, memorizing the way she was looking at him in that moment. "A new start."

"Yes, a new start," she said, slipping her hand around his arm as they walked toward the post office. "What a good idea..."

The dead oak tree slowly came back to life. The dry bark forming back against the hard wood starting at the base and working its way toward the top. Leaves sprung out from the branches, fluttering open and providing shade over bare spots. Moss crept over the roots that dug their way back into the soil. The Gardener of the Dark Forest arched an eyebrow and rapped his knuckles against the tree.

"If Perrom sees that he'll know we were spying on him."

The Dryad emerged from the once rotten tree, stepping out still well hidden behind the thick stand between them and the road. "He only has eyes for Ossonia. Did you see how nervous he was? He reminds me of you."

"You've been breathing in wood fumes for too long."

The Dryad let out a lilting laugh. "I know you too well, Gardener, and love you for it. Our son appears to have found a mate."

"Don't get too far ahead of yourself."

"No, I saw the way he looked at her. Perrom may have to accept he's happy at last."

CHAPTER TWENTY-EIGHT

Correk was sitting in Turner Underwood's study surrounded by oversized, ancient tomes, whose spines were hand sewn with enchanted thread, doing his best to concentrate on learning the new spells. Normally, learning came easily to him, but he was distracted, looking out the window at Leira taking a lesson from Turner. The Fixer was helping her find the limits of the bracelet under controlled circumstances. Correk wanted to go out there and ask her how the date went last night but knew he wasn't going to. "And then what? Tell her good for you? Ask her out yourself? You are a Light Elf from the royal court. Suck it up and concentrate." *Everything was easier before I met you, Leira Berens.* "As Leira would say, you are a fucking liar, Correk," he muttered.

Correk glanced back down at the book and read the same page again. It was in an ancient language and was a spell for bifurcating a road in two to confuse enemies in battle or to help with getting away quickly without being followed. "Divaid paeo," he whispered, not paying enough attention. He looked out the window in time to see the curve of Turner's driveway splitting in two. He jumped up, scanning the page quickly for a way to reverse the spell but there was nothing more. He flipped the pages to the back as he saw the driveway continue to peel back, upending some of Turner Underwood's prized boxwoods.

Turner looked up hurriedly, glancing at the window to the study as he looked back at the driveway, raising his arms, his eyes aglow, yelling, "Baekwod," in the same ancient language. The two spells pushed against each other for a moment, spewing rocks and gravel into the air as the road became rubble.

"Two moons!" Correk slammed his hand on the desk, searching through his memory for any spell he had ever learned that would help fix what he had started.

Turner waved his arms bellowing, "Ad infinitum," stopping the rocks in midair and reassembling them as they fell back into place.

Correk stood very still, taking his hands off the book and saw Leira smile in his direction. The road settled back down with a slight divot running down the side and a bush that was now planted square in the middle. Turner frowned and looked back up at the study, his hands on his hips as Leira shut her eyes and pulled in energy through her feet, setting out an intention.

The road once again lifted, swirling in a counter-clockwise direction, gently depositing the old boxwood back into its rightful spot and repaving the road. Leira looked at Turner, shrugging as Correk got up to go outside and apologize but Turner was already settling back into the lesson, his back to the window.

Correk sat back down and turned the page. "I think it's safe to say I've got that spell down." He looked down at the book, shifting so he couldn't look out the window as easily, and made a point to not even move his lips as he looked at the new spell. Each page was illustrated with hand-painted images of before and after to help with deciphering the spell even if there was a language barrier.

Turner had shown Correk the books, explaining that they were published centuries after the spells were created. "Hand painted by the Gnomes. Very clever people. These are the only remaining editions. Handle them with great care. If even a page is destroyed the spell is lost forever." Turner had rocked back, resting his hands on his cane.

"That would be a good thing with some of these spells." Correk had traced the illustration of an Elf on fire, wondering how often that spell was ever used.

"I've had the same thought myself, many times but over time I came to learn that each spell that exists in the world balances some other spell," the old Fixer had said. "If one were lost then another could run amok. Despite what you may be thinking, every incantation, every bit of magic has its purpose. Dark magic happens when a spell is used to twist magic into causing undo harm. Remember the first thing you learned about magic as a small child. It all runs on feelings. That means magic is fueled by intention. It knows, somehow what we hope it will do and when our motives are twisted, the magic becomes dark. If there weren't purveyors of this nonsense, then all these books could be let loose in the world. But these words are powerful and therefore the consequences stack up higher.

So they are hidden, but must be learned by the Fixer, just in case..."

"I never realized any of these books existed outside of the Oriceran library vault or the Silver Griffins."

"Yes, that's the point. If others knew then they would become a target. Secrecy will be your friend in this job."

Correk had tapped the page of a book. "If this is the only record of a spell, why learn them?"

"A good question. Somewhere out there is the mate to this spell. The one that offsets it in some way we can't even imagine till we see them performed, one after the other. We don't know what that spell is, many of them have thankfully not been performed for thousands of years. But we know from the wisdom that has been passed down that it's out there. You will see many wonders in this role that will take your breath away, day after day. I know rescuing a gargoyle from a witch wasn't very exciting but those are the days I appreciate. There are too many that are much more difficult or dark. But then, there are also the days that are humorous or fun."

Correk's eyes had widened as he got more excited. "In the beginning, the original creators of magic wrote two spells for everything..."

Turner had clapped his hands together. "Yes, you are getting it. That is a piece of information we do not share with others. No need to get someone curious about hunting for a sister spell. But they all must be learned by us. If that spell were to reappear in the wrong hands and was left unanswered, the results could be more than we're willing to pay. So we learn all the spells. Besides, it's cool to know how to create starlight whenever you need to, just ask the ladies." He had given Correk a wink and had tapped the top of one of the piles. "All of magic has a balance to it, a symbiotic relationship. As the Fixer your mission statement is to keep that balance intact. In that way you will protect all the magical beings who rely on it. Got it? Good! I'll leave you to it." He had left the study whistling, a smile on his face.

Correk glanced back at the window and saw Leira walking down toward the lake. "Not whistling a tune now. He loves those boxwood." Correk shook his head, turning the page. He ran his hand over the colorful painting on the large page. It was the spell used over eight-hundred years ago to start the fires in what was supposed to be the last battle with Rhazdon. Correk held his breath as he read the words the old king of Oriceran had said, trying to end the war. The battle where the king had slipped into the world in between.

"Every spell has a counter-weight to it. Rhazdon must have known that too. She was brilliant at mastering them. Unfortunate that she turned out to be such an outstanding bitch."

Correk pulled the book closer, reading the spell again, the reason to learn them all sinking into his bones. He reached up and pulled down the smallest of the books, balanced on the top of the pile. *Incantations Testament and Guide.* The author was unknown.

It was not as old as the others and written in Elven with the text on each page appearing as Correk glanced at the page. The book was meant to serve as a study guide to many of the books, telling their history and when they were used to disastrous or heroic results. There were footnotes provided on how they could have been done better or worse and brought about different results. He pushed the book to the side and went back to the larger spell book. Will have to see if I can take that book home with me.

He read page after page, getting drawn into the spells to tame a dragon or even one to appear invisible for brief periods of time. "Has to be the way Turner disappears so easily. Like a party trick for him. His girlfriends must be very entertained."

"Whose girlfriends?" Leira cocked her head to one side, giving a crooked smile.

Correk started, kicking the table and jostling the books as one pile teetered, and fell over into a landslide. A book skittered off the table and landed at Leira's feet, just inside the doorway.

"I didn't hear you come in."

"Clearly. I thought you were studying the ancient rituals or was there an Elven Playboy edition back then and they were rockin' the ladies. Makes sense. Hey, there's even pictures." Leira came closer and touched the page. "These are kind of beautiful. Rao..."

Correk stood up and put his hand over the rest of the spell. "Just don't say anything out loud."

Leira snorted. "That could have happened to any Fixer in training. It's all back to where it belongs now."

"Thanks to you." Correk gave a crooked smile. "I suppose a little humility is good for me, every once in a while." He carefully restacked the books and found a chair for Leira, pulling it closer to the desk.

"I thought you had the troll with you. Tell me he's not back out crime fighting." Leira sat down next to him and looked at the spines on the books, doing her best to decipher some of the ancient words but not getting very far.

"No, he gave me his word. And if he was here, I'd have to explain to Turner Underwood why there was a tiny orange footprint across one of his ancient, priceless tomes. No thanks. Butchering his driveway will have to stand as my one idiot move... I hope."

"Figuring out these words is harder than learning to read the symbols. There's probably more than one bonehead move in you. Don't worry about it. You've pulled me back from a few and today was nothing. Frankly, even I know repaving the driveway was an easy job. You could have done it. You just startled Turner and you know he doesn't take surprises as well as you'd think he would. That and he's a little obsessed with those bushes. Something about being almost as old as he is, which I think is a little bullshit mixed in with the truth." Leira turned the page and saw an illustration of an Elf doing battle with an apparition. "What is this? Ghosts? Tell me there aren't ghosts that could haunt us."

Correk bent over the book, close to Leira's face. "No, as far as I know there are no ghosts, but I'm only on the second book out of an entire library. I'll let you know. That is a projection that can wield a weapon. According to Turner, not used for thousands of years. Something about letting something loose that you can't put back."

"He likes to be cryptic at times. Part of his cool vibe. Hey, do you think the spell to create a shifter is somewhere in here?" Leira carefully turned the pages, scanning the illustrations. "Maybe even something to undo the harm done to the bionic animals," she said, excited. "Didn't

Turner say that for everything that comes up, a spell has already been created long ago to counter it?"

"Something like that. But magic can't answer everything, at least not without demanding something in return."

"It's easy to forget how old magic really is and how long there's been a constant pull between the opposing sides."

"The ever-present balance. Can't have one without the other." Correk turned to Leira, her face just inches from his as she peered at the book. "You are the living embodiment of that principle." *Never noticed how green your eyes are before.*

"What are you doing? What's that? Why are you scanning me like that?"

Correk covered his surprise by arching an eyebrow and doing his best to look annoyed. "You're seeing things."

Leira narrowed her eyes, looking at Correk. "Yeah, okay... I've got my eye on you," she said, smiling. *Not exactly telling me the truth. That's not like him.* "How's it coming with learning all this?" She looked at the stacks of books.

"This is only a small portion. Apparently, the learning never ends, which means there will be times when I'm carefully rifling through very ancient texts that are irreplaceable trying to find a solution before something melts, oozes or goes kaboom."

"You can do it. I believe in you. I've seen what you can do, and Turner wouldn't have picked you if he didn't think you were up to the job... even after you redesigned his driveway." She slapped Correk on the back, smiling. "How much longer are you trapped here? It's a pretty day and we need to get outside."

"I think we can call it for today. I've taken in all I can absorb. This is going to be a marathon and not a sprint. What did you have in mind?"

"A hike... a hike would be nice through McKinney State Park. It's been too long since I've done that. Hey, aren't you going to ask me about my date last night? Usually, by now you've made at least two pointless jokes and asked a series of nosey questions. Why the silent treatment?"

Correk swallowed hard, hoping he could get the words out. "How was your date last night? Any shots fired?"

"That's more like it. No, and there was no love connection either. Nice guy but it wasn't doing anything for me. There was just something missing. I don't know."

"Too bad, he seemed like a nice guy." Correk followed Leira out to her car, the knot in his stomach dissolving at last. "We have to do something about Fleeker."

"Not today. That will take some finesse if we're going to remove the operation at the roots. Dark ancient magic mixed with an American corporation. This will take strategy and patience."

Correk arched an eyebrow and smiled at Leira. "Not your usual answer."

Leira felt a shudder pass through her. "I felt the darkness come out to greet me and it matched the light. Running at it headfirst may not work and after what happened to Hagan..."

"What if we start with the Dark Wizarding families?"

"I can't believe they're the easier mark." Leira shook her head. "What if we start with looking for Harkin?" She said the words slowly, taking Correk's hand in hers.

He looked down at her hand and up at her face, surprised.

"He may not even be alive."

"You believe he is. That's enough for me. We'll do this together. We're a team."

CHAPTER TWENTY-NINE

R hazdon sat at the bus station, waiting for the announcement over the loudspeaker that the bus heading for Austin, Texas had finally arrived. Her body ached from sitting on the narrow wooden bench and she was looking forward to resting on the padded seat and closing her eyes. She looked up and caught her reflection in a nearby window and shuddered at what she saw. A withered old woman did her best to sit up straighter, hanging on to her cane. Her thinning hair was tied back in a loose bun at the nape of her neck and there were brown spots covering her twisted hands. A long thin scar appeared under her chin and disappeared under the maroon silk top she was wearing.

The battle on Enchanted Rock had drained her of magic and crippled her. She knew she was dying, and time was short. There were things that had to be made right before her time was over. She looked down at her ticket. "Turner Underwood, it's time we met again. There is much to tell you before it's too late if you are to survive the coming menace. After all, I'm the one that set it all loose and tipped the balance into chaos." *And if I play my cards right, maybe I can save myself, yet. Leira Berens will have to play along, but she may be persuaded. Everyone has their soft spots.*

"All aboard for Austin, Texas. Five minutes till the bus pulls out." The announcement blared over the old loud-speakers.

Rhazdon smiled and wearily pulled herself up to a standing position, pain passing through her body and into every bone. "Not long now... The next chapter begins."

CHAPTER THIRTY

Louie sat at the bar in an old pub he liked to frequent near the Dark Market, sipping on a warm beer, his sword strapped to his back and a leather bag full of artifacts lay at his feet. It had been an exceptional day of scavenging and he wanted to stop for a drink before heading home to the cabin. He had managed to ditch the ankle bracelet for a while and make it back to Oriceran for the day. Living on Earth was cramping his style. "There will need to be balance," he said, holding up the foamy glass of beer and wiping off the dirt he found on the other side of the glass. No sense in complaining. The bartender would only spit on it and give it back to him. This was better.

He almost turned around when he walked in after seeing the three Kilomeas huddled at a table near the door but decided to ignore them and sat down anyway. *Besides, this is where I told Ronnie to meet me. Not going to let a few shit for brains Kilomeas run me out of here.* He was sure he recognized one of them from some of his digs. He turned around to get a better look. *Yeah, that's the lazy fuck who likes to chase other scavengers.*

He arched his back, rubbing his shoulder as the toe of his boot nudged the bag and the sound of metal hitting metal could be heard by anyone sitting nearby.

Louie looked up to see who had taken notice, but no one was looking in his direction and the Kilomeas were too involved in arm wrestling each other with one arm and a knife in the other to pay attention to him. Louie watched, amused for a moment but turned back after a while, raising a finger to the bartender to signal for another beer.

He laid half a small gold coin down on the counter and took a long swig, swishing it around in his mouth. The door opened, sending a cold breeze into the small pub and annoying the Kilomeas who let out loud grunts, one of them banging his studded hammer on the table. Ronnie slipped into the bar and quickly made his way past the Kilomeas, taking a seat at the bar on the far side of Louie.

"Hey, hey! Take it outside," yelled the Elven bartender who was drying glasses with a damp rag, frayed at the edges. The bartender sent a warning shot of three small fireballs no bigger than a drop of water sizzling over the tops of the Kilomeas large heads, barely missing a Crystal man sitting at a nearby table. The Crystal retaliated by breaking off a frozen spike and tossing it like a javelin, neatly hitting the bar right in front of where the bartender stood.

Another Kilomea joined in and shook his fist in the direction of the bar but they settled down and went back to making small bets with one another.

"Tell me again why you like this place so much?" Ronnie

settled in at the bar and pushed a coin forward while waving to the bartender. It was a rule in the joint that you showed your money first, then got a drink. There was no food to be had unless one of the patrons bit someone in a fight, which was likely on most nights when it got to be close to closing time.

"It's close to work and cheap and no one bothers you."

"No one bothers you?" Ronnie choked on his beer, sputtering. "Everyone bothers you in here!"

"You know what I mean."

"Oh, so you're some kind of celebrity and you needed to get away from your fans? Or is it the ladies? Boy, that's rich."

"Too many eyes in these parts, these days. This place is full of the kind that don't want anyone knowing where they are..."

"Look out!" Ronnie screeched, sliding off his bar stool, spilling his glass as the Kilomea brought down his large hammer, and Louie leaned back far enough, sliding off the bar and pulling out the sword in one smooth movement.

The Kilomea smiled, showing pieces of a worm still clinging to his teeth. He swung the hammer sideways, attempting to sweep Louie off his feet like a bowling pin.

Lean back and slice the handle of the hammer with the edge of the sword.

The sword was speaking to Louie inside his head. It wasn't the first time. He had grown to trust what it said, acting instinctively whenever he heard it.

The broadsword cut into the thick wood, weakening the handle and splintering it, surprising the Kilomea and enraging him further. He slammed the hammer to the ground and reached out with his hands to throttle Louie as his friends got up from the table to join in the fight.

The bartender quickly grew a larger fireball in his hands this time and sent it screaming in front of the Kilomeas path, cautioning them to stay out of the fight.

"You know the rules," he shouted. "No piling on."

The two beasts stomped out of the bar, roaring with their heads back and mouths wide open as the wind rushed in again.

The Kilomea missed Louie's neck and thought better of it, lunging for the bag still sitting by the bar, a grin returning to his face, large fangs protruding from his mouth.

Bring the flat side down at an angle to his head.

Louie swung, putting all his weight behind it, smashing the Kilomea in the head while he was still bent over. The oversized beast crumpled against the bar, letting out a warm, stale breath of air and rolled backward onto the floor.

"I think he's out." Ronnie picked up a bar stool and nudged him with one of the legs. He let out a soft groan but otherwise didn't move. "Not so bad when they're unconscious."

"Yeah, I don't think that's gonna last long. Come on, we better get out of here."

"Not that way!" yelled the bartender. "His thug friends will be waiting for you out there. Follow me." The bartender lifted a section of the bar and headed for a small room in the back, tossing aside a rug to reveal a hatch in the floor. "Place like this needs an exit strategy, if you know what I mean. Nice sword play. Don't suppose you'd want to trade with it?" The bartender reached up to touch the sword and was sparked with a snap and crackle of electricity.

Louie smiled, opening the hatch and helping Ronnie down into the tunnel. He jumped in after him and tossed the bartender another gold coin. "Thanks for your help."

"Sure... don't like to see those Kilomeas make barbeque out of just anybody. Where'd you find that thing? Never known an artifact to spark like that. That's what it is, isn't it?" He gave Louie a sly look but didn't wait for an answer as he closed the hatch, covered it back over and went back to drying glasses behind the bar, waiting for the next customer and the Kilomea to regain consciousness. "Just another day at the office." He whistled a tune he'd heard the other day and smiled as the potted fern swayed in time with him.

Louie and Ronnie quickly made their way underground, directly under the feet of the behemoths waiting for them outside. The exit to the tunnel was far enough into the Dark Forest where no one could see them exit and it wasn't long before Louie was back in his own cabin, safe and sound and had deposited Ronnie in his favorite tree to sleep in a hammock high off the ground. He preferred it on any day that wasn't raining.

Louie went into the cabin and dropped the bag of artifacts, stripping down to his waist and picking up the sword. He was going to have to head back to the other world soon, before he was missed long enough to really piss someone off. But before he went, he was determined to test out the sword some more. He swung the sword over his head, admiring how well balanced the handle was in his hands.

To the right... crouch down. Turn behind you. Bring the blade up.

The sword was speaking to him, telling him what to do again. *Swing hard to the left, steady your feet.*

He listened to each command, practicing, wanting to see if he could keep up, the muscles rippling in his back. It came to him easily, naturally. He stopped, resting the tip of the wide sword on the floor, breathing hard.

Join forces.

"What?" He picked up his shirt and wiped the sweat off his face, still holding on to the handle of the sword.

Join forces with her. Align with Leira Berens. Fight by her side in the coming battles.

Louie felt a cold sliver of energy pass through him, chilling him to the bone as he picked up his shirt and put it back on. "Time to go back to Earth. Apparently, I'm needed there."

CHAPTER THIRTY-ONE

Leira and Correk stood just outside the Fleeker campus, looking at the grounds from a hidden vantage point of an old covered bus stop.

Leira felt a shudder roll through her body, settling in her belly. Yumfuck sat on her shoulder and let out a miniature shudder as her feelings rolled through him. "This is the place I saw," said Leira. "Looks... kind of friendly. Normal even. Look at all the people getting off the shuttles. They look happy."

"That's how evil works best, when it's disguised as something you want." Correk arched an eyebrow and crossed his arms over his chest.

Leira put her hands on her hips, her stance wide and her jaw set. "Not for long, asshole. We're coming for you, Wolfstan Humphrey." She scooped the troll into her hand and held him up till he was level with her face. "You're a badass, Yumfuck, taking on this place all by yourself. I have respect for that. But we've hit a place where we need to win and if we're going to do that, we'll have to work together from the beginning to the end. That's the only way we all survive. Deal?"

The troll put out his paw and shouted, "All for one!"

Leira gave a crooked smile and put her hand over the troll's paw. "Come on, you too. You've been waiting for me to quit the solo act from the beginning. This is your victory lap."

Correk did his best to smile and laid his hand on top of the pile.

"On three," squeaked the troll. "Three, two, one…"

A swirl of purple light interrupted them, opening up a portal just behind the bus stop. Turner Underwood leaned out, waving the top of his cane. "Come on, Correk. You're needed elsewhere. Now!" Turner abruptly stopped his waving and sniffed the air. "What is that smell? It's rancid magic. Did you step in something?"

"It's kind of behind you. Portals don't really have a back on them." She peered into the portal at the tan stoned building. "I know that place. You're at the old power station on the East side. What's a magical doing there?"

Turner scowled and glanced at Correk. "That's a very complicated answer and no time to give one. Let's get a move on." His nose twitched and he smelled the air once more, this time waving his cane in a figure eight. Gnats appeared in the air, swarming overhead in a hazy circle. It didn't take long for them to form a long line, flitting toward their target.

"That makes sense. They can smell the rot."

"What is back there?" demanded Turner, his bushy eyebrows working up and down.

"The root of all of it. Welcome to Fleeker, home of Wolfstan Humphrey's operations to butcher living things."

Turner grew ashen and he put one foot outside the portal to grab Leira's hand, setting off small sparks that rode up her arm.

"Foolhardy and reckless! Come on, you're going with us," he growled. The troll jumped across, landing on Turner's arm and riding up and down on the wave of exertion.

Leira let herself be pulled into the portal, taking one last look at the sleek corporate building with its tidy grounds. "Hell cleans up pretty well."

"It's still a legitimate hell and a kind of darkness you've never faced before. It's too fucking soon! For both of you!" The gnats returned, hovering just overhead. Turner raised his cane and sucked them in like a vacuum. Turner shook his head, nudging Correk with his cane. "This is bad, very bad. In with you. We have more pressing matters."

"More pressing than hell? Big day." Correk frowned and stepped through the portal and Turner pulled back his cane, creating a whirl of light, shutting it behind them.

Leira dug a toe into the packed dirt. "This was a big hangout place when I was a teenager. Nana used to cruise by here when she wanted me to come home. I appreciated that she never actually stopped and got out." She took a look around at the barren area. "The old plant is more of a refuge for the homeless these days." The three story concrete building was dotted with windows down the two long sides, most of them broken and stretched out along the entire block.

"I had a case here with Hagan a few years back. It's a

convenient place to dump a body. No cameras in the area. I'm surprised it didn't happen more often."

"Who did it?" Yumfuck sat down and pushed off from Turner's shoulder, sledding down to his cuffs and dropping to the ground. He ran to Correk and climbed up his pant leg till Correk picked him up and put the troll on his shoulder.

"The business partner. Hagan called it from the jump."

Correk started walking toward the abandoned building situated across the dry acre. The entire lot was pock-marked by a tired cactus and a patch of tall sunflowers with fast food wrappers clinging around the bottom. Correk was growing restless. Too many loose ends and they were all pointing back toward a dead man, his father. "What was more important than Wolfstan Humphrey?"

He only got a few feet when the ground rumbled beneath him, shaking his legs. The building rattled on its foundation, struggling to stay intact. A fine mist of dirt and dust billowed out from its side as a loud roar erupted from the long rows of windows. Blue sparks of electricity jumped out of the middle windows, snapping against what remained of the glass panes.

"Isn't this place shut down?" Correk took a step back, waiting to see what would happen next. An older man with a long grey beard and bald head in worn baggy jeans and a flannel shirt came barreling out of a doorway, his eyes wide with fear. He saw the trio and waved his arms. "Don't go in there! It's too dangerous. He's crazy!" He didn't wait for an answer and took off running down the street in the opposite direction.

Leira went running past Correk, easily closing the

distance across the acre of open land. Correk wasn't far behind her, the troll bouncing up and down on his shoulder.

The building shook again as they came through the door and Leira saw the cause of the localized earthquake. Peyton in his fury and pain was pushing at a load bearing column, interrupted by his beating on a wall. The illuminated blue lines of electricity jumped all around him, pinging off the walls and leaving small pockmarks in a random pattern.

Turner Underwood had beaten both of them there and was standing only a few yards from Peyton, using the silver head of his cane like a lightning rod to pull in some of the erratic energy.

"How in the hell did you get here first?" Leira took a position to the right of Turner, pulling in energy from the ground and setting an intention. *Calm.*

The blue lines flickered, dancing over Peyton's body, finally smoothing out and running along the floor of the old building to Leira, attracted to her light. She felt the broken magic mixing with her own and saw the fractured images from Peyton's memories, filled with joy, regret and pain. It was almost too much. She gritted her teeth and bent her knees, letting her energy wrap around it, offering refuge for it.

Leira felt the pressure against her ribs and hunched her shoulders, pushing around the unbridled magic as the air was getting forced out of her lungs. The symbols turned over along her arms, picking up speed as she worked at taking in a breath.

The troll jumped down from Correk's shoulder and

grew to his full height of eight feet, growling and swatting at the air, even as his fur took on a blue tinge.

Correk looked on in horror and formed a fireball in his hands, reeling back to launch. A sudden movement overhead caught his eye and he hesitated.

"No, you can't." Harkin leapt down from the rafters, landing easily on his feet and moved between Correk and Peyton. "He doesn't know what he's doing, and he's suffered enough."

Leira squinted from the pain, letting out a gasp. "He looks just like you. Harkin." She was close to passing out when Correk came up behind her, wrapping an arm around her and pulling the energy in through his chest. He never took his eyes off Harkin, an orange fireball still burning in his other hand. Leira sipped in air as the strain eased. Peyton crumpled to the floor, curling up in a ball, breathing hard. His pain had at last subsided.

"What the fuck is going on?" she said with a rush of air, leaning her weight forward against Correk's arm.

Correk held her steady, taking in every detail of the man who had left him a long time ago and was thought to be dead. He looked over at Peyton and the realization slipped over him in a wave that felt like it could knock him down. "That's Peyton, isn't it?" He choked out the words, his eyes shining, even as he kept his muscled arm wrapped around Leira, pulling her closer.

Turner stayed silent, watching the father and son. There was nothing he could do to make this easier for anyone.

"Did you know?" Correk angrily growled at Turner.

"I have wondered from time to time, but I never found

any proof. Someone powerful must have been hiding him and he wisely stayed away from Earth."

Leira's eyes still glowed, the symbols flipping along her arms at a slower pace. She stayed where she was, letting Correk help her ground the volatile energy she was still pulling off Peyton. *Set the intention. Do it for Correk. Calm.*

"What have you done now?" Correk was breathing hard, the fireball casting a glow across Leira's face, warming it. She could feel the slight tremor as he worked at containing his rage and hurt.

"I've wanted to see you a thousand times." It was all Harkin could think to say. Bits of the truth. He didn't take his eyes off his only child. "I checked on you when you were injured and made sure you were alright."

Correk slowly shook his head. "How is that enough? That's not even a beginning. You let me think you were dead." He hurled the fireball in rage as Harkin easily ducked and the flames licked the wall behind him, creeping up toward the windows.

"I wanted to protect you from my mistakes."

Correk's muscles tensed and another fireball appeared in his hand. He threw it and this time with more speed. Harkin dodged backward just in time, the flames singeing his hair.

Still Turner did nothing.

"I wanted to correct my own mistakes."

Correk's anger spilled over and he lit a hundred small fireballs the size of bullets, floating just above his hand. Leira could feel him flex his arm and heard him grunt as he pulled back his arm. "Celeritate ignas aeterni," he thundered.

The shower of flames rained down on Harkin, too many for him to get out of the way. The best he could do was put out the ones that made contact while crying out in pain. Leira lifted her hand to help Harkin and put an end to the one-sided fight but Turner shook his head, tapping his cane hard against the concrete.

Harkin extinguished the flames, soot smudged on his face and the skin along his arm blistering. He was shaking with anger, pain and regret as he raised his arms toward Correk and sang out in the old Oriceran language.

Leira felt Correk's fury melting into an old ache that he had carried for too long. He began to shake violently, the sadness bubbling to the surface. Leira twisted around, wrapping her arms around him and holding him up. "What did he say?"

Correk whispered in her ear through gritted teeth. "What he said to me every night when I was a child. *I will always find my way back to you.* It's just a fairy tale. It's not real."

Leira held him tight. "If there's one thing you've taught me, fairy tales are all based on truth. Hold one to just one idea right now. Your father is alive. We can figure out the rest later."

The story is far from over. Leira's adventure continues in GUARDIANS OF MAGIC.

Get sneak peeks, exclusive giveaways, behind the scenes content, and more. PLUS you'll be notified of special **one day only fan pricing** on new releases.

Sign up today to get free stories.

One of the side things about this pandemic and sheltering in place is it's harder to get away from myself. Usually, I have a lot of activities going on and people around me. Busy, busy, busy. But these past few months, you know, we've all been a bit more quiet. Anybody else feeling it?

And in the house the troll built it's just been me and two dogs. I see neighbors from a distance to chat and even space out our chairs, but still… I've gotten the opportunity to look at a few things.

It's been pointed out to me recently that I don't seem to know my own worth, or value, or achievements – from multiple people who don't even know each other. By the third time I was starting to pay attention and then when the Offspring said, "I look forward to the day when you really see what you've created," I began to wonder something. Why don't I see it the same way?

At first I thought, maybe it's a good thing. I haven't become arrogant or entitled but taken too far and it's something else. I'm not even sure what my reason is, but I can tell you the consequences of it. I haven't always done the best job of advocating for myself, preferring to stay back in the chorus line or along the fringes. I've let others take the spotlight in front of me and downplay my part or even forget I was there. I was hoping that would mean I could stay, right back there and that was at least something.

Turns out, no its not. I didn't have a lot of trust in the universe and how things could turn out if I just put one foot in front of the other and spoke up – not yell or stomp a foot – just speak up. This is mine, I am here, I helped with this. And trust that whoever is supposed to still be there when the dust settles, they'll be there, cheering me on, working alongside me. I realize I'm a bit long in the tooth to be figuring this one out, but let me tell you, still worth it. It's never too late to feel gratitude in an entirely different way and taking a step out there into the unknown to just see what happens. More adventures to follow.

Original: February 28, 2018:

I think I'm finally getting a handle on this marketing thing. I say that knowing full well it's already got an expiration date on it and everything will change by the time you've read this. I'll be pushing buttons, and fixing glitches a week from now on some new googaw, like I was for most of last week (okay, and a little bit today – figured out how to set up giveaways, so there's A LOT of contests in our future. I'm even going to figure out how to get Yumfuck printed on a sun visor for a car for one of the prize packages. That's just too much fun to ignore). Anyway, for now,

I'm rocking and rolling. I'll take it and enjoy it while I've got it.

That's the business these days, maybe every business. Things change rapidly, and it takes a certain amount of courage to plunge ahead knowing full well I'm flying blind for the most part. Armed with a pretty good bullshit detector (honed through paying enough of the wrong people a lot of money over the years), I've learned to listen to that inner voice a lot faster that says when to stay put or when to run.

Besides that, I've been lucky enough to surround myself with really talented, creative, fun people like Michael Anderle and Craig Martelle, who are more like brothers to me at this point. Or Stephen Campbell, the Zen Master who quietly keeps all the plates spinning behind the scenes. That makes the long hours a lot more fun. Well, that and talking to all of you on the Fan Groups. (Everyone out there joined the Peabrain Society yet?)

Truth is, I wouldn't have this life any other way and this past week, I got a nice payoff that showed me exactly why. The Offspring, Louie Carr, is taking his swing at bat and is starting his own venture, Own Path Media Group, managing musical acts and he's already got 3 clients! When I listen to him talk about this turn his life is taking, I remember all the times I was struggling to get ahead and sitting next to me was a small Louie, watching my every move.

There was a long stretch of road where there weren't many cheerleaders in my corner but it never occurred to me to give up or slow down and I made progress till I found the right team, and then connected with all of you, the FANS. Louie has that inner belief burning brightly in him too and it's giving him the strength to just say yes to his dreams. That's my payoff.

Hopefully, my grandchildren will see all this as second nature. Of course, you do what you love. Of course, you keep going until all the pieces fit. Of course, you will eventually succeed. (No, I don't have any grandchildren, yet...) I'm telling you, these days I'm winning on all fronts because in the end it's the connections we make and the people we love and the legacy we leave them with that matters. And on that score, I am very grateful to all of you, the Fans, to LMBPN and all the faces that are wrapped up in that, and to Louie for getting out there and lighting up the world with his gifts. Here we go everyone...

More adventures to follow.

Martha

We really appreciate you reading our stories and allow us the opportunity to do what we love.

Create more stories!

It's a hot summer day here in Henderson as I listen to grasshoppers (or crickets or some type of insect that rubs their legs together to make "that" sound so associated with summer in the South.)

I'm sitting under a fan and Mother Nature is resting, allowing the sun to slowly hide behind the mountains to the west of Las Vegas, my weight being reduced by the minute as the heat leaches the liquid out of my body.

Why not go inside, you ask? Because I'm a glutton for punishment, apparently. I won't allow myself to go do the next thing on my bullet list without getting a few more *Author Notes* done! It seems I am forever behind on these little notes, and I want to make sure my team has these for this week.

In short, I'm late.

Not that being late means I can't be inside in the air

conditioning. It just means that I enjoy the sounds of nature more than the coolness inside.

(Also, I'm not-so-secretly hoping that this kickstarts my body into dropping some weight. That's a thing, right? Sit somewhere hot and sweat off the weight?)

If it isn't a known thing, I'm really hoping it becomes a thing for me. I mean, I like the sound of nature and all, but I'm starting to wonder if I can't just ask Siri or Alexa to play them for me.

Original: February 26, 2018

First, THANK YOU so much for not only reading ALL of our stories in this series, but through to our author notes, as well!

Like Martha, I'm soooooo freaking blessed to be provided the opportunity to provide stories for you, and others like you that like our brand of characters.

Our people, so to speak.

One of my "cool moments" just happened to me about 1 hour ago and I really want to share it with you. For those who read The Kurtherian Gambit, you know the character Nathan Lowell which is in book one, and keeps going into multiple series at one point.

I've mentioned either in other author notes, or maybe on a podcast, that Nathan Lowell is named after an author that I like.

Nathan Lowell (the author) wrote the Ishmael Wong stories that start with Quarter-Share (Traders Tales from the Golden Age of the Solar Clipper - My Book).

So, I'm hanging in the back of this author conference today, and this older gentleman (suit mind you, grey beard,

VERY awesome and completely makes me feel underdressed (because I am…wait, I have on shirt and pants, so underdressed as in very casual.) Anyway, dressing aside, this very polite man waits while a couple of other authors ask me some questions.

When everyone is done, he turns and I notice his name tag says 'Nate'… I got nothing (all names and faces escape me until I've seen people for a lot of times.) So, he introduces himself as NATHAN LOWELL.

I had a fanboy moment (did not squeal). He put out his hand to shake and I might have shocked him by hugging him and being so enthusiastic…

Oops, sorry Nathan.

I answered his question from his fan if my Nathan Lowell was named after him and I confirmed CERTAINLY… I needed a name and I loved his work. Plus, I never expected to become so successful as a writer, (I was a little embarrassed at this point) and I had to admit I riffed off his name for my character.

I think I'm blushing just writing these notes.

Either way, it is SUCH a cool moment for me to meet one of the writers I've admired for at least 7 years or longer. I can't wait to admit to my kids that I've met *THE* Nathan Lowell.

Fucking hell, this is so cool!

Ok, I'll come off my author high now and agree with Martha that we (authors) are so damned blessed to know that we have provided some bright spots in your life.

Let us know on Facebook, or reviews (you are reviewing at least for Yumfuck, right?) how we make you feel in these stories, and know that Martha (and myself) will be traveling more in the next 12 to 18 months.

Hopefully, we will come to an area near you.

Ad Aeternitatem,
Michael Anderle

For Hire: Teachers for special school in Virginia countryside.

Must be able to handle teenagers with special abilities.

Cannot be afraid to discipline werewolves, wizards, elves and other assorted hormonal teens.

Apply at the School of Necessary Magic.

AVAILABLE ON AMAZON RETAILERS

If smart phones and GPS rule the world - why am I hunting a magic compass to save the planet?

Austin Detective Maggie Parker has seen some weird things in her day, but finding a surly gnome rooting through her garage beats all.

Her world is about to be turned upside down in a frantic search for 4 Elementals.

Each one has an artifact that can keep the Earth humming along, but they need her to unite them first.

Unless the forces against her get there first.

AVAILABLE ON AMAZON AND IN KINDLE UNLIMITED!

OTHER SERIES IN THE ORICERAN
UNIVERSE

SOUL STONE MAGE

THE KACY CHRONICLES

MIDWEST MAGIC CHRONICLES

THE FAIRHAVEN CHRONICLES

I FEAR NO EVIL

THE DANIEL CODEX SERIES

SCHOOL OF NECESSARY MAGIC

SCHOOL OF NECESSARY MAGIC: RAINE CAMPBELL

ALISON BROWNSTONE

FEDERAL AGENTS OF MAGIC

SCIONS OF MAGIC

THE UNBELIEVABLE MR. BROWNSTONE

OTHER BOOKS BY JUDITH BERENS

OTHER BOOKS BY MARTHA CARR

**JOIN THE ORICERAN UNIVERSE FAN GROUP ON
FACEBOOK!**